A Garland Series

Foundations of the Novel

Representative Early

Eighteenth-Century Fiction

A collection of 100 rare titles
reprinted in photo-facsimile in 71 volumes

Foundations of the Novel

compiled and edited by

Michael F. Shugrue
Secretary for English for the M.L.A.

with New Introductions for each volume by

Michael Shugrue, *City College of C.U.N.Y.*
Malcolm J. Bosse, *City College of C.U.N.Y.*
William Graves, *N.Y. Institute of Technology*

The Adventures of Rivella

by

Mary de la Rivière Manley

The Adventures and Surprizing Deliverances of James Dubourdieu and his Wife

and

The Adventures of Alexander Vendchurch

by

Ambrose Evans

**with a new introduction
for the Garland Edition by
Malcolm J. Bosse**

Garland Publishing, Inc., New York & London

The new introduction for the

Garland *Foundations of the Novel* Edition

is Copyright © 1972, by

Garland Publishing, Inc., New York & London

All Rights Reserved

Library of Congress Cataloging in Publication Data

Manley, Mary de La Rivière, 1663-1724.
The adventures of Rivella.

(Foundations of the novel)
Original t.p. of the 1st work reads: The adventures
of Rivella; or, The history of the author of the Atalan-
tis ... London; Printed in the year M.DCC.XIV.
Original t.p. of the 2d work reads: The Adventures,
and surprizing deliverances, of James Dubourdieu, and
his wife ... Also, The Adventures of Alexander
Vendchurch ... Written by himself. London: Printed by
J. Bettenham for A. Bettesworth ... 1719.
The text of the 1st part of the 2d work is signed
Ambrose Evans.

Includes bibliographical references.
1. English fiction--18th century. I. Evans,
Ambrose. II. The Adventures and surprizing deliver-
ances of James Dubourdieu and his wife. 1972.
III. Title. IV. Title: The Adventures of Alexander
Vendchurch. V. Series.
PZ1.M3032Ad2   813'.5   72-7419
ISBN 0-8240-0534-1

Introduction

The Adventures of Rivella *was hastily written by Mary Manley, according to the publisher Edmund Curll, to offset and possibly forestall the publication of a philippic directed against her by Charles Gildon, which he was apparently composing at Curll's instigation.*[1] *In her fictionalized autobiography she avoids defending her performance as a political writer and seeks instead to justify her behavior as a woman.*

Born the daughter of Sir John Manley, a loyalist who served from 1667 to 1672 as Lieutenant-Governor of Jersey, she never achieved her rightful social status, possibly because early in her life and continuing until her death Mary Manley was involved in a number of illegal liaisons. Among her acknowledged lovers were her cousin, John Manley, with whom she contracted a bigamous "marriage"; Sir Thomas Skipwith, who produced her first play; John Tilly, warden of Fleet Prison; John Barber, publisher and future mayor of London; and John Tidcombe, who may have served as the model for the narrator of Rivella.[2] *Throughout her life she was a prolific writer whose literary career began with* Letters *in 1696 and in the same year with the production of two plays, a comedy,* The Lost Lover, *and a tragedy,* The Royal Mischief. *Her best known works were scandal chronicles of satiric and political aim in the*

5

form of romans à clef: The Secret History of Queen Zarah *(1705)*, The New Atalantis *(1709), and* Memoirs of Europe *(1710). Of this fiction Professor Koster says, "Considered as literature, the novels should have a secure scholarly place, for they show a considerable range of techniques in the development toward the novel."* [3]

Rivella *begins with a "Translator's Preface," which asserts that the manuscript has been translated from a French original. Although this preface was deleted in the second edition appearing three years later, Mrs. Manley always claimed that her chronicles were translations. Other writers of the period, including Defoe, attempted to achieve some aesthetic distance and verisimilitude by employing the device of a translation of a lost manuscript, but in Mary Manley's case the technique was a means of protecting herself against libel. In an amusing passage she suggests that even such an unconvincing denial of responsibility could keep an author from serious punishment. Questioned by order of the Whig Secretary of State, Charles Sunderland, she pleaded that her characters were imaginary, drawn merely to entertain:*

> *When this was not believ'd, and the contrary urg'd very home to her by several Circumstances and Likenesses; she said then it must be Inspiration, because knowing her own Innocence she could account for it no other way. (p. 113)*

The narrative framework is a dialogue between an amorously inclined young Frenchman, the Chevalier

INTRODUCTION

D'Aumont, and Sir Charles Lovemore, who declares that he has loved Rivella longer and more faithfully than any other man. Mrs. Manley's knowledge of dramatic writing, constantly in evidence throughout her fiction, is put to lively use here, as the two men coolly discuss the physical attributes that women must have to be desirable. The author provides a rather glowing account of her own attractiveness, but ultimately her self-portrait is less a panegyric than a moving confession from a woman whose troubles in life have derived from sensuality, from "the Greatness of her Prepossession" (p. 23).

Although her life story is couched in the form of short romantic episodes, much like those encountered in her novels, what emerges here is a realistic account of female vulnerability to passion and the sad consequences of unfounded optimism. The Adventures of Rivella, *in spite of stylistic crudities and lack of coherent structure, sets forth with admirable clarity the sources in Mary Manley's life for the themes of her fiction. It is therefore an interesting psychological study of a popular novelist who was also an eighteenth-century woman with insight into the wellsprings of her own creativity.*

The Adventures and surprizing Deliverances of James Dubourdieu and his Wife, *published in 1719, contains the portrait of a woman markedly unlike Mrs. Manley or her heroines. The first half of the story is narrated by Martha Rattenberg, wife of James Dubourdieu, who together run a Parisian tavern. To a young Englishman*

7

who dutifully writes down her account, she explains that she had gone into service after being cheated of an inheritance by a wicked brother. First deceived and then married to a polygamist, she had set out for Barbados to change her fortune.

Her practical approach to life indicates that her central trait of character is strength, and the quiet factual prose augments this impression. After she and other passengers are taken prisoner by pirates, they are shipwrecked on a desert island where some of the women fraternize with the buccaneers. Tartly critical of such immorality, she describes the situation with a touch of sarcastic humor:

> *We were indeed all surpriz'd, that a place so adapted for convenient and happy living, should be wholly without inhabitants; and some of us concluded that we were ordain'd to people it; and the young lasses, with whom the pirates had already been familiar, as I told you, seem'd to leave no stone unturn'd to contribute their part towards this work. (p. 44)*

Having maintained her own virtue, she is providentially saved from assault by an earthquake which swallows up all the sinners and leaves her with good people, among them a French surgeon, Mr. Dubourdieu, whom she decides in a typically practical manner to marry. When her husband and a priest fail to return from an exploring expedition, she remains alone for three years on the island. At this juncture in the narrative her husband supplies his own first-person

8

INTRODUCTION

account of what happened to him during their separation, and in so doing shifts the emphasis from adventure to a philosophical discussion of a utopian society. During his exploration of the island he had met and lived with a race of beautiful people whose religion was based on reason and a reverence for life. Finally reunited with his wife, Mr. Dubourdieu returns to civilization thoroughly sobered by his contact with people who call Europeans "the children of wrath" (p. 93). This short narrative, composed of an adventure story and a utopian tale, moves at an admirable pace, and its fanciful content is somewhat offset by a prose style distinguished by clarity and simplicity.

Included with The Adventures of Mr. Dubourdieu and his Wife *is* The Adventures of Alexander Vendchurch, *a travel story of novella length. In picaresque fashion the narrator runs away from home and becomes the servant of a Spanish master who trades at Panama. Falling in love with a Spanish girl, Alexander Vendchurch is dealt with treacherously by her angry father. In one of those incredible coincidences that haunt eighteenth-century fiction, Alexander Vendchurch is shipwrecked and almost immediately reunited with his beloved Elvira, who, returning to Spain, had been shipwrecked on the same island. "Sea lyons" devour other castaways and Alexander lives idyllically with her until her sudden death, after which he returns to England and a large inheritance. The story moves quickly, but it is too lightly developed to compete with another tale that described life on a desert*

9

INTRODUCTION

island – The Life and Strange Surprizing Adventures of Robinson Crusoe – *published in that same year of 1719.*

Malcolm J. Bosse

NOTES

[1] *See Patricia Koster's comprehensive introduction to* The Novels of Mary Delariviere Manley *(Gainesville, Fla., 1971), I, pp. v-xxviii.*

[2] *Koster, p. xxi.*

[3] *Koster, pp. xxi-xxii.*

The Adventures of Rivella

by

Mary de la Rivière Manley

Bibliographical note:

*This facsimile has been made from a copy in the
Yale University Library
(IK M314 714A)*

THE
ADVENTURES
OF
RIVELLA;
OR, THE
HISTORY
Of the AUTHOR of the
ATALANTIS.
WITH

Secret *Memoirs* and *Characters* of feveral
confiderable Perfons her *Cotemporaries.*

Deliver'd in a Converfation to the Young
Chevalier D'Aumont in *Somerfet-Houfe*
Garden, by Sir Charles Lovemore.

Done into Englifh *from the* French.

LONDON:
Printed in the Year M. DCC. XIV.
Price 2 *s*. in Sheep, 2 *s*. 6 *d*. in Calf's Leather.

THE

TRANSLATOR's

PREFACE.

HE French *Publisher* has told his Reader, that ' the Means by ' which he became Master of ' the

' *the following* Papers, *was*
' *by his being* Gentleman of
' the Chamber *to the Young*
' Chevalier D'Aumont *when*
' *he was in* England *with the*
' *Ambaſſador of that Name. He*
' *recounts in his* Preface, *that af-*
' *ter the* Conference *in* Somer-
' ſet-houſe Garden, *thoſe two*
' Perſons *were at Supper toge-*
' *ther, where himſelf attended ;*
' *and that the Young* Cheva-
' lier *laid a* Diſcretion *with*
' *Sir* Charles Lovemore *(who*
' *reproach'd him with not be-*
' *ing attentive to his Relation)*
' *that he would recite to him*
' *upon* Paper *moſt of what he*
' *had diſcours'd with him that*
                         ' *Even-*

' *Evening, as a Proof both of*
' *the Goodneſs of his Memory,*
' *and great Attention:* That
' ſoon *after he, the Publiſh-*
' *er, was employ'd at ſeve-*
' *ral Times, as* Amanuenſis to
' *the ſaid* Chevalier, *by which*
' *Means the Papers remain'd*
' *in his Hands at the Death*
' *of young* D'Aumont, *which*
' *happen'd by a Fever, ſoon af-*
' *ter his Return into* France.'

The Engliſh *Reader is de-*
ſir'd to take Notice that the
Verſes are not to be found in the
French Copy ; *but to make the*
Book more perfect, Care has
been taken to tranſcribe them
with

with great Exactnefs *from the* Englifh *printed* Tragedy *of the fame* Author, *yet extant among us.*

London, June 3d, 1714.

THE

THE
HISTORY
OF
RIVELLA.

✢✢✢✢✢✢✢✢✢✢✢✢✢✢✢✢✢✢✢✢✢✢✢✢✢✢✢✢✢✢✢✢

INTRODUCTION.

N One of thofe fine Evenings
that are fo rarely to be found
in *England*, the Young *Chevalier D'Aumont*, related to the
Duke of that Name, was ta-
king the Air in *Somerfet-Houfe-Garden*,
and enjoying the cool Breeze from the
River; which after the hotteft Day that
had been known that Summer, prov'd
very refrefhing. He had made an Intimacy with Sir *Charles Lovemore*, a Perfon of admirable good Senfe and Knowledge, and who was now walking in the

Gar-

Garden with him, when *D'Aumont* lean-
ing over the Wall, pleas'd with obferving the Rays of the Setting Sun upon
the *Thames*, chang'd the Difcourfe ; Dear
Lovemore, fays the *Chevalier*, now the
Ambaffador is engag'd elfewhere, what
hinders me to have the entire Command
of this Garden ? If you think it a proper
Time to perform your Promife, I will
command the Door-keepers, that they
fuffer none to enter here this Evening,
to difturb our Converfation. Sir *Charles*
having agreed to the Propofal, and Orders
being accordingly given, Young *D'Aumont*
re-affumed the Difcourfe : Condemn not
my Curiofity, faid he, when it puts me
upon enquiring after the ingenious Women of your Nation : Wit and Senfe is
fo powerful a Charm, that I am not afhamed to tell you my Heart was infenfible
to all the fine Ladies of the Court of
France, and had perhaps ftill remain'd fo,
if I had not been foftned by the Charms
of Madam *Dacier*'s Converfation ; a Woman without either Youth or Beauty, yet
who makes a Thoufand Conquefts, and
preferves them too. I have often admir'd
her Learning, anfwer'd *Lovemore*, and to
fuch a Degree, that if the War had not
prevented me, I had doubtlefs gone to
France to have feen amongft other Curi-
ofities, a Lady who has made her felf admired

mired by all the World: But I do not imagine my Heart would have been in any Danger by that Vifit, her Qualifications are of the Sort that ftrike the Mind, in which the Senfe of Love can have but little Part: Talking to Her is converfing with an admirable Scholar, a judicious Critick, but what has That to do with the Heart? If fhe be as *unhandfom* as Fame reports her, and as *learned*, I fhould never raife my Thoughts higher than if I were difcourfing with fome Perfon of my own Sex, great and extraordinary · in his Way. You are, I find, a Novice, anfwer'd *D'Aumont* in what relates to Women; there is no being pleas'd in their Converfation without a Mixture of the Sex which will ftill be mingling it felf in all we fay. Some other Time I will give you a Proof of this, and do my felf the Honour to entertain you with certain Memoirs relating to Madam *Dacier*, of the Admiration and Applaufe fhe has gain'd, and the Conquefts fhe has made; by which you will find, that the *Royal Academy* are not the only Perfons that have done her Juftice; for whereas they beftow'd but the Prize of Eloquence, others have beftow'd their Heart: I muft agree with you, that her Perfections are not of the Sort that infpire immediate Delight, and warm the Blood with Pleafure, as thofe do who treat well of Love: I have not known any of the Moderns in that Point come up to your famous Author of the *Atalantis.* She has carried the Paffion farther than could be readily conceiv'd: Her *Germanicus on the Embroider'd Bugle Bed, naked out of the Bath :—* Her *Young and innocent Charlot,* tranfported with the powerful *Emotion of a juft kindling Flame, finking with Delight and Shame upon the Bofom of her Lover in the Gallery of Books:* Chevalier Tomafo *dying at the Feet of Madam* de Bedamore, *and afterwards pof-feffing Her in that* Sylvan *Scene of Pleafure the Garden;* are fuch Reprefentatives of Nature, that muft warm the coldeft Reader; it ráifes high Ideas of the Digni-ty of Human Kind, and informs us that we have in our Compofition, wherewith to tafte fublime and tranfporting Joys: After perufing her Inchanting Defcripti-ons, which of us have not gone in Search of Raptures which fhe every where tells us, as happy Mortals, we are capable of tafting. But have we found them, *Chevalier,* anfwer'd his Friend? For my Part, I believe they are to be met with no where elfe but in her own Embraces. That is what I would experience, reply'd *D'Aumont,* if fhe have but half fo much of the Practic, as the Theory, in the Way of Love, fhe muft certainly be a moft ac-

complifh'd

complifh'd Perfon : You have promifed to
tell me what you know of her Life and
Conduct; I would have her Mind, her
Perfon, her Manner defcrib'd to me; I
would have you paint her with as mafterly
an Hand, as fhe has painted others, that I
may know her perfectly before I fee
her.

IS not this being a little too particular,
anfwer'd Sir *Charles*, touching the Form
of a Lady, who is no longer young, and
was never a Beauty? Not in the leaft,
briskly reply'd the Chevalier, provided her
Mind and her Paffions are not in Decay.
What youthful Charmer of the Sex ever
pleas'd to that Height, as did Madam the
Dutchefs of *Mazarin*, even to her Death;
tho' I am told fhe was near twice *Rivella's*
Age? Were not all Eyes, all Hearts, devoted to her, even to the laft? One of the
moft lovely Princes of the Court reduc'd
himfelf almoft to Beggary, only, to fhare
with others, in thofe Delights which fhe
was capable of difpenfing? Laft Night I
heard Mr. *C*— difcourfing of her Power;
he was marry'd, as you know, to a Lady
perfectly Beautiful, of the Age of Sixteen,
who has fet a Thoufand Hearts on Fire;
and yet he tells you, one Night with Madam *Mazarin* made him happier, than
the whole Sex could do befides; which
pro-

proceeded only (as himſelf remarks) from her being entirely Miſtreſs of the Art of Love; and yet ſhe has never given the World ſuch Teſtimonies of it, as has *Rivella*, by her Writings: Therefore, once more, my deareſt Friend, as you have, by your own Confeſſion, been long of her intimate Acquaintance, oblige me with as many Particulars relating to her Life and Behaviour as you can poſſibly recollect. By this time, the two *Cavaliers* were near one of the Benches; upon which repoſing themſelves, Sir *Charles Lovemore*, who perceiv'd young *D'Aumont* was prepar'd with the utmoſt Attention to hearken to what he ſhould ſpeak, began his Diſcourſe in this manner.

THE

THE

HISTORY

OF

RIVELLA.

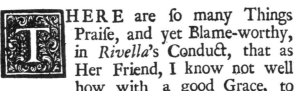

THERE are ſo many Things Praiſe, and yet Blame-worthy, in *Rivella*'s Conduct, that as Her Friend, I know not well how with a good Grace, to repeat, or as yours, to conceal, becauſe you ſeem to expect from me an Impartial Hiſtory. Her Vertues are her own, her Vices occaſion'd by her Misfortunes; and yet as I have often heard her ſay, *If ſhe had been a Man, ſhe had been without Fault:* But the Charter of that Sex being much more confin'd than ours, what is not a Crime in Men is ſcandalous and unpardonable in Woman, as ſhe her
ſelf

ſelf has very well obſerv'd in divers Places, throughout her own Writings.

HER Perſon is neither tall nor ſhort;
from her Youth ſhe was inclin'd to Fat;
whence I have often heard her Flatterers
liken her to the *Grecian Venus*. It is certain, conſidering that Diſadvantage, ſhe
has the moſt eaſy Air that one can have;
her Hair is of a pale Aſh-colour, fine, and
in a large Quantity. I have heard her
Friends lament the Diſaſter of her having
had the Small-pox in ſuch an injurious manner, being a beautiful Child before that Di-
ſtemper; but as that Diſeaſe has now left
her Face, ſhe has ſcarce any Pretence to it.
Few, who have only beheld her in Publick, could be brought to like her; whereas none that became acquainted with her,
could refrain from loving her. I have heard
ſeveral Wives and Miſtreſſes accuſe her of
Faſcination: They would neither truſt
their Husbands, Lovers, Sons, nor Bro-
thers with her Acquaintance upon Terms
of the greateſt Advantage. Speak to me
of her Eyes, interrupted the *Chevalier*,
you ſeem to have forgot that Index of the
Mind; Is there to be found in them, Store
of thoſe animating Fires with which Her
Writings are fill'd? Do Her Eyes love as
well as Her Pen? You reprove me very juſtly, anſwer'd the Baronet, *Rivella* would
have

have a good deal of Reafon to complain of
me, if I fhould filently pafs over the beft
Feature in her Face. In a Word, you
have your felf defcribed them : Nothing
can be more tender, ingenious and bril-
lant with a Mixture fo languifhing and
fweet, when Love is the Subject of the
Difcourfe, that without being fevere, we
may very well conclude, the fofter Paffions have their Predominancy in Her Soul.

H O W are Her Teeth and Lips, fpoke
the *Chevalier?* Forgive me, dear *Lovemore,* for breaking in fo often upon your
Difcourfe ; but Kiffing being the fweeteft
leading Pleafure, 'tis impoffible a Woman
can charm without a good Mouth. Yet,
anfwer'd *Lovemore,* I have feen very great
Beauties pleafe, as the common Witticifm
fpeaks, *in fpight of their Teeth :* I do not
find but Love in the general is well natur'd and civil, willing to compound for
fome Defects, fince he knows that 'tis
very difficult and rare to find true Symmetry and all Perfections in one Perfon :
Red Hair, Out - Mouth, thin and livid
Lips, black broken Teeth, courfe ugly
Hands, long Thumbs, ill form'd dirty
Nails, flat, or very large Breafts, fplay
Feet ; which together makes a frightful
Compofition, yet divided amongft feveral,
prove no Allay to the ftrongeft Paffions :

C But

But to do *Rivella* Juftice, till fhe grew fat, there was not I believe any Defect to be found in her Body : Her Lips admirably colour'd ; Her Teeth fmall and even, a Breath always fweet ; Her Complexion fair and frefh ; yet with all this you muft be us'd to her before fhe can be thought thoroughly agreeable. Her Hands and Arms have been publickly celebrated ; it is certain, that I never faw any fo well turned : Her Neck and Breafts have an eftablifh'd Reputation for Beauty and Colour : Her Feet fmall and pretty.   Thus I have run thro' whatever Cuftom fuffers to be vifible to us ; and upon my Word, *Chevalier,* I never faw any of *Rivella*'s hidden Charms.

PARDON me this once, faid *D'Aumont,* and I affure you, dear Sir *Charles,* I will not haftily interrupt you again, What Humour is fhe of ? Is her Manner Gay or Serious ? Has fhe Wit in her Converfation as well as Her Pen ? What do you call Wit, anfwer'd *Lovemore ·* If by that Word, you mean a Succeffion of fuch Things as can bear Repetition, even down to Pofterity ? How few are there of fuch Perfons, or rather none indeed, that can be always witty ? *Rivella* fpeaks Things pleafantly ; her Company is entertaining to the laft ; no Woman except one's Miftrefs wearies one fo little as her felf : Her Knowledge

ledge is univerſal; ſhe diſcourſes well, and agreeably upon all Subjects, bating a little Affectation, which nevertheleſs becomes her admirably well ; yet this thing is to be commended in her, that ſhe rarely ſpeaks of her own Writings, unleſs when ſhe wou'd expreſly ask the Judgment of her Friends, inſomuch that I was well pleas'd at the Character a certain Perſon gave her (who did not mean it much to Her Advantage) that one might diſcourſe Seven Years together with *Rivella*, and never find out from her ſelf, that ſhe was a *Wit*, or an *Author*.

I HAVE one Pardon more to ask you, cry'd the *Chevalier* (in a Manner that fully accus'd himſelf for Breach of Promiſe) Is ſhe genteel? She is eaſy, anſwer'd his Friend, which is as much as can be expected from the *en bonne Point :* Her Perſon is always nicely clean, and Her Garb faſhionable.

WHAT we ſay in reſpect of the fair Sex, I find goes for little, perſu'd the *Chevalier*, I'll change my Promiſe of Silence with your Leave, Sir *Charles*, into Conditions of interrupting you when ever I am more than ordinarily pleas'd with what you ſay, and therefore do now begin with telling you, that I find my ſelf reſolved to

C 2   be

be in Love with *Rivella*. I eafily forgive
Want of Beauty in her Face, to the
Charms you tell me are in her Perfon : I
hope there are no hideous Vices in her
Mind, to deform the fair Idea you have
given me of fine Hands and Arms, a
beautiful Neck and Breaft, pretty Feet,
and, I take it for granted, Limbs that make
up the Symmetry of the whole.

RIVELLA is certainly much indebted, continu'd *Lovemore*, to a Liberal Education, and thofe early Precepts of Vertue
taught her and practifed in her Father's
Houfe. There was then fuch a Foundation laid, that tho' Youth, Misfortunes, and
Love, for feveral Years have interrupted
fo fair a Building, yet fome Time fince,
fhe is returned with the greateft Application to repair that Lofs and Defect ; if not
with relation to this World (where Women have found it impoffible to be reinfta-
ted) yet of the next, which has merciful-
ly told us, *Mankind can commit no Crimes
but what upon Converfion may be forgiven.*

RIVELLA's natural Temper is haughty, impatient of Contradiction : She is
nicely tenacious of the Privilege of Her
own Sex, in Point of what Refpect ought
to be paid by ours to the Ladies ; and as fhe
underftands good Breeding to a Punctuali-
ty,

ty, tho' the Freedom of her Humour often difpenfes with *Forms*, fhe will not eafily forgive what Perfon foever fhall be wanting in that which Cuftom has made her Due : Her Soul is foft and tender to the Afflicted, her Tears wait upon their Misfortunes, and there is nothing fhe does not do to affwage them. You need but tell her a Perfon is in Mifery to engage her Concern, her Purfe, and her Intereft in their Behalf: I have often heard her fay, that fhe *was an utter Stranger to what is meant by Hatred and Revenge;* nor was fhe ever known to perfue hers upon any Perfon, tho' often injured, excepting Mr. *S——le,* whofe notorious Ingratitude and Breach of Friendfhip affected her too far, and made her think it the higheft Piece of Juftice to expofe him.

NOW I have done with her Perfon, I fear you will think me too particular in my Defcription of her Mind : But *Chevalier* there lies the intrinfick Value; 'tis that which either accomplifhes or deforms a Perfon. I will in few Words conclude her Character; fhe has lov'd Expence, even to being extravagant, which in a Woman of Fortune might more juftly have been term'd Generofity: She is Grateful, unalterable in thofe Principles of Loyalty, derived from her Family : A little too vainglorious

glorious of thofe Perfections which have been afcribed to her ; fhe does not however boaft of what Praife, or Favours, Perfons of Rank may have conferr'd upon her : She loves *Truth*, and has too often given her felf the Liberty to *fpeak*, as well as *write* it.

SHE was born in *Hampfhire*, in one of thofe Iflands, which formerly belong'd to *France*, where her Father was Governour ; afterwards he enjoy'd the fame Poft in other Places in *England.* He was the Second Son of an Ancient Family ; the better Part of the Eftate was ruin'd in the Civil War by adhering to the *Royal Family*, without ever being repair'd, or fcarce taken Notice of, at the Reftoration : The Governour was Brave, full of Honour, and a very fine Gentleman : He became a Scholar in the Midft of a Camp, having left the Univerfity at Sixteen Years of Age, to follow the Fortunes of K. *Charles* the Firft. His Temper had too much of the Stoick in it for the Good of his Family.   After a Life the beft Part fpent in Civil and foreign War, he began to love Eafe and Retirement, devoting himfelf to his Study, and the Charge of his little Poft, without ever following the Court : His great Vertue and Modefty render'd him unfit for folliciting fuch Perfons, by whom Preferment was there to be gain'd ; fo that his

De-

Deferts feem'd bury'd and forgotten. In his Solitude he wrote feveral Tracts for his own Amufement ; his *Latin Commentaries* of the *Civil Wars of England*, having pafs'd through *Europe*, may perhaps have reach'd your Notice, which is all that I fhall mention to you of his Writings, becaufe you are unacquainted with our *Englifh* State of Learning ; and yet upon recollection, fince the *Turkifh-Spy* has been tranflated into other Languages, I muft likewife tell you that our Governour was the Genuine Author of the firft Volume of that admir'd and fuccefsful Work. An Ingenious *Phyfician*, related to the Family by Marriage, had the Charge of looking over his Papers amongft which he found that Manufcript, which he eafily referved to his proper Ufe ; and both by his own Pen, and the affiftance of fome others, continu'd the Work until the Eighth Volume, without ever having the Juftice to Name the Author of the Firft.

BUT this is little relating to the Adventures of *Rivella*, who had the Misfortune to be Born with an indifferent Beauty, between two Sifters perfectly Handfom ; and yet, as I have often thought my felf, and as I have heard others fay, they had lefs Power over Mankind than had *Rivella*. *Maria* the eldeft, was unhappily
beftow'd

beftow'd in Marriage, (at her own Requeft, by her Father's fondnefs and af-
fent to his Daughter's Choice) on a Wretch
every way unworthy of Her, of her Fortune, her Birth, her Charms or Tendernefs.

MY Father's Eftate lay very near *Rivella*'s Father's Government. I was then
a Youth, who took a great deal of Delight
in going to the Caftle, where Three fuch
fair Perfons were inclofed.

THE eldeft was now upon her Marriage. *Cordelia* the youngeft fcarce yet
thought of. *Rivella* had juft reach'd the
Age of Twelve, when I beheld the wonderful Effects of Love upon the Heart of
young and innocent Perfons. I had ufed
to pleafe my felf in talking Romantick
Stories to her, and with furnifhing her
with Books of that Strain. The Fair *Maria* was fix Years elder, and above my
Hopes; I was a meer Lad, as yet unfafhion'd; I beheld her with Admiration,
as we do a glorious Sky ; it is not yet our
Hemifphere, nor do we think of fhining
there. *Rivella* was nearer to my Age
and Underftanding, and tho' four Years
younger than my felf, was the Wittieft
Girl in the World: I would have kifs'd
her, and embrac'd her a thoufand Times
over,

over, but had no Opportunity. Never
any young Ladies had fo fevere an Education: They had loft their Mother when
very young, and their Father, who had
paft many Years abroad, during the Ex-
ile of the *Royal Family* had brought
into *England* with him all the Jealoufy and Diftruft of the *Spaniard* and *Italian.* I have often heard *Rivella* regret her
having never gone to School, as lofing the
innocent Play and Diverfions of thofe of
her own Age. A fevere *Governante,* worfe
than any *Duenna,* forbid all Approaches
to the Appartment of the Fair; as young
as I was, I could only be admitted at
Dinner or Supper, when our Family vifited; but never alone: She was fond of
Scribling: Tho' in fo tender an Age, fhe
wrote Verfes, which confidering her Youth
were pardonable, fince they might very
well be read without Difguft; but there
was fomething furprizing in her Letters,
fo natural, fo fpirituous, fo fprightly, fo
well turned, that from the firft to the laft
I muft and ever will maintain, that all
her other Produ&ions however fuccefsful they have been, come fhort of her
Talent in writing Letters: I have had
Numbers of them; my Servant us'd to
wait on her as if to bring her Books to read,
in the Cover of which I had contrived always to fend her a Note, which fhe re-

D   turn'd

turn'd in the fame Manner. But this was perfect Fooling; I lov'd her, but fhe did not return my Paffion, yet without any affected Coynefs, or perfonating a Heroine of the many Romances fhe daily read. *Rivella* would let me know in the very beft Language, with a bewitching Air of Sincerity and Manners, that fhe was not really cruel, but infenfible; that I had hitherto fail'd of infpiring her with new Thoughts: Since her young Heart was not confcious of any Alteration in my Favour; but in return to that generous Concern I exprefs'd for her, fhe would inftruct it as much as poffible to be gratefull; 'till when my Letters, and the Pleafure of writing to me again, was a Diverfion more to her Tafte than any fhe met with befides; and therefore would not deny her felf the Satisfaction of hearing from, or of anfwering me, as often as fhe had an Opportunity.

BUT all my Hopes of touching her Heart were fuddenly blafted. To bring my felf back to what I was juft now telling you of the ftrange Effects of Love in youthful Hearts, I muft acquaint you that upon the Report of an Invafion from *Holland*, a Supply of Forces was fent to the Garrifon, amongft which was a *Subaltern* Officer, the moft beautiful Youth I remember

ber

ber to have ever feen, till I beheld the Chevalier *D'Aumont* ; Monfieur *D'Aumont* told
Sir *Charles*, with a Smile, his Compliment
fhould not procure him a Paufe in his relation, and therefore conjur'd him to proceed.

THIS Young Fellow, purfu'd *Lovemore*, had no other Pretences but thofe of
his Perfon, to qualify him for being my
Rival ; neither of himfelf did he dream of
becoming fuch ; he durft not prefume to
lift up his Eyes to the Favourite Daughter
of the *Governour* ; but alas ! hers defcend-
ed to fix themfelves on him : I have heard
her declare fince, that tho' fhe had read
fo much of Love, and that I had often
fpoke to her of it in my Letters, yet fhe
was utterly ignorant of what it was, till
fhe felt his fatal Power ; nay after fhe had
felt it, fhe fcarce guefs'd at her Difeafe, till
fhe found her Cure : Young *Lyfander*, for
fo was my Rival call'd, knew not how to
receive a good Fortune, which was become
fo obvious, that even her Father and all
the Company perceiv'd her Diftemper better than her felf : Her Eyes were continually fix'd upon this young Warrior, fhe
could neither eat nor fleep ; fhe became
Hedtick, and had all the Symptoms of a
dangerous Indifpofition. They caus'd her
to be let Blood, which joyn'd to her Ab-
ftinence from Food made her but the weak-

er,

er, whilft her Diftemper grew more ftrong.
The Gentleman who had newly married
her Sifter, was of Counfel with the Family how to fupprefs this growing Misfortune; he fpoke roundly to the *Youth,*
who had no Thoughts of improving the
Opportunity, and charg'd him not to give
in to the Follies of the young Girl; he told
him he would fhoot him thro' the Head
if he attempted any thing towards footh-
ing *Rivella's* Prepoffeffion, or rather Mad-
nefs. *Lyfander* who was paffionately in
Love elfewhere, eafily affured them he had
no Defigns upon that very young Lady,
and would decline all Opportunities of entertaining her; but as the *Governour's* hof-
pitable Table made moft Perfons welcom,
he forbore not to purfue his firft Invitation, and came often to Dinner where the
dear little Creature faw him conftantly,
and never removed her Eyes from his
Face : His Voice was very good ; the
Songs then in Vogue amorous, and fuch as
fuited her Temper of Mind ; fhe drank
the Poyfon both at her Ears and Eyes,
and never took Care to manage, or conceal her Paffion; poffibly what fhe has
fince told me in that Point was true, That
*She knew not what fhe did, as not having
Freewill, or the Benefit of Reflection ; nor
could fhe confider any Thing but* Lyfander,
tho' amidft a Croud.

THE

THE *Governour* was a wife Man, and forbore faying any Thing to the Girl which might acquaint her with her own Diftemper, much lefs caufe her to fufpect that himfelf and others were acquainted with it: He carefs'd her more than ufual, footh'd and lamented her Indifpofition, propofed Change of Air to her; fhe fell a weeping, and begg'd fhe might not go to be fick from under his Care, for that would certainly break her Heart: He thought gentle Methods were the beft, and therefore order'd her Sifters, and their Governefs, to do all they could to divert, but never to leave her alone with young *Lyfander.*

IN the mean Time, by the Intereft the *Governour* made at Court, he procured that Battalion to be recall'd, and another to be deputed in Place of what had given him fo much Uneafinefs. The Day before their Marching Orders came ; he propofed playing after Dinner for an Hour or Two at *Hazard* ; moft of the Gentlemen prefent were willing to entertain the *Governour.* *Lyfander* excufed himfelf, as having loft the laft Night, all his fmall Stock at *Back-Gammon* ; his little Miftrefs heard this with a vaft Concern; and as fhe afterwards told me, could have readily beftow'd

upon

upon him all fhe had of value in the World. Her Father, who beheld her in a deep *Reſvery*, with her Eyes fix'd intently upon *Lyſander*, call'd her to him, and giving her a Key where his Money was kept, order'd her to fetch him a certain Sum to Play with; fhe obey'd, but no fooner beheld the glittering Store, (without reflecting on what might be the Confequence, or indeed any Thing elfe but that her Dear *Lyſander* wanted Money) than fhe dipt her little Hand into an Hundred Pound Bag full of Guineas, and drew thence as much as it would hold : Upon her return fhe met him in the Gallery ; (feeing the Company ingag'd in Play he was ftolen off, poffibly with an intent to follow *Rivella*, and have a Moment to fpeak to her in without Witneffes ; for the Regards he gave her from his Eyes, when he durft encounter Hers, fpoke him wiling to be Grateful) . She bid him hold out his Hat and fay nothing, then throwing in the Spoil, fhe. briskly pafs'd on to the Company, brought her Father the Money he wanted ; return'd him the Key, and fet her felf down to overlook the Gamefters.

THIS Story I have had from her felf, by which Action fhe was fince convinc'd of the Greatnefs of her Prepoffeffion, being perfectly Juft by Nature, Principle, and
Edu-

Education, nothing but Love, and that in a high degree could have made her otherwife. The Awe fhe was in of her Father was fo great, that upon the higheft Emergency fhe would not, durft not have wrong'd him of a fingle Shilling. Whether the *Governour* never mifs'd thofe Guineas, as having always a great deal of Money by him for the Garrifon's Subfiftence; or that he was too wife to fpeak of a Thing that would have reflected upon his Daughter's Credit; *Rivella* was fo Happy as to hear no more of it?

MEAN time my Affair went on but Ill; She anfwer'd none of my Letters, nay forgot to read them; when I came to vifit her, fhe fhew'd me a Pocket full which fhe had never open'd; this vex'd me exceffively, and the more, when fhe fuffer'd me with extream Indifference to take them again: I would have known the Reafon of this Alteration; fhe cou'd not account for it, fo that I left her with outward Rage, but inwardly my Heart was more her Slave than before: Whether it be the vile and fordid Nature of the God of Love to make us moftly doat upon ungenerous Ufage, and at other Times to caufe us to return with equal Ingratitude the Kindnefs we meet from others.

THE

THE next Day I ingag'd my Sifter to make a Vifit to the Caftle; we took the Cool of the Morning, fhe was intimate with *Maria* before her Marriage, and fuffer'd her felf to be perfuaded to let me wait on her; we were drinking Chocolate at the *Governour*'s Toilet, where *Rivella* and her Sifters attended; when the Drums beat a loud Alarm, we were prefently told we fhould fee a very fine Sight, the New Forces march in, and the Old ones out, if they can properly be call'd fo, that had not been there above Eighteen Days; at the News my Miftrefs, who had heard nothing of it before, began to turn pale as Death; fhe ran to her *Papa*, and falling upon his Bofom. wept and fob'd with fuch Vehemence, that he apprehended fhe was falling into Hyfterick Fits. Her Father fent for their Governefs to carry her to her Bed-Chamber, but fhe hung upon him in fuch a Manner, that without doing her a great deal of Violence, they could not remove her thence. I ran to her Affiftance with a Wonder great as my Concern, but fhe more particularly reje&ed my Touches, and all that I could fay for her Confolation.

MEAN time the Commander in chief, followed by moft of his Officers (amongft
which

which the lovely *Lyſander* appeared with
a languiſhing Air full of Diſappointment,
which yet added to his Beauty) came up
to the *Governour*, and told him his Men
were all under Arms and ready to march
forth, whenever he pleas'd to give the Word
of Command. At the ſame Time entred
another Gentleman equally attended, whom
the *Governour* ſtept forth to welcome : He
aſſured him the Forces that obey'd him were
all drawn up upon the *Counterſcarp*, and
thought themſelves happy, more particularly himſelf, to have the good Fortune of
being quarter'd where a Perſon of ſuch
Honour and Humanity was *Governour.*

TO conclude, poor *Rivella* fell from
one Fainting into another without the leaſt
immodeſt Expreſſion, Glance or Diſcovery
of what had occaſion'd her Fright : She
was remov'd, and we had the Satisfaction
of ſeeing the military Change of Forces,
and poor *Lyſander* depart without ever beholding his Miſtreſs more.

METHINKS, Monſieur *le Chevalier*,
continu'd *Lovemore*, I am too fond of
ſuch Particularities as made up the firſt
Scene of my Unhappineſs : I call it ſo,
when I remember how dangerouſly ill that
poor Girl grew, and how my Soul ſickned
at her Danger. What avails it to renew
paſt Pains or Pleaſures ? *Rivella* recover'd,

E   and

and begg'd fhe might be remov'd for fome
Time to any other Place, which would
perhaps better agree with her than the
Air wherein I breath'd. In a Word, without ever having been belov'd, my Importunities now caufed me to be for fome
Time even hated by Her.

THE Lady had a younger Brother who
was penfion'd at a *Hugenot* Minifter's
Houfe on the other Side of the Sea and
Country, about eighteen Miles farther
from *London*, a Solitude rude and barbarous : *Rivella* begg'd to be fent thither,
that fhe might improve Time, and learn
French : She would not have any Servant
with her for fear of talking *Englifh* ; nor
would fhe ever fpeak to her Brother in
that Language : What fhall I fay, fo incredible was her Application, tho' fhe had
a Relapfe of her former Diftemper, that
in three Months Time fhe was inftructed
fo far as to read, fpeak and write *French*
with a Perfection truly wonderful ; infomuch that when her Father came to take
her home, finding the Air had very much
impair'd her Health, the good *Minifter*,
her Mafter, who was a learned and modeft Perfon, begg'd the *Governour* to leave
Mademoifelle with him, and he would engage in twelve Months, counting from the
Time fhe firft came, to make her Miftrefs
of

of thofe Four Languages of which he was Mafter, *viz. Latin, French, Spanifh* and *Italian.*

THE next Day after her Return, I came to pay my Duty to her, and welcome her back; fhe was lefs averfe, but not more tender: The Refpeẟ I had for her, made me forbear to reproach her with the Paffion fhe had fhewn for *Lyfander*; my Sifters tattling with her Sifters, had gain'd the Secret, and very little to my Eafe imparted the Confidence to me: We began an Habit of Friendfhip on her Side, tho' on mine it never ceafed to be Love: And I may very truly tell you, *Chevalier*, that fuch was the Effeẟ of that early Difappointment, as has for ever hinder'd me from knowing the true Pleafures of Paffion, becaufe I have never felt a Concern for any other Woman, comparable to what I felt for *Rivella.*

AFTER this fhort Abfence, I found my felf condemn'd to a more lafting one: My Father defign'd to fend me abroad with an Intent that I might fpend fome Years in my Travel. At the fame Time *Rivella* had the Promife of the next Vacancy for Maid of Honour to the Queen: I congratulated her good Fortune, acquainting her with my ill Fortune in being condemn'd to feparate my felf from her.

Tho'

Tho' I was never happy in her Love, yet I was jealous of lofing her Friendſhip, a-midſt the Diverſions of a Court, and the Dangers of Abſence : Who does not know the Fervency of our early Paſſions? I begg'd to ſecure her to me, by a Marriage unknown to our Parents, but I could not prevail with her; ſhe fear'd to diſpleaſe her Father, and I durſt not ask the Conſent of mine : I had flatter'd my ſelf that it was much eaſier to gain their Pardon than procure their Approbation, becauſe we were both ſo young : But *Rivella* was immoveable, notwithſtanding all I could ſay to her. How often for her Sake, have I lamented her Diſdain, and little Foreſight, for refuſing to marry me, which had ſhe agreed to, all thoſe Misfortunes that have ſince attended her, in Point of Honour and the World's Opinion, had probably been prevented, which ſhews there is ſomething in what the vulgar conceive, of *its being once in our Lives in our own Power to make or aſſiſt our Fortune.*

I departed for *Italy*; the *Abdication* immediately came on, the Queen was gone to *France*, and *Rivella* thereby diſappointed of going to Court. Her Father was what he term'd himſelf, truly loyal; he laid down his Command and retired with his Family, to a private Life, and a ſmall
Country-

Country-Houſe, where the Misfortunes of his Royal Maſter ſunk ſo deep into his Thoughts, that he dy'd ſoon after, in mortal Apprehenſion of what would befall his unhappy Country.

H E R E begins *Rivella's* real 'Misfortunes; it would be well for her, that I could ſay here ſhe dy'd with Honour, as did her Father : I muſt refer you to her own Story, under the Name of *Delia*, in the *Atalantis*, for the next Four miſerable Years of her Life : My ſelf did not return from Travel in three Years : My Father was alſo dead, and left me a fair Eſtate without any Incumbrance; my Siſter having been married ſome time before. I heard this News when I was upon my return, reſolving to offer *Rivella* my whole Fortune, as ſhe was already poſſeſſed of my Heart : Abſence, nor the Converſation of other Women had not ſupplanted her in my Eſteem. When I thought of her Genius and ſprightly Wit, Compariſon indear'd her to me the more ; but I was extreamly griev'd and diſappointed, when I learn'd her ruin. I will not tell you how much I was touch'd with it. I ſought her out with Obſtinacy ; but could not tell where to meet her : I was almoſt a Year in the Search, and then gave it over ; till one Night I happen'd to call in at Madam *Mazarin's*, where I ſaw *Rivella* introduc'd **by**

by *Hilaria*, a Royal Miftrefs of one of our
preceding Kings. I fhook my Head in beholding her in fuch Company. I was fo
much improv'd by Travelling, that, as fhe
told me afterwards, She did not know me
'till I had fpoken to her : I could not fay
the fame thing of her. She was much impair'd ; her fprightly Air, in which lay her
greateft Charm, was turn'd into a languifhing Melancholy ; the white of her Skin,
degenerated into a yellowifh Hue, occafion'd by her Misfortunes, and three Years
Solitude ; tho' quickly after fhe recover'd
both her Air and her Complexion.

HOW confus'd and abafh'd fhe was
at my addreffing to her ! The Freedom of
the Place gave me Opportunity to fay what
I pleas'd to her : She was not one of the
Gamefters, but begg'd me I would be
pleas'd to retire, and fpare her the Shame of
an *Eclaircifment* in a Place no way proper
for fuch an Affair. I obey'd, and accepted
the Offer fhe made me of fupping with her
at *Hilaria*'s Houfe, where at prefent fhe
was lodg'd ; that Lady having feldom the
Power of returning home from Play before
Morning, unlefs upon a very ill Run, when
fhe chanced to lofe her Money fooner than
ordinary.

NE-

NEVER was there a more defolate
Meeting than between my felf and *Rivella*:
She told me all her Misfortunes with an
Air fo perfectly ingenuous, that, if fome
Part of the World who were not acquainted
with her Vertue, ridicul'd her Marriage,
and the Villany of her Kinfman; I, who
knew her Sincerity, could not help believing
all fhe faid. My Tears were Witneffes of
my Grief; it was not in my Power to fay
any thing to leffen her's: I therefore left
her abruptly, without being able to eat or
drink any thing with her for that Night.

TIME, which allays all our Paffions,
leffen'd the Sorrow I felt for *Rivella*'s Ruin,
and even made me an Advocate to affwage
hers: The Diverfions of the Houfe fhe
was in were dangerous Reftoratives: Her
Wit, and Gaity of Temper return'd, but
not her Innocence.

HILARIA had met with *Rivella* in
her folitary Manfion, vifiting a Lady who
liv'd next Door to the poor Reclufe. She
was the only Perfon that in three Years *Rivella* had convers'd with, and that but
fince her Husband was gone into the Country: Her Story was quickly known. *Hilaria*, paffionately fond of new Faces, of
which Sex foever, us'd a thoufand Arguments

ments to diffuade her from wearing away her Bloom in Grief and Solitude. She read her a learned Lecture upon the Ill-nature of the World, that wou'd never reftore a Woman's Reputation, how innocent foever fhe really were, if Appearances prov'd to be againft her; therefore fhe gave her Advice, which fhe did not difdain to Practife; the *Englifh* of which was, *To make her feif as happy as fhe could without valuing or regretting thofe, by whom it was impoffible to be valu'd.*

THE Lady, at whofe Houfe *Rivella* firft became acquainted with *Hilaria*, perceiv'd her Indifcretion in bringing them together. The Love of Novelty, as ufual, fo far prevail'd, that herfelf was immediately difcarded, and *Rivella* perfwaded to take up her Refidence near *Hilaria's* ; which made her fo inveterate an Enemy to *Rivella*, that the firft great Blow ftruck againft her Reputation, proceeded from that Woman's malicious Tongue : She was not contented to tell all Perfons, who began to know and efteem *Rivella*, that her Marriage was a Cheat, but even fent Letters by the Penny-Poft to make *Hilaria* jealous of *Rivella's* Youth, in refpect of him who at that time happen'd to be her Favourite.

R I-

RIVELLA has often told me, That from *Hilaria* she receiv'd the first ill Impreſſions of Count *Fortunatus,* touching his Ingratitude, Immorality, and Avarice; being her ſelf an Eye-Witneſs when he deny'd *Hilaria* (who had given him Thouſands) the common Civility of lending her Twenty Guineas at *Baſſet*; which, together with betraying his Maſter, and raiſing himſelf by his Siſter's Diſhonour, ſhe had always eſteem'd a juſt and flaming Subject for Satire.

RIVELLA had now reign'd ſix Months in *Hilaria*'s Favour, an Age to one of her inconſtant Temper; when that Lady found out a new Face to whom the old muſt give Place, and ſuch a one, of whom ſhe could not juſtly have any Jealouſie in point of Youth or Agreeableneſs; the Perſon I ſpeak of, was a Kitchin-maid married to her Maſter, who had been refug'd with King *James* in *France.* He dy'd, and left her what he had, which was quickly ſquander'd at Play; but ſhe gain'd Experience enough by it to make Gaming her Livelihood, and return'd into *England* with the monſtrous Affectation of calling her ſelf a *French-woman*; her Dialect being thence-forward nothing but a ſort of broken *Engliſh*: This paſſed upon the Town,

F be-

becaufe her Original was fo obfcure, that they were unacquainted with it. She generally ply'd at Madam *Mazarin*'s *Baſſet*-Table, and was alfo of ufe to her in Affairs of Pleafure ; but whether that Lady grew weary of her Impertinence, and ftrange ridiculous Airs, or that fhe thought *Hilaria* might prove a better Bubble ; fhe profited of the Advances that were made her, and accepted of an Invitation to come and take up her Lodging at *Hilaria*'s Houfe, where in a few Months fhe repay'd the Civility that had been fhewn her, by clapping up a clandeftine Match between her Patronefs's eldeft Son, a Perfon tho' of weak Intellects, yet of great Confideration, and a young Lady of little or no Fortune.

B U T to return to *Rivella*. *Hilaria* was tir'd, and refolv'd to take the firft Opportunity to be rude to her : She knew her Spirit would not eafily forgive any Point of Incivility or Difrefpect.

H I L A R I A was *Querilous, Fierce, Loquacious,* exceffively fond, or infamoufly rude: When fhe was difgufted with any Perfon, fhe never fail'd to reproach them with all the Bitternefs and Wit fhe was Miftrefs of, with fuch Malice and Ill-nature, that fhe was hated not only by all the World, but by her own Children and Fa-

Family; not one of her Servants, but what would have laugh'd to fee her lie dead amongſt them, how affecting foever fuch Objects are in any other Cafe. The Extreams of *Prodigality*, and *Covetoufnefs*; of *Love* and *Hatred*; of *Dotage* and *Averfion*, were joyn'd together in *Hilaria's* Soul.

RIVELLA may well call it her fecond great Misfortune to have been acquainted with that Lady, who, to excufe her own Inconſtancy, always blaſted the Character of thofe whom ſhe was grown weary of, as if by *Slander* and *Scandal*, ſhe could take the Odium from her felf, and fix it upon others.

SOME few Days before *Hilaria* was refolved to part with *Rivella*, to make Room for the Perfon who was to fucceed her; ſhe pretended a more than ordinary Paffion, caufed her to quit her Lodgings to come and take part of her own Bed. *Rivella* attributed this *Feint* of Kindnefs to the Lady's Fears, left ſhe ſhould fee the Man *Hilaria* was in Love with, at more Eafe in her own Houfe than when ſhe was in hers; tho' that beloved Perfon had always a Hatred and Diſtruſt of *Rivella*. He kept a Miſtrefs in the next Street, in as much Grandeur as his Lady : He fear'd
ſhe

she would come to the Knowledge of it by this new and young Favourite, whose Birth and Temper put her above the Hopes of bringing her into his Interest, as he took care all others should be that approached *Hilaria.* He resolved, how dishonourable soever the Procedure were, to ruin *Rivella,* for fear she should ruin him ; and therefore told his Lady she had made Advances to him, which for her Ladyship's sake he had rejected ; this agreed with the unknown Intelligence that had been sent by the Penny-Post ; but because she was not yet provided with any Lady that would be her Favourite in *Rivella's* Place ; she took no notice of her Fears, but politickly chose to give her a great and lovely Amusement ; it was with one of her own Sons, whom she caress'd more than usual to draw him oftner to her House, leaving them alone together upon such plausible Pretences, as seem'd the Effect of Accident not Design : What might have proceeded from so dangerous a Temptation, I dare not presume to determine, because *Hilaria* and *Rivella's* Friendship immediately broke off upon the Assurance the former had receiv'd from the broken *French-woman,* that she would come and supply her Place.

THE last Day she was at *Hilaria's* House, just as they sat down to Dinner,
Ri-

Rivella was told that her Sifter *Maria*'s Husband was fallen into great Diftrefs, which fo fenfibly affected her, that fhe could eat nothing; fhe fent Word to a Friend, who could give her an Account of the whole Matter, that fhe would wait upon her at Six a Clock at Night, refolving not to lofe that Poft, if it were true that her Sifter was in Misfortune, without fending her fome Relief. After Dinner feveral Ladies came in to Cards; *Hilaria* ask'd *Rivella* to play; fhe begg'd Her Ladyfhip's Excufe, becaufe fhe had Bufinefs at Six a Clock; they perfuaded her to play for Two Hours, which accordingly fhe did, and then had a Coach fent for and return'd not till Eight: She had been inform'd abroad that Matters were very well compos'd touching her Sifter's Affairs, which extreamly lightned her Heart; fhe came back in a very good Humour, and very hungry, which fhe told *Hilaria*, who, with Leave of the firft Dutchefs in *England* that was then at Play, order'd Supper to be immediately got ready, for that her dear *Rivella* had eat nothing all Day: As foon as they were fet to Table, *Rivella* repeated thofe Words again, that fhe was very hungry; *Hilaria* told her, fhe was glad of it, *There were fome Things which got one a good Stomach*: *Rivella* ask'd her Ladyfhip what thofe things were?

Hilaria

Hilaria anſwer'd, ' Don't you know what?
' That which you have been doing with
my ——— [and named her own Son,]
' Nay, don't bluſh *Rivella*; 'twas doubt-
' leſs an Appointment, I ſaw him to Day
' kiſs you as he lead you thro' the dark
' Drawing-Room down to Dinner. Your
' Ladyſhip may have ſeen him attempt it,
' anſwer'd *Rivella*, [perfectly frighted
with her Words,] ' and ſeen me refuſe the
' Honour: But why [reply'd *Hilaria*] did
' you go out in a Hackney-Coach, with-
' out a Servant? Becauſe [ſays *Rivella*]
' my Viſit lay a great Way off, too far
' for your Ladyſhip's Chairmen to go: It
' rain'd, and does ſtill rain extreamly; I
' was tender of your Ladyſhip's Horſes
' this cold wet Night; both the Footmen
' were gone on Errands; I ask'd below
' for one of them, I was too well Man-
' ner'd to take the *Black*, and leave none
' to attend your Ladyſhip; eſpecially when
' my Lady Dutcheſs was here: Beſides,
' your own Porter paid the Coachman,
' which was the ſame I carried out with
' me; he was forc'd to wait ſome Time at
' the Gate, till a Guinea could be chang'd,
' becauſe I had no Silver; I beg all this
' good Company to judge, whether any
' Woman would be ſo indiſcreet, knowing
' very well, as I do, that I have one Friend
' in this Houſe, that would not fail exa-
                                    ' mining

' amining the Coachman where he had
' carried me, if it were but in hopes of
' doing me a Prejudice with the World
' and your Ladyſhip.'

THE Truth is, *Hilaria* was always
ſuperſtitious at Play; ſhe won whilſt *Rivella* was there, and would not have her
remov'd from the Place ſhe was in, thinking ſhe brought her good Luck: After ſhe
was gone, her Luck turn'd; ſo that before
Rivella came back, *Hilaria* had loſt above
two hundred Guineas, which put her into a Humour to expoſe *Rivella* in the Manner you have heard; who briskly roſe up
from Table without eating any Thing,
begging her Ladyſhip's Leave to retire,
whom ſhe knew to be ſo great a Miſtreſs
of Senſe, as well as of good Manners, that
ſhe would never have affronted any Perſon at her own Table, but one whom ſhe
held unworthy of the Honour of ſitting
there.

NEXT Morning ſhe wrote a Note to
Hilaria's Son, to deſire the Favour of
ſeeing him; he accordingly obey'd: *Rivella* deſir'd him to acquaint my Lady
where he was laſt Night, from Six till
Eight; he told her at the Play in the
ſide Box with the Duke of---- whom he
would bring to juſtify what he ſaid: I
chanc'd

chanc'd to come in to drink Tea with the
Ladies; *Rivella* told me her Diſtreſs; I
was mov'd at it, and the more, becauſe
I had been my ſelf at the Play, and ſaw
the Perſon for whom ſhe was accus'd, ſet
the Play out: In a Word *Rivella* waited
till *Hilaria* was viſible, and then went
to take her Leave of her with ſuch an Air
of Reſentment, Innocence, yet good Manners, as quite confounded the haughty *Hilaria.*

FROM that Day forwards ſhe never
ſaw her more; too happy indeed if ſhe
had never ſeen her: All the World was
fond of *Rivella*, and enquiring for her of
Hilaria ſhe could make no other Excuſe
for her own abominable Temper, and de-
teſtable Inconſtancy, but that ſhe was run
away with —— her Son, and probably
would not have the Aſſurance ever to
appear at her Houſe again.

BUT I who knew *Rivella*'s Innocency, beg'd ſhe wou'd retire to my Seat in
the Country, where ſhe might be ſure to
command with the ſame Power as if it
were her own, as in effect it muſt be,
ſince my ſelf was ſo devoted to her Service:
I made her this Offer becauſe it could no
longer do her an Injury in the Opinion of
the World which was ſufficiently preju-
dic'd againſt her already; ſhe excus'd her
ſelf,

felf, upon telling me fhe muft firft be in
Love with a Man before fhe thought fit
to refide with him; which was not my
Cafe, tho' fhe had never fail'd in Refpect,
Efteem and Friendfhip for me. She told
me her Love of Solitude was improved by
her Difguft of the World; and fince it was
impoffible for her to be publick with Reputation, fhe was refolv'd to remain in it
conceal'd : She was forry that the War hinder'd her to go to *France*, where fhe had
a very great Inclination to pafs her Days;
but fince that could not be help'd, fhe faid
her Defign was to wafte moft of her
Time in *England* in Places where fhe was
unknown. To be fhort, fhe fpent Two
Years in this Amufement; in all that Time
never making her felf acquainted at any
Place where fhe liv'd. 'Twas in this Solitude, that fhe compos'd her firft Tragedy,
which was much more famous for the Language, Fire and Tendernefs than the Conduct. Mrs. *Barry* diftinguifh'd her felf as
much as in any Part that ever fhe play'd.
I have fince often heard *Rivella* laugh and
wonder that a Man of Mr. *Betterton*'s
grave Senfe and Judgment fhould think
well enough of the Productions of a Woman of Eighteen, to bring it upon the
Stage in fo handfom a Manner as he did,
when her felf could hardly now bear the
reading of it.

G   B E

BEHOLD another wrong Step towards ruining *Rivella's* Character with the World; the Incenfe that was daily offer'd her upon this Occafion from the Men of Vogue and Wit: Her Appartment was daily crouded with them. There is a Copy of Verfes printed before her *Play*, faid to be writ by a great Hand, which they agreed to make their common Topick when they would addrefs to her. have heard them fo often recited, that I ftill remember them, which are thus in *Englifh*. If you don't thorougly underftand it, I'll give you the Words in *French*.

What! all our Sex in one fad Hour un-
                                    (done?

Loft are our Arts, our Learning, our Renown,

Since Nature's Tide of Wit came roulling
                                    (down:

Keen were your Eyes we knew, and fure
                                    (their Darts;

Fire to our Soul they fend, and Paffion to
                                    (our Hearts!

Needlefs was an Addition to fuch Arms,

When all Mankind were Vaffals to your
                                    (Charms:

                                        That

That Hand but *seen, gives Wonder and De-
(fire,*

*Snow to the Sight, but with its Touches
(Fire!*

Who *sees thy* Yielding Queen, *and would
(not be*

On *any Terms the bleft, the happy He;*

Entranc'd we fancy all his Extafie.

Quote Ovid *now no more ye amorous
(Swains,*

Delia *than* Ovid *has more moving Strains.*

Nature in Her alone exceeds all Art;

*And Nature fure does neareft touch the
(Heart.*

Oh *! might I call the bright Difcoverer mine,*

The whole. fair Sex unenvy'd I'd refign;

Give all my happy *Hours to* Delia's
(Charms,

She who by writing thus our Wifhes warms,

*What Worlds of Love muft circle in her
(Arms?*

I had ftill fo much Concern for *Rivella,*
that I pitied her Conduct, which I faw

muft

muft infallibly center in her Ruin: There was no Language approached her Ear but Flattery and Perfuafion to Delight and Love. The Cafuifts told her a Woman of her Wit had the Privilege of the other Sex, fince all Things were pardonable to a Lady *who could fo well give Laws to others, yet was not obliged to keep them her felf.* Her Vanity was now at the Height, fo was her Gaiety and good Humour, efpecially at Meat; fhe underftood good Living, and indulged her felf in it: *Rivella* never drank but at Meals, but then it was no way loft upon her, for her Wit was never fo fparkling as when fhe was pleas'd with her Wine. I could not keep away from her Houfe, yet was ftark mad to fee her delighted with every Fop, who flatter'd her Vanity: I us'd to take the Privilege of long Acquaintance and Efteem to correct her ill Taft, and the wrong Turn fhe gave her Judgment in admitting Adulation from fuch Wretches as many of them were; tho' indeed feveral Perfons of very good Senfe allow'd *Rivella's* Merit, and afforded her the Honour of their Converfation and Efteem: She look'd upon all I faid with an evil Eye; believing there was ftill Jealoufy at the Bottom. She did not think fit to correct a Conduct which fhe call'd very innocent, for me whofe Paffion fhe had never valu'd: I ftill preach'd,
and

and fhe ftill went on in her own Way,
without any Regard to my Doctrine, till
Experience gave her enough of her Indifcretion.

A certain Gentleman, who was a very
great Scholar and Mafter of abundance of
Senfe and Judgment, at her own Requeft,
brought to her Acquaintance one Sir *Peter
Vainlove*, intending to do her Service as
to her Defign of writing for the Theater,
that Perfon having then Intereft enough
to introduce upon one Stage whatever
Pieces he pleas'd : This Knight had a very good Face, but his Body was grown fat:
He was naturally fhort, and his Legs being
what they call fomewhat bandy, he was
advis'd to wear his Cloaths very long, to
help conceal that Defect; infomuch that
his Drefs made him look fhorter than he
was: He was following a handfom Lady
in the *Mall*, after a World of Courtfhip,
and begging her in vain to let him know
where fhe liv'd; feeing fhe was prepared
to leave the *Park* he renew'd his Efforts,
offering to go down upon his Knees to
her, to have her grant his Requeft; the
Lady turn'd gravely upon him, and told
him fhe thought, *he had been upon his
Knees all this Time :* The Knight confcious of his duck Legs and long Coat, retired in the greateft Confufion, notwithftanding his natural and acquired Affurance.

rance. Sir *Peter* was fuppofed to be towards Fifty when he became acquainted with *Rivella*, and his Conftitution broken by thofe Exceffes, of which in his Youth he had been guilty: He was Married young to a Lady of Worth and Honour, who brought him a very large Joynture; never any Woman better deferved the Charaƈter of a good Wife, being univerfally obliging to all her Husband's Humours; the great Love fhe had for him, together with her own Sweetnefs of Temper, made him infinitely eafy at Home; but he was deteftably vain, and lov'd to be thought in the Favour of the Fair, which was indeed his only Fault, for he had a great deal of Wit and good Nature; but fure no Youth of Twenty had fo vaft a *Foible* for being admired. He wrote very pretty wellturned *Billet-deuxs*; he was not at all fparing of his Letters when he met a Woman that had any Knack that Way: *Rivella* was much to his Tafte, fo that prefently there grew the greateft Intimacy in the World between them; but becaufe he found fhe was a Woman of Fire, more than perhaps he could anfwer, he was refolved to deftroy any Hopes fhe might have of a nearer Correfpondence than would conveniently fuit with his prefent Circumftances, by telling her his Heart

was

was already prepoſſeſs'd. This ſerved him
to a double Purpoſe, *Firſt*, To let her
know that he was reciprocally admired:
And *Secondly*, That no great things were
to be expeſted from a Perſon who was engaged, or rather devoted to another. He
made *Rivella* an entire Confident of his A-
mour, naming fine Mrs. *Settee*, then of the
City, at the Head of her Six tall Daughters,
not half ſo beautiful as their Mother: This
Affair had ſubſiſted Ten Years, according
to the Knight's own Account. The Lady
had begun it her ſelf (falling in Love with
him at the *Temple-Revels*) by Letters of
Admiration to him; after ſome Time, cor-
reſponding by amorous high-flown *Billets*,
ſhe granted a Meeting, but was three
Years before ſhe would let him know who
ſhe was, tho' there were moſt Liberties
but that of the Face allow'd. Afterwards
they met without any of that Reſerve:
It coſt the Knight according to his own
Report three Hundred Pounds a Year (beſides two Thouſand Pounds worth of Jew-
els preſented at Times) to ſee her but once
a Week, and give her a Supper: He ma-
naged this Matter ſo much to his own vain
falſe Reputation, that it was become a
Proverb amongſt his Friends, *Oh 'tis* Fri-
day *Night, you muſt not expeſt to ſee
Sir* Peter! He put a Relation of his own
into a Houſe, and maintain'd her there,
only

only for the Conveniency of meeting his
Miſtreſs. This Creature in ſome Time
proving very Mercenary, and the Knight
unwilling to be impos'd upon, ſhe dogg'd
the Lady home, and found out who ſhe
was; when once ſhe had got the Secret,
ſhe made Sir *Peter* pay what Price ſhe
pleas'd for her keeping it; not that his
Vanity was at all difpleas'd at the Town's
knowing his good Fortune, for he privately boaſted himſelf of it to his Friends,
but this Baggage threatned to ſend the
Husband and his own Lady News of their
Amour.

BEHOLD what a fine Perfon *Rivel-
la* choſe to fool away her Reputation with:
I am ſatisfy'd that ſhe was provoked at
the Confidence he put in her, and thought
her ſelf *piqued* in Honour and Charms to
take him from his real Miſtreſs: She was
continually bringing in the Lady's Age,
in Excufe of which the Knight often ſaid,
*Settee was one of thoſe laſting Beauties
that would have Lovers at Fourſcore*; he
often admir'd the Delicacy of her Taſte,
upon which *Rivella* was ready to burſt with
Spleen, becauſe ſhe would not permit her
Husband any Favours after ſhe was once
engaged with his *Worſhip*, her Conduct
and nice Reaſoning forcing the *good plain
Man* to be contented with ſeparate Beds.

Sir

Sir *Peter* was however exactly scrupulous
in doing Justice to the Lady's Honour ;
protesting that himself had never had the
Last Favour, tho' she Lov'd him to Di-
straction, for fear of Consequences; yet
she never scrupled to oblige him so far,
as to undress and go even into the naked
Bed with him once every Week, where
they found a way to please themselves as
well as they could.

RIVELLA was wild at being always
entertain'd with another Woman's Charms.
Vainlove used to show her Mrs. *Settee's*
Letters, which were generally as long as
a Taylor's Bill, stuff'd with the *faux Bril-
lant*; which yet fed the Knight's Vanity,
and almost Intoxicated his Brain. He
had found an agreeable Way of entertaining himself near *Rivella*, by talking incessantly of his Mistress; he did
not pass a Day without visiting and
showing her some of her *Billet-deuxs*.
Mean time he was so assiduous near *Rivella*, that Mrs. *Settee* took the Alarm.
He always sat behind her in the Box at
the Play, led her to her Chair, walk'd
with her in the *Park*, introduced her to
his Lady's Acquaintance, and omitted no
sort of Opportunity to be ever in her
Company. *Rivella* put on all her Arts to
ingage him effectually, tho' she would

never

never hear that fhe had any fuch Defign;
but what elfe could fhe mean by a Song
which I am going to repeat to you, made
upon the Knight's dropping a Letter in her
Chamber, writ by his darling Miftrefs,
wherein fhe complain'd of his Paffion for
Rivella? It began thus; *It is in vain you
tell me that I am worfhip'd and ador'd when
you do things fo contrary to it*; *Rivella* immediately fent it back to him enclofed with
thefe Verfes,

I.

Ah dangerous Swain, tell, tell me no more

Of the bleft Nymph you worfhip and adore;

When thy fill'd Eyes are fparkling at her Name

I raving wifh that mine had caus'd the Flame.

II.

If by your Fire for her, you can impart

Diffufive heat to warm another's Heart;

Ah dang'rous Swain! what wou'd the ruin be,

Shou'd you but once perfuade you burn for me?

THO' poffibly this might be only one
of the thoughtlefs Sallies of *Rivella's* Wit
and Fire, yet it was of the laft Confequence to her Reputation: The Knight
was perfectly drunk with *Vanity* and *Joy*,
upon

upon receiving fuch agreeable Proofs of his
Merit: He caufed the Words to be fet to
Notes, and then fung them himfelf in all
Companies where he came: His Flatterers, who were numerous, and did not
now want to learn his weak Side, gave
him the Title of *the dangerous Swain,*
which he prided himfelf in; till his Miftrefs grew down right uneafy, and would
have him vifit *Rivella* no longer. He ca-
pitulated, as Reafon good, and would be
paid his Price for breaking fo tender a
Friendfhip, and what fo agreeably flatter'd his Vanity, which in fhort was, as
the fcandalous Chronicle fpeaks, that his
Miftrefs fhould go to Bed to him without
Referve: Either the Weaknefs of his Conftitution, or the Greatnefs of his Paffion,
was prejudicial to his Health: He grew
proud of the Diforder, and went into a
publick Courfe of Phyfick, as if it were
a worfe Matter; finding it extreamly for
his Credit, that the Town fhould believe
fo well of him (for upon Report of a fair
young Lady whom he brought to tread
the Stage, that he had pafs'd three Days
and Nights fucceffively in Bed with her
without any Confequence, he was thought
rather dangerous to a Woman's Reputation
than her Vertue) he would fmile and never difabufe his Friends, when they ral-
lied him upon his Diforder: For fome Time
poor *Rivella*'s Character fuffer'd as the

Perfon

Perſon that had done him this Injury,
till ſeeing him equally aſſiduous and fond
of her in all publick Places, join'd to what
the *Operator* diſcover'd of his pretended
Diſeaſe; the World found out the Cheat,
deteſting his Vanity and *Rivella*'s Folly;
that cou'd ſuffer the Converſation of a
Wretch ſo inſignificant to her Pleaſures,
and yet ſo dangerous to her Reputation.

THIS ſhort liv'd-report did not do *Rivella* any great Prejudice, amongſt the
Crowd of thoſe who follow'd and flatter'd
her with pretended Adoration: She would
tell me that her Heart was ſtill untouch-
ed, bating a little Concern from her Pride
to move old *Vainlove*'s, who ſo obſtinately
defended it for another : 'Tis true, ſhe often
hazarded Appearances by indulging her
natural Vanity, and ſtill continued to do
ſo, tho' perhaps with more Innocency
than Diſcretion; till the Perſon came, who
indeed fix'd her Heart : I am going to
ſhew you a Gentleman of undoubted Merit, accompliſh'd both from without and
within : His Face was beautiful, ſo was his
Shape, till he grew a little burly. He was
bred to Buſineſs, as being what you call in
France, one of the long Robe : His natural
Parts prodigious, which were happily join'd
by a learned and liberal Education : His
Taſte delicate, in reſpeɛ of good Authors;
remark-

remarkable for the Sweetnefs of his Temper, and in fhort, every way qualified for being Beloved, where ever he fhould happen to Love.

VALUING my felf as I do upon the Reputation of an Impartial Hiftorian, neither blind to *Rivella*'s Weakneffes and Misfortunes, as being once her Lover, nor angry and fevere as remembring I cou'd never be Beloved ; I have join'd together the juft, and the tender, not expatiated with Malice upon her Faults, nor yet blindly overlooking them : If I have happen'd, by repeating her little Vanities, to deftroy thofe firft Inclinations you may have had to efteem what was valuable in her Compofition ; remember how hard it is in Youth, even for the ftronger Sex to refift *the fweet Poyfon of Flattery, and well directed Praife or Admiration.*

DURING the fhort Stay *Rivella* had made in *Hilaria*'s Family, fhe was become acquainted with the Lord *Crafty*: He had been Ambaffador in *France*, where his Negotiations are faid to have procured as much Advantage to your King, as they did Difhonour to his own Country. He had a long Head turn'd to Deceit and over-reaching : If a thing were to be done two Ways, he never lov'd the plain, nor
valu'd

valu'd a Point if he could easily carry it:
His Perfon was not at all beholding to Nature, and yet he had poffeffed more fine
Women than had the fineft Gentleman,
not lefs than twice or thrice becoming his
Mafter's Rival. When *Hilaria* was in
France he found it extreamly convenient
for his Affairs to be well with her, as fhe
was Miftrefs, and himfelf Ambaffador:
For fome Time 'tis fuppofed that he lov'd
her out of Inclination, her own Charms being inevitable; but finding fhe was not very
regular, he reproach'd her in fuch a Manner, that the haughty *Hilaria* vow'd his
Ruin: She would not permit a Subject to
take that Freedom fhe would not allow a
Monarch, which was, prefcribing Rules
for her Conduct: In fhort, her Power
was fuch over the King, tho' he was even
then in the Arms of a new and younger
Miftrefs, and *Hilaria* at fo great a Di-
ftance from him, as to yield to the Plague
of her Importunity with which fhe fill'd
her Letters. He confented that Lord *Craf-*
ty fhould be recall'd, upon fecret Advice
that fhe pretended to have received of
his Corruption and Treachery. The Ambaffador did not want either for Friends
in *England,* nor in *Hilaria*'s own Family,
who gave him very early Advice of what
was defign'd againft him: He had the
Dexterity to ward the intended Blow, and
turn

turn it upon her that was the Aggreſſor;
Hilaria's own Daughter betray'd her to
the Ambaſſador: He had corrupted not
only her Heart, but ſeduced her from her
Duty and Integrity: Her Mother was
gone to take the *Bourbon* Waters, leaving
this young Lady the Care of her Family,
and more immediately of ſuch Letters as a
certain Perſon ſhould write to her, full of
amorous Raptures for the Favours ſhe had
beſtow'd. Theſe fatal Letters, at leaſt ſeveral of them with Anſwers full of Tenderneſs under *Hilaria*'s own Hand, the Ambaſſador proved ſo lucky as to make himſelf
Maſter of: He return'd with his *Credentials*
to *England* to accuſe *Hilaria* and acquit
himſelf: The Miſtreſs was ſummon'd from
France to juſtify her ill Conduct: What
could be ſaid againſt ſuch clear Evidences of
her Diſloyalty? 'Tis true, ſhe had to deal
with the moſt merciful Prince in the World,
and who made the largeſt Allowances for
human Frailty, which ſhe ſo far improv'd,
as to tell His Majeſty, there was nothing
criminal in a Correſpondence deſign'd only for Amuſement, without preſuming to
aim at Conſequences; the very *Mode* and
Manner of Expreſſion in *French* and *En-*
gliſh, were widely different; that which in
one Language carried an Air of extream
Gallantry, meant no more than meer Civility in t'other. Whether the Monarch
were,

were, or would feem perfuaded, he appear'd fo, and order'd her to forgive the Ambaffador; to whom he return'd his Thanks for the Care he had taken of his Glory, very much to *Hilaria*'s Mortification, who was not fuffer'd to exhibit her Complaint againft him, which was look'd upon as proceeding only from the Malice and Revenge of a vindictive guilty Woman.

LORD *Crafty* made a very fuccefsful Embaffy touching his own Intereft, tho' he fail'd of bringing the Court altogether into thofe Meafures which the *French* King defired. His Paternal Eftate was not more than Five thoufand Pound a Year, which he extreamly improv'd, as you may know by the *Rent-Roll*, deliver'd in upon his Son's Marriage, which doubled that Sum fix.Times over, all due to his own Contrivance, wherein he was affifted often by the Ladies, which made him have a very great Opinion of their Management: This Lord us'd to value himfelf upon certain Rules in Policy, of trufting no Perfon with his real Defigns: What Part he gave any one in his Confidence when they were to negotiate an Affair for him, was in his own Expreffion but tying 'em by the Leg to a Table, they cou'd not go farther than the Line that
held

held them. He was incapable of Friendſhip but what made for his Intereſt, or of
Love but for his own proper Pleaſures:
Nature form'd him a Politician, and Experience made him an Artiſt in the Trade
of Diſſimulation; but the beſt that can be
ſaid of thoſe great Parts, which he put to
ſo bad an uſe, is, that there was a wrong
Turn in his Birth, Fortune that caus'd him
to be Born the Heir of a good Family
miſtook his Bent; ſhe had done much better in making him an Attorney, for there
was no Point how difficult or knotty ſo-
ever, but what he could either untie or
evade.

H E was married to the Reliɗ of one
who had been the richeſt Merchant in
England; ſhe brought along with her not
only a very large Jointure, but a larger
Law-ſuit, which hit Lord *Crafty*'s Genius;
he became much more in Love with That
than her Perſon: Mr. *Double* her Huſband was Childleſs, and had contraɗed an
inviolable Friendſhip with Baron *Meanwell*, inſomuch that they had interchang-
ably made each other their Heir by Deed
of Gift. Mr. *Double*'s Affairs call'd him
Abroad to the Plantations, which Opportunity his Wife took to revenge her ſelf
upon the Baron, for adviſing her Huſband
to pull down a very large Houſe and to ſell

I   the

the Ground and Materials to the Builders:
This Lady, who was remarkable for her
Pride, regretted so fine a Seat, and was resolved to punish Lord *Meanwell* for the
Loss of it. She perfuaded her Spoufe to
make a Will in the *Indies*, whereby she
relinquish'd one Quarter part of her Joynture, conditionally that Lord *Meanwell*'s
Pretenfions might be ftruck out; and young
Double, who had no Relation to the Merchant but the Name, appointed Heir to
the Eftate. *During* King *Charles* the Firft's
Troubles, Merchant *Double*'s Father refided at a Seat he had in *Effex* near the
Sea-fide, he was walking one Evening upon the Strand, regarding feveral poor half
naked, half ftarv'd Paffengers that were
getting out of a Ship lately come into the
Road; thefe miferable Wretches were ef-
caped from the *Maffacre* in *Ireland*, amongft
them was a well look'd Woman with a Boy
in her Hand, habited *'en Peafant*: Mr.
Double ask'd her feveral Queftions, which
she anfwer'd to his Satisfaction, amongft
the reft that her Name and her Sons were
Double, but her Husband had been kill'd
by the *Rebels*, which affected him fo much,
that he order'd her Home to his own
Houfe, where she remain'd the reft of her
Life: Her Son was made Mr. *Double*'s
Gardener; thriving under a flourifhing Family he married very well, and alfo left
a Son,

a Son, whom old *Double* put into the Army, where he rofe to be a Lieutenant Colonel; but did not die rich, leaving a Widow and feveral Children; the eldeft of which, Merchant *Double*'s Lady had picked out, as an Heir worthy to revenge her Quarrel againft the Lord *Meanwell:* Her Husband died in the *Indies* not long after he had obliged his Wife in a Point fo much to his Difhonour, confidering the Deed he had executed in Favour of the Baron : Some Perfons who knew the little regard he had for that worthlefs Brood of the *Doubles*, thought he yielded to his Lady's Importunities only for a quiet Life, thinking he did little more than make her an infignificant Compliment, becaufe two Days before he went to the *Indies*, he had added a *Codicel* which was affix'd to the *Deed*, whereby he for ever incapacitated himfelf to revoke the faid *Deed*, but in the Prefence of fix Witneffes; two whereof were to be *Prelates* of the Church of *England* ; dying in the *Indies* as he did, whatever Will he could make There, muft be defective in that main Article. His Lady return'd with all the Pomp and Splendour of an Eaftern Queen; but her Pride working to an exceffive Height, foon turn'd her Brain; whereby young *Tim Double* was deprived of a powerful Patronefs to carry on thofe Pretenfions fhe had brought

I 2   over

over from the *Indies* in his Favour ; and Baron *Meanwell* in all Probability likely to enjoy for himself, and his Heirs for ever, the use Fruit of the foremention'd Deed of Gift.

FORTUNE that loves to mingle her self in all Events, thrust between the *Baron* and his great Hopes the most powerful, most cunning, and most dexterous Adversary that she could possibly have rais'd ; it was the Lord *Crafty*, who had swallow'd in his Imagination all *Double*'s Estate : He knew himself blest with a Purse and a Capacity equal to the Work ; He therefore bought the Merchant's Widow of her two Women, his own Chaplain married them together ; but the Lady being suppofed *Non Compos*, it is said one of her Female Directors was, in effect the Bride, lying behind the Pillows, and making proper Answers for the Lunatick ; whereby she got to her self the Management of that old Fox, and to the Day of his Death us'd to carry whatever Point she had in Hand, by only threatning to take upon her self, the Title and Quality of his Wife.

LORD *Crafty*, as Reason good, immediately affumed the Management of his Lady's Affairs, and commenced a Suit in young *Tim*'s Name against the Baron ; the
Progress

Progrefs of that Suit, would make an honeft Man for ever deteft going to Law;
the Point *Crafty* contended for, was to in-
validate the *Codicel*, which he attempted
to prove fpurious. How many *Verdicts*
were there given and reverfed? What
number of Witneffes convicted of Perju-
ry? How much Treafure expended in
the Purfuit and the Defence? Our Courts
of Judicature rung of nothing elfe; in the
mean time the Caufe, was a fat Caufe,
and the Lawyers contrived how to pro-
long it whilft none were Gainers but themfelves: Baron *Meanwell* almoft beggar'd
himfelf; Lord *Crafty* was indeed better
circumftanced, but feeing the Delays of
the Courts of Juftice, and the Tricks of
young *Tim Double*; he began to breathe an
Air of Accommodation as well as the *Baron*: But *Tim*'s Pretenfions being the diffi-
culteft Point to be adjufted, they were at a
lofs how to find a Method by which all
things might be fettled in that Calm, which
the Exigency of both their Affairs feem'd
to require,

T I M *Double* prov'd not only a Sot,
but the moft diffolute, fenfelefs, obftinate
Wretch, that a Man could deal with. His
Education and natural Parts were both
mean, his Temper extravagant and vain;
he valu'd himfelf extreamly upon his Province

vince of Diffimulation, as having practis'd
under a very great Mafter. At the Age
of Sixteen he was trapan'd when he was
Drunk, to marry the Daughter of a poor
Petty-pan Merchant; the Girl was Pretty
and Ingenious enough; fhe made him a
very good Wife, and often by her Management prevented his being undone by
Sharpers, to vhom he was naturally ad-
dicted : But he hated her, and ftudied nothing fo much as how to get rid of her;
tho' to her Face he affected fo prodigious
a Paffion, that he could not breathe without mixing Eyes, preffing and kiffing her
Hands and Neck ; nor would he touch a
Bit of Meat but what fhe cut; nay, he
muft fit by her at Table, and often eat
off of no Plate but hers : This was a ful-
fom Sight to all who knew he had brought
his Marriage into Parliament, where it
was likely to have been difannul'd, had not
Lord *Crafty* by his underhand Practices
prevented it, leaft *Tim*, becoming a fingle
Man, fome rich powerful Family might
efpoufe his Caufe, and by Virtue of his
Title to fo great an Eftate, give his Lordfhip an unexpected Diverfion, in the Views
he had of gaining it all to himfelf.

LORD *Crafty* had from time to time
fupplied him with feveral large Sums of
Money, whereby he pretended to purchafe
his

his Title to the whole Eftate; but the
Point being yet undecided, that was look'd
upon no better than *Champarty* and *Main-
tainance.* *Tim* executed feveral Deeds,
whereby he divefted himfelf of all Pretenfions to the Eftate, when it fhould be recover'd; which, when he had done, Lord
Crafty brought him in a Bill of Threefcore
Thoufand Pounds; fome for Monies receiv'd, and the reft for vaft Sums expended
in the Law-Suit. *Tim* enter'd into Bonds
and Judgments, by which he acknow-
ledg'd himfelf Debtor to my Lord *Crafty*;
after which, he was left at Liberty to go
where he pleas'd; his Lordfhip before, never fuffering him to ftir, but under the
Conduct of fome Perfon he could confide
in. *Tim*'s Riots were fo great, that Lord
Crafty would no longer fupply him with
Money; he ran in Debt where-ever he
could, till at length he was arrefted and
forc'd to furrender himfelf a Prifoner at
Weftminfter-Hall, before the *Lord Chief
Juftice of the Common-pleas.*

I T was perfectly neceffary that I fhould
enter into this long Digreffion, to inform
you of the true State of Things, before
I give you Knowledge of an Affair, by
which *Rivella* was prefented with frefh
Occafion to renew the Complaint fhe fo
juftly

juftly had againft Fortune, for turning all her Profpects of Good into Evil.

AT that Time *Rivella* liv'd in a pretty Retirement, fome few Miles out of Town, where fhe diverted her felf chiefly with walking and reading. One Day *Califta*, her Sifter Authorefs (with whofe Story I may hereafter entertain you, as well as with the other writing Ladies of our Age) came, as ufual, to make her a Vifit; fhe told her that *Cleander*, a Friend of hers, one of the moft accomplifh'd Perfons living, was in Cuftody of a *Serjeant of Arms* for fome Misdemeanours, which were nothing in themfelves, but as he had been of Council on Lord *Crafty*'s Side, againft Lord *Meanwell*, and was fuppos'd to have had the chief Conduct of the laft Trial, Matters were like to be partially carried, becaufe *Ofwald* (poor *Rivella*'s Kinfman and Husband, tho' fhe always hated his being call'd fo) was appointed Chairman of the Committee order'd to examine *Cleander*; and *Ofwald* being long known a Champion for Lord *Meanwell*, in refpect of his Caufe, it was very juftly fear'd, that he would joyn Revenge and Retaliation to his own native Temper of Choler and Fury, by which Means *Cleander* was to expect very fevere Ufage, if not a worfe Misfortune.

TO

T O conclude; after *Califta* had rais'd
Rivella's Pity, Wonder and Curiofity, for
the Merit, Beauty, and Innocence of the
Gentleman under Profecution; fhe propofed a real Advantage to her felf, if fhe
could influence her Kinfman to ftand neu-
ter in the Caufe; or if that was not to
be expected, that fhe would fo far ingage
him, that he fhould keep away on the Day
which was appointed for *Cleander*'s Exa-
mination.

R I V E L L A, was always inclin'd to
affift the Wretched; neither did fhe believe it Prudence to neglect her own Intereft, when fhe found it meritorious to
perfue it : She told *Califta*, that being only
her Friend was enough to ingage her to
endeavour at ferving this *Cleander* whoever he were; but that fince fhe had taken
Care to add Intereft to Friendfhip, which
were Motives her Circumftances were no
way qualified to refufe, fhe was refolved
upon that double Confideration, to attempt doing whatever was in her Power
for both their Services; but becaufe fhe
was not willing to embark without fome
Profpect of a fortunate Voyage, fhe defired
to fpeak with *Cleander* in Perfon, as well
to inform her felf of the Merits of the
Caufe, as to be acquainted with a Gentle-

K   man

man of whom fhe had given fo advantagious a Defcription.

CALISTA blufh'd at the Propofal,
which *Rivella* obferving, immediately ask'd
her, if he were her Lover, which would
be enough to ingage her to ferve him
without any other Motive; and thereupon
faid, that fhe would be contented to take
Minutes from *Califta* only, without concerning her felf any further about being
acquainted with *Cleander.*

CALISTA who was the moft of a
Prude in her outward Profeffions, and the
leaft of it in her inward Practice, unlefs
you'll think it no *Prudery* to allow Free-
doms with the Air of Reftraint; ask'd *Rivella* with a fcornful Smile, What it was
fhe meant? *Cleander* was a married Man,
and as fuch, out of any Capacity to engage
her. fecret Service; her Friendfhip was
meerly with his Wife, and as fuch if fhe
would affift him, fhe fhould be oblig'd to
her for her Trouble. *Rivella* who hates
Diffimulation, efpecially amongft Friends,
was refolved to pique *Califta* for her Infin-
cerity, and therefore faid, fince it was fo;
fhe infifted upon feeing and informing her
felf from *Cleander*'s own Mouth, or elfe
fhe would not ingage in the Bufinefs.

THE

T H E next Day *Cleander* fent a Gentle-
man to wait upon *Rivella*, and beg her
Intereft in his Service, together with the
Promife and Affurance of a certain Sum of
Money if fhe fhould fucceed.

T H E S E Preliminaries fettled, the Day
after *Cleander* fent the fame Perfon (who
happen'd to be a fort of an infignificant.
Gentleman, acquainted long fince both with
Rivella and himfelf) in a Chariot, with an
unknown Livery to bring her to Town,
and even to the *Serjeant at Arms*'s Houfe,
where *Cleander* was at that time confin'd.

R I V E L L A had formed to her felf
what it was going to fpeak to a Man of
Bufinefs in Private, that fhe muft at leaft
wait till the Croud were difmifs'd, and
therefore took a Book in her Pocket, that
fhe might entertain her felf with reading
whilft fhe waited for Audience : She chofe
the Duke *de Rochfoucaut*'s Moral Reflections ; fhe had not attended long, before
Cleander came to Wait on her, tho' but for
two or three Moments till he could difmifs
his Company, praying her to be eafy till
he might have the Honour to return ; during this fhort Compliment, *Rivella* had
thrown her Book upon the Table, *Cleander*
whilft he was fpeaking took it up, as not

heeding

heeding what he did, and departed the Room with the Book in his Hand : Who that has ever dipp'd into thofe Reflections, does not know that there is not a Line there, but what excites your Curiofity, and is worth being eternally admired and remembred? *Cleander* had never met with it before : He form'd an Idea from that Book of the Genius of the Lady, who chofe it for her Entertainment, and tho' he had but an indifferent Opinion hitherto of Woman's Converfation, he believ'd *Rivella* muft have a good Tafte from the Company fhe kept. He found an Opportunity of confirming himfelf, before he parted, in *Rivella*'s Senfe, and Capacity for Bufinefs as well as Pleafure; which were agreeably mingled at Supper, none but thofe two Gentlemen and *Rivella* being prefent. Behold the beginning of a Friendfhip which endured for feveral Years even to *Cleander*'s Death. He was married Young, but as yet knew not what it was to Love : His Studies and Application to Bufinefs, together with the Defire of making himfelf great in the World, had employ'd all his Hours : Neither did his Youth and Vigour ftand in need of Diverfions to relieve his Mind; he was civil to his Lady, meant very well for her Children, and did not then dream there was any thing in her Perfon defective to his Happinefs, that was in

the

the Power of any other of that Sex to beftow.

E A R L Y in the Morning *Rivella* went
to *Weſtminſter-Hall*, ſhe took up her Poſt
at the *Bookſellers-Shop*, by the Foot of thoſe
Stairs which go up to the Parliament-houſe :
She had not waited long but ſhe ſaw her
Kinſman ; he was cover'd with Bluſhes
and Confuſion, not imagining what Buſineſs ſhe had there, unleſs to expoſe him ;
he had not even ſeen her Face in ſome Years
nor ſhe his, having ſought nothing ſo much
as to avoid one another.

R IV E L L A advanced to ſpeak with
him, he bluſh'd more and more, ſeveral
Members coming by to go to the Houſe,
and obſerving him with a Lady in his Hand,
he thought it was beſt to take her from
that publick Place, and therefore led her
the back Way out of the *Hall*, call'd a
Coach put her in it, and afterwards got in
himſelf without having Power to ask her
what Buſineſs brought her to enquire after
him in a Place ſo improper for Converſation, at the ſame Time ordering the Coachman to drive out of Town.

T H U S was that important Affair ne-
glected, they choſe another *Chairman* for
the *Committee*, which ſat that Morning :
Cleander was acquitted, with the uſual Re-
primand,

primand, and order'd to be set at Liberty,
very much to the Regret of *Oswald* when
he came coolly to consider how scanda-
loufly he had abandon'd an Affair of that
Importance, and which Lord *Meanwell* had
left wholly to his Management.

BEFORE *Rivella* parted with her
Spoufe, she told him, what was her defign'd Requeft, and the Motive. He seem'd
very well pleas'd that nothing but Intereft
had engag'd her : He bid her be sure to
cultivate a Friendfhip with *Cleander*, who
would doubtlefs come to return his Thanks
for the Service she had done him ; recommending to her at the fame Time, *Firft*,
not to receive the Money which had been
promifed her, becaufe there were better
Views, and which would be of more Importance to her Fortune; and *Secondly*, to
leave her Houfe in the Country for fome
Time, to come and take Lodgings in *London*, where he would wait upon her to
direct her in the Management of fome
great Affair.

BEHOLD *Rivella* in a new Scene,
that of Bufinefs; in which however Love
took Care to fave all his own Immunities :
He befpoke the moft confiderable Place for
Cleander, who often vifited her with a
Pleafure new and furprizing to his hither-
                                                    to

to infenfible Breaft: I was lately come
to Town: *Rivella*'s Converfation always
made Part of my Pleafure, if not my
Happinefs; fo that whenever fhe allow'd
me that Favour, I never omitted waiting
on her: Some Prefentiment told me this
agreeable Gentleman would certainly fucceed: I faw his Eyes always fix'd on her
with unfpeakable Delight, whilft hers lan-
guifh'd him fome Returns: He approv'd
rather than applauded what fhe faid, but
would always fhift Places, till he got one
next her, omitting no Opportunity to touch
her Hand, when he could do it without
any feeming Defign: I told her fhe had
made a Conqueft, and one that fhe ought
to value her felf upon; for *Cleander* was
affuredly a Man of Worth as well as Beauty: She laugh'd, and faid he was fo awk-
ard, and fo unfafhion'd as to love; that
if he did bear her any great good Will,
fhe was fure he neither durft, nor knew
how to tell it her: I perceiv'd the Pleafure fhe took in fpeaking of him: Wherefore I came in with my old Way of Caution and Advice, bidding her have a Care:
One Affair with a married Man did a
Woman's Reputation more Harm than
with Six others: Wives were with reafon
fo implacable, fo invenom'd againft thofe
who fupplanted them, that they never forbore to revenge themfelves at the Expence

of

of their Rival's Credit; for if nothing elſe
enſu'd, a total Deprivation of the World's
Eſteem, was ſure to be the Conſequence
of an injur'd Wife's Reſentment: *Cleander*
was too handſom a Man to be loſt with
any Patience; his Wife was much older
than himſelf, and much a Termagant,
therefore nothing but Fire and Fury could
be expected from ſuch a Domeſtick Evil:
The Deprivation of a charming Husband's
Heart, being capable to rouſe the moſt in-
ſenſible: *Rivella* laugh'd, and thank'd me
for my Advice, but how ſhe profited by
it a very little Time will ſhew us.

HER Kinſman (I chuſe to call him
ſo, rather than by that hateful Name her
Husband) careſs'd her with the utmoſt
Blandiſhments; he told her it was now
in her own Power to redeem all the Miſ-
management they had both been guilty of
in reſpect of her Fortune: *Cleander* was
the Perſon that could do Miracles in Point
of Accommodation between Lord *Crafty*
and Baron *Meanwell* : He empower'd her
to make him very advantagious Offers, if
he would but uſe his Intereſt towards
compoſing that Affair. She founded *Cleander* upon that Head: He anſwer'd her
as a Perſon who could refuſe nothing to
a Woman he lov'd, but at the ſame Time
told her they were all miſtaken; he had
not

not any Part of Lord *Crafty*'s Confidence
which he was now very glad of, becaufe
he muft either difoblige her, or, which was
a worfe Evil, betray my Lord : Nay more,
his Lordfhip had been wanting in doing
him little Services during his Confinement,
which he would nor eafily forgive ; that
true indeed he had been of *Council* for him
in the laft Trial ; but not *trufted* ; tho' that
very Sufpicion had drawn upon him Lord
Meanwell's Difpleafure, and *Ofwald*'s Per-
fecution, notwithftanding which, Lord
Crafty had fail'd of Generofity enough to
ftand by him, perhaps not efteeming him
of fufficient Confequence to his Service :
Rivella reported this back to her *Principal* ; he would not believe *Cleander*, which
made her likewife diftruft his Integrity ;
he never came to vifit her, but fhe always
teiz'd him with thefe Words, *You can oblige me ! you can retrieve my broken Fortune ! you can give Peace to* Weftminfter-
Hall, *between thofe mighty Potentates that
have fo long divided it ! and you refufe to
do it ! did I ferve you with fuch an Ill-will,
or by halves? Ceafe profeffing your Gratitude and Friendfhip to me when it rifes no
higher than common Effects ; you had better
never vifit, than difoblige me.* Cleander
was quite vanquifh'd by her Reproaches
and Importunity ; the Evil was in his

L Heart,

Heart, he could not refrain feeing her, and took this Opportunity to declare himfelf, by telling her his Opinion, was, *that no Lover either could, or ought to refufe what was ask'd him by the Perfon he lov'd.* In fhort, he gave her to underftand, that he had not any Obligation to Lord *Crafty*, and he was very glad of it, but that he thought the Baron's Way did not lie towards an Accommodation with that Lord, but with Mr. *Timothy Double*, becaufe if Matters were agreed between them two, and the *Deed* and the *Will* joyn'd, what had Lord *Crafty* to do in it any further than to expect to find his Wife's Jointure well paid : Double *is a Prifoner*, faid *Cleander*, *where I command*; *if you,* Madam, *were fecur'd, fo that our Intereft could become mutual, and we not make our felves the* Baron's, *or your* Kinfman's *Tools, I don't find there would be any great Difficulty in bringing this Matter to bear.*

R I V E L L A immediately gave Part of her Secret to her Coufin, and he to the *Baron*; they could not help wondring at their own Blindnefs which had till then mifs'd fo obvious a Mark. The *Baron* admitted *Cleander*'s Genius for Bufinefs, and order'd *Rivella* to meet his Lordfhip at a Third Place, there to take his Inftructions :

ons: He began with affuring her of his entire Confidence in her Honour and Capacity, bidding her make it *Cleander's* Intereft to conclude this Project of Reconciliation, for which when it was accomplifh'd they fhould have between them Eight Thoufand Pounds paid down upon the Nail; it was her Bufinefs, either to come in for half, or to make what Terms fhe could with *Cleander*; that in the mean Time *Tim Double* fhould be introduc'd to her Lodgings, where they would have her entertain and carefs him to all the Height of his own extravagant Humour: In a few Days they fhould be able to fee whether the Project would bear, which if it did not, *Rivella* fhould have a Prefent of an Hundred Guineas, to defray what Expence fhe might be at, and over and above his Lordfhip's Acknowledgment and Protection as long as he liv'd. *Cleander*, to oblige *Rivella*, agreed to thefe Propofals, becaufe he could not refufe what fhe fo earneftly infifted on; but he bid her remember it was only to pleafe her, not thro' any great Profpect he had of advantaging himfelf, becaufe the Perfons they had to deal with, he fear'd, had not all the Honour that was requir'd in fuch an Affair, where much more was to be left to the *Bona Fide* than to any Security, that could, as Matters
ftood,

ſtood, be made obligatory or binding in Law.

THUS was *Timothy Double* introduc'd to *Rivella*'s Appartment; but before he could make his Appearance there, poor *Cleander* was forc'd to accouter him at his own Coſt; he was horribly out of Humour becauſe he was very much out of Repair. Therefore he ſent him his Taylor, of whom *Tim* immediately beſpoke Two Suits that came to more than Sixſcore Pound, full of Gold and Silver. The Perriwig-maker furniſh'd him upon *Cleander*'s Credit, with two Perriwigs upwards of Thirty Guineas apiece: Lace and Linnen made another improving Article; ſo that before *Cleander* durſt ask him a Queſtion, he was dipp'd above Three Hundred Pound for his Service, without putting one Piece into his Pocket: He would not truſt him with ready Money, left he ſhould elope, and fall again into ſome of the Hands of his old Comrades the Sharpers. *Cleander* did not fail to hint to *Rivella* the Expence he had been at to pleaſe her Humour; at the ſame Time making her obſerve Lord *Meanwell*'s Parſimony, that would venture no more than an Hundred Guineas, and that not paid down, to gain ſo vaſt an Advantage to himſelf as an Accommodation with *Tim*, asking her with

a Smile, how one of her great Soul, could
fo earneftly engage her Cares and Intereft
for the Service of him, who had fo little
a Soul?

TIM ftuck full of Gold and Silver Lace,
made a tolerable Figure, he was neither
ugly nor conceited; his Habit having fo
much of the fine Gentleman, the worft of
it was, his. Converfation did not well a-
gree with his Drefs; but he had been long
enough with Lord *Crafty* to learn an outward Civility, his Behaviour was feeming-
ly modeft and full of Bows; *Cleander*
brought him to *Rivella*, as an injur'd
Gentleman, who had been ruin'd by that
Lord's Refinements: *Tim* prefently re-
counted feveral pleafant Acts of Management, which would make no ill Figure in
fecret Hiftory. *Cleander* was obliged to
endure this Booby for feveral Days, to
drink with him, nay, to fleep with him,
till he had gotten into his Confidence; in
all that Time never naming Lord *Meanwell*'s Name; that Task was left to *Rivella*, of whofe good Senfe and Honour he
gave *Tim* a very advantagious Character:
They ufed generally to Dine with her, fhe
did Pennance enough, being obliged to deny her felf to all other Company, and to
lengthen out Dinner till it came to Supper
Time, from whence *Tim* muft always go to
the

the Tavern before he went to Bed. Miferable *Cleander* kept him Company, for fear he fhould get fome of his old Gang, who were Spies gain'd by Lord *Crafty*: In Conclufion he began to talk freely with *Rivella* by way of unlading his Grievances, the Wretchednefs of his Circumftances; great Debts and Incumbrance with Lord *Crafty*, did not make him half fo uneafy as the Difficulty of being rid of his Wife: Tho' he was fure he could ftill be divorced from her, if he had any Friend to ftand by him, who would be kind enough to affift him with his Purfe: This naturally introduced Lord *Meanwell*, of whofe Vertues *Rivella* made a pompous Differtation, which much furprized *Tim* who had been ufed to hear the *Baron* treated as the greateft *Fourb* in Nature: The firft thing inftill'd into him was the Forgery of the Claufe, which had been annexed to old *Double*'s Deed. *Rivella* endeavour'd to fet him right as to that fufpicious Circumftance, and with much more eafe and Juftice difplay'd Lord *Crafty* in his political Capacity; *Tim* could help her in her Task, and did not fcruple to give her many Inftances relating to himfelf, particularly one Night when Lord *Crafty* got *Tim* behind a Table with Deeds and Conveyances before him, to which end he had kept him clofe up for feveral Days, *Tim*'s Nofe fell a Bleeding, he rofe to fetch a Hand-

Handkerchief, my Lord would not let him
go but prefented him his own, which being quickly wet, the Lawyer and his Witneffes fupplied him with theirs; in Conclufion they would have fuffer'd him to bleed
to Death, rather than ftir till he had fign'd
and feal'd, according to his Lordfhip's
own Heart's Defire.

B Y thefe Practices *Tim* was ruin'd to all
Intents and Purpofes and condemn'd to perifh in Prifon, without he could relieve himfelf by fome other Method than had yet
been taken. He had coft *Cleander* juft Five
hundred Pound when *Rivella* propofed to
him an Accommodation with Lord *Meanwell*, in which the young Man was at firft
very fincere : But here the Parcimony of
that Lord, or the Folly of his Manager *Ofwald* fpoil'd all ; *Rivella* was of *Tim*'s fide,
and, Reafon good, ftrove to make as advantagious a Bargain for him as fhe could ; nothing would ferve *Tim* but to be made a
Lord, he had all the Time of *Crafty*'s
Management been flatter'd with a much
greater Title when the Eftate fhou'd be
once recovered: That which ftuck hardeft with *Tim*, was a Point which Lord
Meanwell ftrenuoufly infifted upon, nay,
would do nothing without, *viz.* parting
with the fuperbious chief Seat of the
Doubles, which the *Baron* wanted to fettle
upon

upon his fecond Son whom he lov'd extreamly. *Tim* was told that as Matters
ftood, it was infinitely too large for any
Expence he could ever hope to make, but
in Exchange he fhould have the Lord *Meanwell*'s own Houfe, with all the Furniture,
which was a much more modern Structure,
and where he conftantly refided when he
was in Town, and with it, the Houfe-keeper's Place belonging to one of the King's Pa-
laces where *Tim* would have occafion to
commence Courtier, a Province he exceffively long'd for, befides frequent Opportunities to oblige the Maids of Honour in the
Choice of their Lodging, which weigh'd
very much with *Tim*'s amorous Temper:
He defired to view the Infide of the Houfe,
to know whether it was a Habitation fit
for a Man of fo great a Soul; this was a
difficult Point, which yet he infifted on fo
far, that he would treat no further unlefs
he lik'd the Houfe, that which he was to
refign in Lieu of it, being the Idol of his
Fancy, tho' no way fuitable to any but an
overgrown Eftate: The *Baron* very well
knew Lord *Crafty* had Spies in his Family
who would foon carry the Report to him
of *Tim Double*'s being to vifit his Houfe,
which muft certainly ruin the whole Treaty; they were at their Wits end to get him
to pafs over that Circumftance, but *Tim*
was obftinate and would not be perfuaded;

at

at length, Women being good at Invention, *Rivella* found a Method how to gratify *Tim's* Curiofity, and in a Way which hit his Vein, having a great Inclination to be dabling with Politicks and Intrigues; the next *Sunday* the *Baron* and all his Family were purpofely to dine abroad, Leave fhou'd be given to the Servants to do what they would with themfelves, which, if not given them, they are apt enough to take when their Attendance is not required at home: His Chaplain he could fo far confide in, as to tell him two Clergymen from the *U-niverfity* had a Curiofity to fee the Houfe *incognito*, which for certain Reafons he defired him to fhow: A Servant whom the *Baron* had long trufted was to let in the *Oxonians*, and introduce them to the Chaplain.

T W O Clergymen's Habits were fent to *Rivella's* Lodgings, where the Pious Gentlemen were to take Orders; fhe had fent the Landlady and all the Family to divert themfelves at her Country Houfe, and left no Soul with her felf but an under Servant, whom fhe difpatch'd to Church: It fell a Raining with great Violence for the reft of the Day; the Sparks came after Dinner, and were foon metamorphofed into fpruce *Clergymen*: *Tim* had a *French* Brocade Veft under his Habit which neverthe-

lefs

lefs durft not appear ; the Difficulty of getting a Coach on *Sundays*, and efpecially in rainy Weather, made them keep theirs : *Tim* had contracted fuch an ill Habit of Swearing, that he could neither leave it off nor knew when he did it ; *Rivella* call'd the Coachman in, and told him the Perfons he brought thither had fent him his Money, having no occafion to go farther : But there were two Minifters above that wanted a Coach, the Fellow brufh'd up his Seats, and in they got, *Cleander* gave him Directions where to go, which he not taking readily, *Tim* fell a fwearing at him for a Blockhead and a Dunce; the Man ftared, got up nimbly into his Coach-box, fnapt his Whip, and fwore as loud as *Tim* had done, that he never faw fuch *Pafons* in his Life.

A L L things were difplay'd to the beft Advantage at Lord *Meanwell*'s; *Tim* liked it well enough when his Thoughts had no Return of that Glorious Seat in the Country, which often coft him many a Pang to forgo; but to comfort himfelf, he would needs fee the Cellars, the Chaplain waited on him down, and civilly offer'd him his Choice, either of *Champaign* or *Burgundy*; *Tim* liked both, and in he fat for it, *Cleander* winked at him in vain, jogg'd his Knee, no Notice took honeft *Tim*,

the

the Glaſs went about, the Chaplain was
diſpoſed to ſtare, ſeeing him ſwallow down
the Liquor ſo greedily; at length, *Cleander* told *Tim* in his Ear, it was neceſſary
they ſhould be gone before Church was
done : *Tim* anſwer'd aloud, that might be,
But where was there ſo good *Burgundy* to
be had after Church? *Cleander* was at his
Wits end at the Incivility of the Brute; *Tim*
laid about him, as if all the Wine in the
Cellar was his own, becauſe the Houſe and
Furniture were to be ſo if he pleas'd. *Cleander* grew wild to get him away, and
told him, with that Reverend Gentleman's leave, they would take ſome Bottles
with them in the Coach to drink when
they came home. The Chaplain's Com-
miſſion did not extend ſo far, his Lord was
a good Husband of his Wines, and yet he
knew not how to refuſe; in ſhort, he
yielded that they ſhould have half a dozen
Bottles : But when they came to the Gate
the Coachman was gone unpaid ; probably the Fellow knew they were the ſame
Perſons he had carried before in a Lay-
Habit, and did not know what to make of
them, yet not daring to mutter, ſeeing
them go into ſuch a Houſe : *Tim* was half
bouzy, and without any Reſpect to his
Cloth, with a Bottle in each Hand, ſtood
in the Street calling *Coach! Coach!* the
Rain ſtill continuing no Coach came; the

Chaplain

Chaplain and *Cleander*, likewife with each
their two Bottles in Hand, were fomething
abafhed, and did not call *Coach! Coach!*
fo loud as did *pot valiant Tim*; at length,
the Expedient was found of fending the *Ba-*
ron's Servant for two Chairs: *Tim* would
have all the fix Bottles along with him in
his own Chair, they were carried back a-
gain to *Rivella*'s, where they unrob'd and
ended this troublefom Adventure.

TIM having at length agreed to an Exchange of Houfes, being perfuaded to allow in Point of Grandeur for the difference
of Town and Country, the Treaty went
on; he was promifed to be relieved from
all his Ingagements to Lord *Crafty*. He
demanded two thoufand Pounds a Year to
be fettled upon him and his Heirs for e-
ver; to be affifted in his Divorce, and if
that could be effected, that he might have
leave to Court one of the *Baron*'s Daughters; to receive ten Thoufand Pounds in
ready Money, and be made a Lord; this
laft Article was readily complied with, a
Patent for a *Barony* valu'd at ten Thoufand Pound being found in the Family,
granted by the late King for Services done,
the other two Articles they thought too
large, and therefore offer'd but one Thoufand Pound a Year, and fix in Money.

LORD

LORD *Meanwell*'s Overfight lay in
not fixing *Tim*'s inconftant Temper whilft
he might have done it; the Squire quickly wanted a Change of Place, Circumftances and Diverfion: The Baron ought to
have clos'd with *Tim*'s Terms, when he
could have had them, and not loft irreco-
verable Time in ftriving to beat down the.
Market, tho' he confefs'd it was cheap,
and what he would gladly give rather
than go without: Befides, his worthlefs
Plenipo, *Ofwald*, who pretended to his
Lordfhip that he ferved for nought, when
he faw Matters were juft beginning to
bear, told *Riveila* that he underftood *Cleander* had confented that fhe fhould divide with him the Eight Thoufand Pound,
which himfelf very unworthily expected
to divide with her. He would have Two
Thoufand for his own Ufe, and the other
Two Thoufand fettled after her Death,
upon a Son which had been the Product
of their Marriage.

RIVELLA anfwer'd him, that provided the Baron were acquainted with
thefe Conditions, fhe would agree with
them, how remote foever from what had
been firft promifed her; but if otherwife,
fhe would not be any longer impos'd upon by *Ofwald*'s Pretences: This caus'd bad
Blood

Blood between them; he began to be jealous of *Tim*, without fufpecting *Cleander*: He put himfelf into Paffions and Difgufts, and wore out the Time in Complaints and Expoftulations, yet took Part of all thofe fine Dinners that were every Day feen at *Rivella*'s; for which, when fhe defir'd him to reprefent to the Baron the Expence fhe was unavoidably put to, he once brought her the paultry Sum of Three Pound, which, as fhe faid, would not furnifh one *Defert*; and this was all the Money ever tender'd her from the *Baron* in that Affair, tho' fhe reafonably prefum'd his Lordfhip, according to his own Propofal, had trufted larger Sums for her Ufe into the Hands of his Treafurer *Ofwald*.

BUT whilft *Ofwald* was contriving how to reduce *Tim*'s Demands, fecure Two Thoufand Pound to himfelf without the Baron's Knowledge, and get the other Two Thoufand Pound fettled in reverfion upon his Son, an unforefeen, and as one fhould think an inconfiderable Accident, let all of them fee the Vanity of pretending to divide the Spoil before the Prey was fecur'd.

THERE was a Girl about Seventeen or Eighteen, nam'd *Bella*, who fometimes frequented the Play-houfe, but as yet could get no Salary; for a Year or Two together fhe us'd to come to *Rivella*'s when fhe

was

was in Town, to beg her to fpeak to the
Managers, that fhe might be receiv'd into Pay: She was a poor Woman's Daughter in the Neighbourhood, which ingaged
Rivella to promife her what little Intereft fhe had: *Bella* us'd fometimes to come
to Dinner there, as fhe did at other Places, offering her Service in making up
Heads, and thofe little Offices wherein
the Girl was tolerably handy: When there
was no Company, *Rivella* had fometimes
the Goodnefs to make her fit down at the
Table with her, otherwife fhe us'd to be
glad to get a Meals Meat with Mrs. *Flip-*
panta, *Rivella*'s Woman: That Wench,
was perfectly *Mercurial*, and had the greateft Propenfity to Intrigue, and bringing
People together; tho' her Lady was not
then acquainted with her Talent, no more
than her other Qualification of Diffimulation; for fhe was perfectly demure before her Miftrefs: *Bell* was greatly in her
Favour, becaufe fhe us'd at fpare Times
to entertain her with Scraps of Plays and
amorous Speeches in Heroicks: The Landlady and another Woman who lodg'd in
the Houfe where *Rivella* lodg'd, were
fond of the fame Amufement: *Bell* was
much oftner there than *Rivella* knew, and
when fhe was abroad, the Wench was always repeating in a Theatrical Tone and
Manner.

LORD

LORD *Meanwell's* Phlegm, or Irrefo-
lution, made the Treaty hang long, together with *Ofwald's* very ill Humour about
the Four Thoufand Pounds, which he had
fwallow'd in his Imaginations, joyn'd to
his pretended Jealoufy of *Tim*, fo that *Rivella* was grown weary, and glad to go
abroad for a little Relief, leaving the Houfe
to *Tim* and *Ofwald* to drink in; as for *Cleander*, I prefume he was but feldom there;
when *Rivella* was not, Mrs. *Flippanta*
made a Figure in her Lady's Abfence, and
Bella by this Means came to be feen by
Tim; he fell in Love with her according
to his Way of loving: The Girl had a
round Face, not well made, large dull
Eyes, but fhe was young, and well enough
complexion'd, tho' fhe wanted Air, and
had a Defect in her Speech, which were
two Things they objected againft as to
her coming into the Play-Houfe. *Tim*
bribed *Flippanta* to get the Girl's Company in her Lady's Abfence, as he would
have done for any Girl that came in his
Way. They were grown very well acquainted, before *Tim* told the News of his
growing Flame to *Cleander*; which he
fpoke of as a Thing indifpenfibly neceffary to his Happinefs: *Tim* fancied himfelf fome mighty confiderable Perfon, he had
three very great Affairs upon his Hands,

to

to end with my Lord *Meanwell*, get rid
of his Wife, and poffefs himfelf of *Bell*'s
Favours: *Cleander* told *Rivella* what a
Scrape they were brought into, and conjur'd her not to oppofe him; for if *Tim*
was crofs'd in his Humour, all was at an
End: He was already dipp'd feveral Hundred Pounds; for that fine 'Squire, 'tis fuppos'd, could not be kept all this Time without Money in his Pocket, and a great
deal too. The Affair had been fo long
depending, that his Wife found out his
Haunt at *Rivella*'s, of which fhe immediately gave Notice to Lord *Crafty*: She was
fix'd immoveably to his Lordfhip's Service, notwithftanding her Husband's Intereft, which *Tim* had honeftly told *Cleander* in the Beginning, and therefore begg'd
he might remain conceal'd from his Wife
till all was concluded with the Baron:
Lord *Crafty* knew fo much of *Rivella*'s
Temper, that fhe would not have en-
dur'd fuch a Booby as *Tim*, and have made
great Expence upon him without better
Views: He heard of *Tim*'s Bravery, and
what Airs he gave himfelf: Lord *Crafty*
had never been fo defective in any Point
of Policy as in abandoning of *Tim*; it
muft coft him confiderable to retrieve
that falfe Step: It was no hard Matter to
find his Lodging by dogging him from
Rivella's Houfe, which when once done,

N   he

he fent a Perfon to him, call'd old *Simon*,
who had long been Lord *Crafty*'s Creature,
and by humouring *Tim* in his Vices and
Vanities, had gain'd an abfolute Afcendant
over him ; but when *Tim* grew poor and
no longer of Confequence to Lord *Crafty*,
Mr. *Simon* forfook him with the reft, yet
foon regain'd his former Station by Flattery ; and finding the Place of a Favourite
vacant, he reaffum'd it as formerly. *Tim*
ask'd *Cleander* to intercede with *Rivella*
that Mr. *Simon* might be permitted to
make one of the Company : *Rivella* told
them they were undone from that Minute,
he was a Creature of my Lord *Crafty*'s
and the whole Defign would certainly
come to nothing: *Tim* affur'd *Cleander*
that *Simon* was a Convert and hated my
Lord's ill Ufage of him as much as they
did : *Rivella* knew *Tim*'s Tallent at Dif-
fembling, which he openly valu'd himfelf
upon, and therefore did not much regard
what he faid ; fhe fent to the *Baron* to give
him Notice of this Accident: Then his
Lordfhip's and *Ofwald* began to put themfelves upon the Frett , *Tim* had fometime
fince funk his Pretenfions, of two Thoufand to fifteen Hundred Pounds a Year,
and was come to clofe with their own offer
of fix Thoufand Pound in Money, which
thefe fhallow, or greedy Politicians finding, thought to fink him further, and in
that

that View kept the Affair fo long in hand
that it got Wind ; but then Lord *Meanwell*
began to beftir himfelf too late, he order'd
Rivella to tell the Squire, that he did agree
to all his Demands, and was accordingly
feeing the Writings perfected ; in the mean
Time, the Articles were drawing up for
Tim to fign, upon which, he was to receive eight Hundred Pound overplus for
his prefent Neceffities : *Simon* had leave
given to make one at *Rivella*'s, and fhe
had Orders to affure him of a Prefent of
five Hundred Pound for his own Occafions.

MEAN Time, *Tim*'s Flame for *Bella*
daily increas'd, *Rivella* call'd her to her,
and bid her keep away from her Houfe ;
for fhe would not charge her felf with
the Confequences, Squire *Tim* being a married Man : The Girl did not fcruple to tell
her, that her Defign of going to the Play-
houfe was in hopes of finding fome body
to keep her, fhe had often feen in the
Dreffing Room, what great Refpect Mrs.
Barry and the reft, ufed to pay to Mrs.
Alyfe when fhe ufed to come thither, and
how fine they all liv'd, which fhe was
fure they cou'd not do upon their Pay. *Rivella* was amaz'd at her Confidence, which
fhe thought no way fuitable to a Maid :
She then fpoke to *Tim* to give over the Purfuit, fince that Girl could not poffibly be of

N 2   any

any Confequence to a Man like him, and to ruin her, would be an eternal Reproach to the whole Company; *Tim* fwore he would marry her to morrow, or as foon as he was divorced, and old *Simon* thought this a very good Handle, he made his Court in the Squire's name more artfully to the Girl. He affured her that *Rivella* was her mortal Enemy, and envied her leaft fhe fhould come to be greater than herfelf: For *Tim* had indeed told *Rivella*, as I faid before, that if he could be divorced he would marry *Bella*; this gain'd his Point with the Girl: She affumed very haughty Airs towards *Rivella*, and very tender ones towards *Tim*: Old *Simon* had likewife fucceeded his Court to *Flippanta*, by making believe he was fmitten with her Beauty: Poor decay'd *Flip* was proud of a Conqueft, and readily entered into a Confederacy againft her Miftrefs: To conclude, *Bella* was become the Head of the Company, neither durft *Rivella* contradict her. She thought fome fmall Time longer would put an end to her Suffering, and betray'd as little Uneafinefs as poffible. *Simon* perfuaded *Tim* that he had no other way to preferve *Bella*'s Favour, but by breaking that difhonourable Treaty he had been drawn into with the Lord *Meanwell*; *Bella* affured him of the fame thing: *Simon* told him, that Lord *Crafty* heartily repented the Neglect

glect had been fhown whilft his Lordfhip
was in the Country, and to make appear
that he was fincere, offer'd to give him up
all his Ingagements, and to profecute the
Suit againft the *Baron*, till he had put him
in Poffeffion of the whole Eftate. *Tim* did
not know which Part to chufe, when he
was with *Bell* and *Sim*, he was Theirs,
when he was with *Cleander* and *Rivella*
he was for Them; at length, the long
look'd for Hour came, when he was to fign
the Articles and receive his eight Hundred
Pounds Bounty Money : The *Baron* would
needs have him come alone to the Tavern
where they were to meet, that fo the Act
might look voluntary; but, the Difficulty
was how to get him there; they durft not
fo much as tell him, leaft he fhould give
Part of the Intelligence to Mr. *Simon*; in
fhort, it was left to *Rivella*'s Management, fhe took him out in a Coach with
her to the appointed Place, upon Pretence
of meeting a Gentleman who had a Mind
to part with a Diamond Buckle for his Hat,
and if *Tim* lik'd it, he might become a
Proprietor in the Buckle, and have fix
Month's Credit given him; this was fomething that hit the *Squire*'s Vanity; but as
they were going thither, *Rivella* told him
the real Defign; but that fince the utmoft
Secrefy was neceffary, fhe had ufed that
Artifice to prevent Mr. *Simon*, and confequently

quently Lord *Crafty* from knowing his good
Fortune till it was beyond their Power to
prevent: She faid, that faithful *Cleander* attended with the Lord *Meanwell's* Lawyer,
who for his own Honour, as well as out of
Refpect and friendfhip for *Tim*, would take
care to have all poffible Juftice done him
in an Affair that was going to make fuch
a Noife in the World: To be fhort, *Rivella* fortified him fo well that he promifed
to go in and perform what he had cove-
nanted; fhe fet him down two Doors,
fhort of the Tavern, he kifs'd her Hand
with an Air entirely fatisfied, and told her
fhe fhou'd always command that Fortune,
which fhe had been fo good to procure for
him; and that the next Day at Dinner, he
would do himfelf the Honour to wait upon her to pay his Acknowledgments more
at large: Thus was that great Affair dif-
patched; and the eighth Day after appointed for executing the Deeds; and putting
the Squire in Poffeffion of what Eftate and
Money had been ftipulated for him.

OLD *Simon* revell'd with the Money
Tim brought home, who had never the
Honefty to repay *Cleander* the leaft Part
of what he had borrow'd of him; as to
Rivella's Expences, they were come to a
Sum fo much beyond what the *Baron* had
promis'd her, in cafe that Affair did not
fucceed,

fucceed, that fhe never demanded any Money from him; throwing *at all*, as in a defperate Game; where nothing lefs can repair the former Lofs.

THE eighth Day did come; the Lord and his Agent, the Deeds and the Lawyers were ready; but not ·the Squire: Old *Simon* and Mr. *Timothy*, Madam *Bell* and *Mademoifelle Flippanta* filently diflodged 'without Beat of Drum, and left *Cleander* and *Rivella* to repent of their grand expenfive Negotiation; by which in the end, no Perfons happened to be Gainers, but the Lord *Crafty* and Mr. *Simon*.

I WILL not tire you with many more Particulars: *Tim* was infatuated by *Bell*'s Perfuafions who now lodged with him as his Lady, but *incog*, for Fear of the *Baron* and *Cleander*: Lord *Crafty* let them fpend together the Money *Tim* had fo bafely acquired, and then fent him away to *Flanaers* under *Sim*'s Conduct, who took care to confine him to a Houfe they had taken, not fuffering him to converfe with any Company, but three or four Rakes that they had gotten purpofely to drink with him from Morning till Night, keeping him perpetually flufter'd, leaft his cooler Senfe fhould make him confider what he had done, and put him upon ftealing away
from

from them to return back into *England,*
there to perform Articles with the Lord
Meanwell. Treacherous *Bell* was likewife
over-reach'd, fhe was put for fometime to
Penfion by a feign'd Name at a poor Woman's Houfe in an obfcure Part of the
Town, with daily Promifes of being fent
into *Flanders* to her Beloved, who had ftipulated with Lord *Crafty's* Agent that fhe
fhould follow him; telling *Rivella* and o-
thers that he was married to her, which
whether true or falfe fignified little, fince
Bell very well knew, unlefs he could make
his former Marriage null, *Tim* was in no
Capacity to marry again.

HERE that infignificant treacherous
Creature grew Poor and was forgotten;
for when *Bell* no longer ferved their Ends,
Lord *Crafty* and his *Managers* remembred
her no more than if fhe never had been
born; a very quick Return for her Perfidy,
Folly and Ingratitude; had fhe not feduced
Tim Double from his Engagements, *Cleander* would have taken care of her Interefts
fo far (fince her higheft Ambition was
only to be a Miftrefs) as that the *Squire*
fhould have done fomething for her above
that extream Contempt which her Vices
have fince brought upon her; whence moft
who have heard even her own Pretences,
have been uncharitable enough to conclude,
that

fo vile a Nature as hers could hardly ever have been otherwife; fince extream Corruption does not all at once, but rather gradually feize upon fuch who have any Degree of Vertue in their Compofition.

SOON after thefe Difappointments, *Rivella* receiv'd an anonymous Letter by the Penny-Poft, to beg her to be next Day at twelve a Clock, all alone, in a Hackney-Coach, in the upper *Hyde-Park* near the Lodge: She ask'd *Cleander*'s Opinion; he affur'd her it was the Hand-writing of Lord *Crafty*, which was fo particular that no body could be miftaken that had once feen it; he advifed her to go to the Appointment, for that Lord had too much Refpect for the fair Sex to do an Outrage to any Lady; accordingly fhe went and found that very Perfon alone in another Hackney-Coach; he alighted and came into hers: After the firft Forms were over, he did not fcruple to value himfelf upon defeating their well laid Defign. He affur'd her they fhould never recover *Tim* again, and therefore advifed her, fince fhe underftood fo much of this Matter, to make up her Difappointments by indeavouring an Accommodation between the *Baron* and himfelf, to which end, his Lordfhip gave her Power to a certain Point, how to proceed.

THE

THE *Baron* approv'd of the Project, he gave *Rivella* leave to treat with the Lord *Crafty*, with an Aſſurance of Two Thouſand Pound for her ſelf if they ſhould, by her means, agree; and to ſhew his Lord-ſhip that *Cleander* and her ſelf were *Truſt-worthy*, and very well deſerved his Favour, ſhe brought *Tim*'s only Brother, the next Heir in caſe *Tim* ſhould have no Sons, to his Lordſhip; this poor young Man want-ed Food, Raiment and Education, his Parts and Honeſty much exceeded the Squires; he ſold his Reverſion to the *Baron* for an Annuity of an Hundred and Fifty Pounds a Year; and thought himſelf very happy to be able to ſecure a preſent Maintenance out of his imaginary future Hopes.

THIS was a Circumſtance Lord *Craf-ty* could hardly forgive himſelf; looking up-on *Tim* or his Lady to be fruitful Perſons, tho' the Males all died, he never once conſi-der'd his Brother might prove of Conſe-quence: In ſhort, his Lordſhip and *Rivella* often met, he did all that was in his Power to ſhake her Fidelity to the *Baron*; told her he laid Eighteen Thouſand Pound a Year at her Feet, all his good Fortune had come by Ladies, but he had never found any of ſo great Ability as her ſelf. He endeavour'd to make it her Intereſt to cor-
rupt

rupt *Ofwald* to incline the *Baron* to eafier
Terms of Accommodation; when he faw
fhe was not to be fhaken, he confented to
treat with the Lord *Meanwell* in Perfon,
a Circumftance he had hitherto refufed her
whenever fhe propofed it. They accordingly met where Lord *Crafty* extoll'd *Rivella* in fuch an artful Manner, that made
the *Baron* fufpect fhe was in his Intereft,
telling him he was fo well fatisfied in her
Honour and Capacity, (for no Lawyer they
had ever employ'd knew the Caufe fo well)
that he would refer the whole Matter to the
Decifion, and peremptorily offer'd to put it
upon that very Iffue. The *Baron* at that
Touch fhrank himfelf all in a Heap, like the
fenfible Plant; he told *Ofwald*, that *that*
very artful Lord had corrupted *Rivella*'s
Truth, elfe how was it poffible he durft leave
a Matter of fuch vaft Confequence to her
Decifion: *Ofwald* had a better Opinion of
her, and begg'd his Lordfhip, as a Proof
that he would but feem to agree to *Crafty*'s
Propofal, and then he would quickly find
that what he faid was nothing but Pretence and Artifice : The *Baron* was not of
his Opinion, believing himfelf wifer than
all the World, and perhaps willing to fave
the Money he had promifed *Rivella*, tho'
it coft him much more the other way ; he
clapt up an hafty Agreement with *Crafty*,
without any farther confulting *Ofwald* in

the

the Matter, by which, out of old *Double's*
Eſtate, he gave *The* Lord Threeſcore and
Twelve Thouſard Pound, and yet ſtill remain'd liable to perform Conditions with
Tim, when ever he ſhould think fit to force
him to it; but very much to his Mortification on one ſide, and Joy on the other,
he heard that *Tim* was kill'd with drinking, a juſt and miſerable Return for his
Debauchery, Folly and Villany: If the
Baron had known of his Death before the
Agreement, it would have ſaved him ſeveral Thouſand Pounds; but ſince the Agreement was made, he was very glad 'twas
now become out of *Tim's* Power to call
his Lordſhip to an Account for that which
he had made with him.

THUS my dear *D'Aumont*, continued
Sir *Charles*, I have finiſh'd the Secret Hiſtory of that tedious Law Suit, which I juſtly
fear has likewiſe tir'd your Patience. My
Buſineſs was to give you *Rivella's* Hiſtory on thoſe Occaſions that have to her Prejudice, made moſt Noiſe in the World;
ſince ſhe has writ for the *Tories*, the *Whigs*
have heighten'd this Story, and too ſevere-
ly reflected upon her for *Bella's* Misfortunes, tho' they were all occaſion'd by her
own Viciouſneſs, Forwardneſs and Treachery, in which *Rivella* had not any Part.
Rivella never ſaw nor applied her ſelf to
the

the *Baron* any more, nor converfed with *Ofwald.* If that Lord ever made her an Acknowledgment, it was directed to mifcarry, as coming thro' *Ofwala's* Hands, and fhe with Reafon, reckons that Family to be much her Debtors : Poor *Cleander* was a great deal of Money out of Pocket, but he lov'd *Rivella* too well to reproach her with it.

D U R I N G their mutual Intelligence and Friendfhip, *Califta,* after a long Difufe, came to vifit *Rivella* ; *Cleander* was then in the Room, they both look'd fo amazed and confounded, that *Rivella* took the firft Occafion to withdraw, to permit them an Opportunity to recover their Concern. If you remember *Chevalier, Califta* was the Lady who firft ingaged *Rivella* to ferve *Cleander,* tho' fhe excufed her felf upon being his Wife's Acquaintance, and not *Cleander's* : When fhe had ended her Vifit, *Rivella* would know what had occafion'd their mutual Confufion; he laugh'd and defended himfelf a long Time ; at length, he confefs'd *Califta* was the firft Lady that had ever made him unfaithful to his Wife : Her Mother being in Misfortunes and indebted to him, fhe had offer'd her Daughter's Security, he took it, and moreover the Blefling of one Night's Lodging, which he never paid her back again.

Rivella

Rivella laugh'd in her Turn, becaufe *Ca-lifta* had given her felf Airs of not vifiting *Rivella*,now fhe was made the Town Talk by her fcandalous Intriegue with *Cleander* ; *Rivella* defired him to give her the Bond, which he promifed and perform'd.

MUCH about that Time, *George* Prince of *Hefs Darmftad*, came the fecond Time into *England*; he had been *Vice-Roy* of *Catalonia*, towards the latter End of *Charles* the Third's Reign : The Inclination his Highnefs had of returning into *Spain*, his Adorations for the *Dowager*, his Relation being no Secret, made him keep up his Correfpondence with the *Catalans*; principally with the Inhabitants of *Barcelona*, who continually follicited him to Aid them with Forces, whereby they might be enabled to declare themfelves a-gainft *Philip* of *Bourbon*, whom they un-willingly obey'd : The Prince of *Hefs* re-prefented this to the Court of *England*, as a Matter of very great Importance ; he produced feveral Letters from the chief Perfons of *Catalonia* : His Highnefs was recommended to a Merchant in the City, whom he pray'd to introduce him into the Acquaintance of fome of the moft ingeni-ous Ladies of the *Englifh* Nation ; this Merchant was acquainted with a Gentle-woman that was newly fet up to fell *Milli-ner's*

ner's Ware to the Ladies and Gentlemen;
she was well born, and incouraged by several Persons who laid out their Money
with her in Consideration of her Misfortunes: The Merchant desir'd she would
speak to the Lady *Rivella*, who was her
Customer, and two Ladies more, to come
one Evening to Cards at her House, where
himself would introduce the Prince incog.
His Highness understood nothing of *Loo*,
which was the Game they play'd at; he
could not speak a Word of *English*, nor the
other Ladies a Word of *French*. They
knew his Quality, tho' they were to take
no notice of it, and thought to win his
Money, which is all that most Ladies care
for at Play: *Rivella* sat next the Prince,
and for the Honour of the *English* Women
would not let him be cheated, she assisted
him in his Game, and in conjunction with
his good Luck, order'd the Matter so well,
that his Highness was the only Person who
rose a Winner: From that Time he conceiv'd the greatest Esteem for *Rivella*, the
Prince presented her with his Picture at
length, and continued a Correspondence
with her till the Day before his Death:
Cleander did not believe there was any mixture of Love in it, because it was well
known, the Prince had engaged his Heart
in *Spain*, and his Person in *England*, by
way of Amusement to a certain celebrated

ted Lady, who had made a great Figure in
F..anders, and was more known by the
Name of the *Electress* of *Bavaria*, than
her own.

RIVELLA tasted some Years the Pleasure of Retirement, in the Conversation of
the Person beloved ; but a tedious and an
unhappy Law-Suit straitned *Cleander's* Cir-
cumstances and put him under several Difficulties. In the mean time his Wife died ;
Rivella was complimented upon her Loss
even by *Cleander* himself, for all the World
thought he lov'd her so well as to marry
her ; she receiv'd his Address with such
Confusion and Regret, that he knew not
what to make of her Disorder, till at
length bursting forth into Tears, she cry'd
I am undone from this Moment! I have
lost the only Person, who secured to me the
Possession of your Heart! *Cleander* was
struck with her Words, I came into the
Room, and *Rivella* withdrew to hide her
Concern : *Cleander* felt himself so wounded by what she had spoken, that I shall never forget it ; he confess'd her to be the
greatest Mistress of Nature that ever was
born ; she knew, he said, the hidden Springs
and Defects of Human-kind ; Self-love was
indeed such an inherent Evil in all the
World, that he was afraid *Rivella* had spoken
something that look'd too like Truth ; but
what

what ever happened he ſhould never be acquainted with a Woman of her Worth, neither could any thing but extream Neceſſity, force him to abandon her Innocence and Tenderneſs.

NOT long after *Cleander* was caſt at Law, and condemn'd in a great Sum to be paid by the next Term ; he conceal'd his Misfortunes from *Rivella,* but ſhe learn'd them from other Perſons : One muſt be a Woman of an exalted Soul to take the Part ſhe did : The Troubles of the Mind caſt her into a Fit of Sickneſs ; *Cleander* gueſs'd at the Cauſe, and endeavour'd to reſtore her at any Price, having aſſur'd her of it ; ſhe ask'd him if he would marry her ; he immediately anſwer'd he would, tho' he were ruin'd by it ; ſhe told him that was a very hard Sentence, ſhe could not conſent to his ruin with half ſo much eaſe as to her own ; then enquired if there was any Way to ſave him ? He explain'd to her his Circumſtances, and the Propoſals that had been made to him of courting a rich young Widow, but that he could not think of it : *Rivella* pauſ'd a long Time, at length pulling up her Spirits, and fixing her Reſolution, ſhe told him it ſhould be ſo ; he ſhould not be undone for her ſake ; ſhe had receiv'd many Obligations from him, and he had ſuffer'd ſeveral

P   Incon-

Inconveniences on her Account; particularly in the Affair of Mr. *Timothy Double:* She was proud it was now in her Power to repay part of the Debt she ow'd; therefore she conjur'd him to make his Addresses to the Lady, for tho' he might be so far influenced by his Bride as afterwards to become ingrateful, she would much rather that should happen, than to see him Poor and Miserable, an Object of perpetual Reproach to her Heart and Eyes; for having preferr'd the Reparation of her own Honour, to the Preservation of his.

I SHOULD move you too far, Generous *D'Aumont*, in relating half that Tenderness and Reluctance, with which it was concluded they should part: I was the Confident between them; but tho' I had Esteem and Friendship for *Cleander*, there was something touch'd my Soul more nearly for *Rivella*'s Interest; therefore I would have disswaded her from that Romantick Bravery of Mind, by advising her to marry her Lover, who was so bright a Man, that he could never prove long unhappy, his own Capacity being sufficient to extricate him; but as she had never taken my Advice in any Thing, she did not begin now; there was a Pleasure she said in becoming Miserable, when it was to make a Person happy, by whom she
had

had been fo very much obliged, and fo long and faithfully beloved!

CLEANDER's handfom Perfon immediately made Way to the Widow's Heart ; it is not my Bufinefs to fpeak much of her, tho' the Theam be very ample ; I have heard him fay, that he might have fucceeded to his Wifh, if he could have had the Confidence to believe a Woman could have been won fo quickly : Her Relations got notice of the Courtfhip, and reprefented the Difadvantage of the Match, which occafion'd Settlements and Security of her own Fortune to her own Ufe. *Cleander* trufted to the Power he hoped to gain over her Heart ; thinking when once they were married, fhe might be brought to recede, but he was miftaken : *The wooing lafted but a Month; with all the Obftacles her Friends could raife*, which perhaps was a Fortnight longer than the Date of her Paffion afterwards. Fears and Jealoufies enfu'd; they pafs'd many uneafy Hours of Wedlock together. He teiz'd the Lady about Cards, and fhe him for *Rivella* who feldom faw him ; for fhe led her Life moftly in the Country, and never appear'd in Publick after *Cleander*'s Marriage; which with four Years Uneafinefs concluded in the Lofs of his Senfes, and in three more of his Life ; whether the

Want

Want of *Rivella*'s Converfation, which he
had fo long been us'd to contributed, or the
Uneafinefs of his Circumftances; for his
Marriage had not anfwer'd the fancied
End, or fomething elfe, which I am not
willing to fay, where very much may be
faid ; tho' as *Rivella*'s Friend, I have no
Reafon to fpare *Cleander*'s Lady, becaufe
fhe always fpeaks of her with Language
moft unfit for a Gentlewoman, and on all
Occafions, has us'd her with the Spite and
ill Nature of an enraged jealous Wife.

AFTER that Time, I know nothing
memorable of *Rivella*, but that fhe feem'd
to bury all Thoughts of Gallantry in *Cleander*'s Tomb; and unlefs fhe had her felf
publifh'd fuch melting Scenes of Love, I
fhould by her Regularity and good Behaviour have thought fhe had loft the Memory of that Paffion. I was in the Country when the Two firft Volumes of the
Atalantis were Publifh'd, and did not
know who was the Author, but came to
Town juft as the Lord S——d had granted
a Warrant againft the *Printer* and *Pub-
lifher* : I went as ufual, to wait upon *Rivella*, whom I found in one of her Heroick Strains; fhe faid fhe was glad I was
come, to advife her in a Bufinefs of very
great Importance; fhe had as yet confulted

ed with but one Friend, whose Counsel
had not pleas'd her; no more would
mine, I thought, but did not interrupt
her; in Conclusion she told me that her
self was Author of the *Atalantis*, for
which three innocent Persons were taken
up and would be ruin'd with their Families; that she was resolv'd to surren-
der her self into the *Messenger's* Hands,
whom she heard had the Secretary of
State's Warrant against her, so to difcharge those honest People from their Im-
prisonment: I stared upon her and thought
her directly mad; I began with railing
at her Books; the barbarous Design of exposing People that never had done her
any Injury; she answer'd me she was
become *Misanthrope*, a perfect *Timon*, or
Man-Hater; all the World was out of
Humour with her, and she with all the
World, more particularly a *Faction* who
were busy to enslave their Sovereign, and
overturn the Constitution; that she was
proud of having more Courage than had
any of our Sex, and of throwing the first
Stone, which might give a Hint for other
Persons of more Capacity to examine the
Defects, and Vices of some Men who took
a Delight to impose upon the World, by the
Pretence of publick Good, whilst their true
Design was only to gratify and advance
themselves. As to exposing those who had
never

never injured her, fhe faid fhe did no more by others, than others had done by her (*i.e.*) Tattle of Frailties; the Town had never fhewn her any Indulgence, but on the contrary reported ten fold againft her in Matters of which fhe was wholly Innocent; whereas fhe did but take up old Stories that all the World had long fince reported, having ever been careful of glancing againft fuch Perfons who were truly vertuous, and who had not been very carelefs of their own Actions.

RIVELLA grew warm in her Defence, and obftinate in her Defign of furrendring her felf a Prifoner: I ask'd her how fhe would like going to *Newgate?* She anfwer'd me very well; fince it was to difcharge her Confcience; I told her all this founded great, and was very Heroick; but there was a vaft Difference between real and imaginary Sufferings: She had chofe to declare her felf of a Party moft Supine, and forgetful of fuch who ferved them; that fhe would certainly be abandon'd by them, and left to perifh and ftarve in Prifon. The moft fevere Criticks upon *Tory* Writings, were *Tories* themfelves, who never confidering the Defign or honeft Intention of the Author, would examin the Performance only, and that too with as much Severity as they
would

would an Enemy's, and at the fame Time
value themfelves upon their being impartial, tho' againft their Friends : Then as
to Gratitude or Generofity, the *Tories* did
not come up to the *Whigs*, who never
fuffer'd any Man to want Incourage-
ment and Rewards if he were never fo
dull, vicious or infignificant, provided he
declar'd himfelf to be for them; whereas
the *Tories* had no general Intereft, and
confequently no particular, each Perfon
refufing to contribute towards the Benefit of the whole; and when it fhould
come to pafs (as certainly it would) that
fhe perifh'd thro' Want in a Goal, they
would fooner condemn her Folly, than pit-
ty her Sufferings; and cry, *fhe may take it
for her Pains: Who bid her write? What
good did fhe do? Could not fhe fit quiet as
well as her Neighbours, and not meddle
her felf about what did not concern her?*

RIVELLA was ftartled at thefe
Truths, and ask'd me, What then would
I have her do? I anfwer'd that I was ftill
at her Service, as well as my Fortune :
I would wait upon her out of *England*,
and then find fome Means to get her fafe
into *France*, where the Queen, that was
once to have been her Miftrefs, would
doubtlefs take her into her own Protection; fhe faid the Project was a vain
one,

one, that Lady being the greateſt Bigot
in Nature to the *Roman* Church, and
ſhe was, and ever would be, a *Proteſtant*,
a Name ſufficient to deſtroy the greateſt
Merit in that Court. I told her I would
carry her into *Switzerland*, or any Country that was but a Place of Safety, and
leave her there if ſhe commanded me;
ſhe aſk'd me in a haſty Manner, as if
ſhe demanded Pardon for heſitating upon the Point, what then would become
of the poor *Printer*, and thoſe two other
Perſons concern'd, the *Publiſhers*, who with
their Families all would be undone by her
Flight? That the Miſery I had threaten'd
her with, was a leſs Evil than doing a
diſhonourable Thing: I aſk'd her if ſhe
had promis'd thoſe Perſons to be anſwer-
able for the Event? She ſaid no, ſhe had
only given them leave to ſay, if they were
queſtion'd, *they had receiv'd the Copy from
her Hand!* I us'd ſeveral Arguments to ſatisfy her Conſcience that ſhe was under
no farther Obligation, eſpecially ſince the
Profit had been theirs; ſhe anſwer'd it
might be ſo, but ſhe could not bear to
live and reproach her ſelf with the Miſery that might happen to thoſe unfortunate People: Finding her obſtinate, I
left her with an angry Threat, of never beholding her in that wretched State, into
which ſhe was going to plunge her ſelf.

RIVELLA

RIVELLA remain'd immovable in a Point which fhe thought her Duty, and accordingly furrender'd her felf, and was examin'd in the Secretary's Office : They us'd feveral Arguments to make her difcover who were the Perfons concern'd with her in writing her Books; or at leaft from whom fhe had receiv'd Information of fome fpecial Facts, which they thought were above her own Intelligence : Her Defence was with much Humility and Sorrow, for having offended, at the fame Time denying that any Perfons were concern'd with her, or that fhe had a farther Defign than writing for her own Amufement and Diverfion in the Country; without intending particular Reflections or Characters : When this was not believ'd, and the contrary urg'd very home to her by feveral Circumftances and Likeneffes; fhe faid then it muft be *Infpiration*, becaufe knowing her own Innocence fhe could acount for it no other Way : The Secretary reply'd upon her, that *Infpiration* us'd to be upon a good Account, and her Writings were ftark naught ; fhe told him, with an Air full of Penitence, that might be true, but it was as true, that there were evil Angels as well as good; fo that neverthelefs what fhe had wrote might ftill be by *Infpiration*.

Q   NOT

NOT to detain you longer, dear attentive *D'Aumont*, the gathering Clouds beginning to bring Night upon us, this poor Lady was clofe fhut up in the *Meffenger's* Hands from feeing or fpeaking to any Perfon, without being allow'd Pen, Ink and Paper; where fhe was moft tyranically and barbaroufly infulted by the Fellow and his Wife who had her in keeping, tho' doubtlefs without the Knowledge of their Superiors; for when *Rivella* was examin'd, they ask'd her if fhe was civilly us'd? She thought it below her to complain of fuch little People, who when they ftretch'd Authority a little too far, thought perhaps that they ferv'd the Intention and Refentments, tho' not the Commands of their Mafters; and accordingly chofe to be inhuman, rather than juft and civil.

RIVELLA's Council fued out her *Habeas Corpus* at the *Queen's Bench-Bar* in *Weftminfter* Hall; and fhe was admitted to Bail. Whether the Perfons in Power were afhamed to bring a Woman to her Trial for writing a few amorous Trifles purely for her own Amufement, or that our Laws were defective, as moft Perfons conceiv'd, becaufe fhe had ferv'd her felf with Romantick Names, and a feign'd Scene of Action? But after feveral

veral Times expofing her in Perfon to walk crofs the Court before the Bench of Judges, with her three Attendants, the *Printer* and both the *Publifhers*; the *Attorny General* at the End of three or four Terms dropt the Profecution, tho' not without a very great Expence to the Defendants, who were however glad to compound with their Purfes for their heinious Offence, and the notorious Indifcretion of which they had. been guilty.

THERE happen'd not long after a total Change in the Miniftry, the Perfons whom *Rivella* had difoblig'd being removed, and confequently her Fears diffipated; upon which that native Gaiety and good Humour fo fparkling and confpicuous in her, return'd; I had the hardeft Part to act, becaufe I could not eafily forego her Friendfhip and Acquaintance, yet knew not very well how to pretend to the Continuance of either, confidering what I had faid to her upon our laft Seperation the Night before her Imprifonment: Finding I did not return to wifh her Joy with the reft of her Friends upon her Inlargement, fhe did me the Favour to write to me, affuring me that fhe very well diftinguifh'd that which a Friend out of the Greatnefs of his Friendfhip did advife, and what a Man of Ho-

nour

nour could be fuppos'd to endure, by giving Advice wherein his Friend or himfelf muft fuffer, and that fince I had fo generoufly endeavour'd her Safety at the expence of my own Character, fhe would always look upon me as a Perfon whom nothing could taint but my Friendfhip for her. I was afham'd of the Delicacy of her Argument, by which fince I was prov'd guilty, tho' the Motives were never fo prevalent, ftill my Honour was found defective, how perfect foever my Friendfhip might appear.

RIVELLA had always the better of me at this Argument, and when fhe would infult me, never fail'd to ferve her felf with that falfe one, *Succefs*, in return, I brought her to be afham'd of her Writings, faving that Part by which fhe pretended to ferve her Country, and the ancient Conftitution; (there fhe is a perfect *Bigot* from a long untainted Defcent of Loyal Anceftors, and confequently immoveable) but when I would argue with her the Folly of a Woman's difobliging any one Party, by a Pen equally qualified to divert all, fhe agreed my Reflection was juft, and promis'd not to repeat her Fault, provided the World would have the Goodnefs to forget thofe fhe had already committed, and that henceforward

forward her Bufinefs fhould be to write of
Pleafure and Entertainment only, wherein
Party fhould no longer mingle ; but that
the *Whigs* were fo unforgiving they would
not advance one Step towards a *Coalition*
with any Mufe that had once been fo indif-
creet to declare againft them : She now a-
grees with me, that Politicks is not the Bufinefs of a Woman, efpecially of one that can
fo well delight and entertain her Readers
with more gentle pleafing Theams, and has
accordingly fet her felf again to write a
Tragedy for the Stage. If you ftay in *England*, dear *Chevalier*, till next Winter, we
may hope to entertain you from thence,
with what ever *Rivella* is capable of performing in the *Dramatick* Art.

BUT has fhe ftill a Tafte for Love,
interrupted young Monfieur *D'Aumont* ?
Doubtlefs, anfwer'd Sir *Charles*, or whence
is it that fhe daily writes of him with fuch
Fire and Force ? But whether fhe does
Love, is a Queftion? I often hear her Exprefs a Jealoufy of appearing fond at her
Time of Day, and full of Rallery againft
thofe Ladies, who fue when they are no
longer fued unto. She converfes now with
our Sex in a Manner that is very delicate,
fenfible, and agreeable; which is to fay,
knowing her felf to be no longer Young,
fhe does not feem to expect the Praife and
Flat-

Flattery that attend the Youthful: The greateſt Genius's of the Age, give her daily Proofs of their Eſteem and Friendſhip; only one excepted, who yet I find was more in her Favour than any other of the Wits pretend to have been, ſince he in Print has very lately told the World, 'twas his own Fault he was not Happy, for which Omiſſion he has publickly and gravely ask'd her Pardon. Whether this Proceeding was ſo *Chevalier* as is ought, I will no more determine a- gainſt him, than believe him againſt her ; but ſince the charitable Cuſtom of the World gives the Lie to that Perſon, whoſo- ever he be, that boaſts of having receiv'd a Lady's Favour, becauſe it is an Action unworthy of Credit, and of a Man of Honour; may not he by the ſame Rule be disbeliev'd, who ſays he might and would not receive Favours; eſpecially from a Sweet, Clean, Witty, Friendly, Service- able and young Woman, as *Rivella* was, when this Gentleman pretends to have been *Cruel*; conſidering that in the Choice of his other Amours, he has given no ſuch Proof of his Delicacy, or the Niceneſs of his Taſte? But what ſhall we ſay, the Pre- judice of *Party* runs ſo high in *England,* that the beſt natured Perſons, and thoſe of the greateſt Integrity, ſcruple not to ſay Falſe and Malicious Things of thoſe who differ from them in Principles, in any Caſe

but

but Love ; Scandal between *Whig* and *Tory*, goes for nothing ; but who is there befides my felf, that thinks it an impoffible Thing a *Tory* Lady fhould prove frail, efpecially when a Perfon (tho' never fo much a *Whig*) reports her to be fo, upon his own Knowledge.

THUS generous *D'Aumont*, I have endeavour'd to obey your Commands, in giving you that part of *Rivella*'s Hiftory, which has made the moft Noife againft her ; I confefs, had I fhown only the bright Part of her Adventures ; I might have Entertain'd you much more agreeably, but that requires much longer Time ; together with the Songs, Letters and Adorations, innumerable from thofe who never could be Happy. Then to have rais'd your Paffions in her Favour ; I fhould have brought you to her Table well furnifh'd and well ferv'd ; have fhown you her fparkling Wit and eafy Gaiety, when at Meat with Perfons of Converfation and Humour : From thence carried you (in the Heat of Summer after Dinner) within the Nymphs Alcove, to a Bed nicely fheeted and ftrow'd with *Rofes*, *Jeffamins* or *Orange-Flowers*, fuited to the variety of the Seafon ; her Pillows neatly trim'd with Lace or Muflin, ftuck round with *Junquils*, or other natural Garden Sweets, for fhe ufes no Perfumes,

and

and there have given you leave to fancy your self the happy Man, with whom she chose to repose her self, during the Heat of the Day, in a State of Sweetness and Tranquility : From thence conducted you towards the cool of the Evening, either upon the *Water*, or to the *Park* for Air, with a Conversation always new, and which never cloys ; *Allon*'s let us go my dear *Lovemore*, interrupted young *D'Aumont*, let us not lose a Moment before we are acquainted with the only Person of her Sex that knows how to *Live*, and of whom we may say, in relation to Love, since she has so peculiar a Genius for, and has made such noble Discoveries in that Passion, that it would have been a *Fault in her*, *not to have been Faulty.*

FINIS.

The Adventures
and Surprizing Deliverances
of James Dubourdieu
and his Wife

and

The Adventures of Alexander Vendchurch

by

Ambrose Evans

Bibliographical note:

This facsimile has been made from a copy in the Beinecke Library of Yale University (IK SW5.5 R719)

THE
ADVENTURES,
AND
SURPRIZING DELIVERANCES,
OF
JAMES DUBOURDIEU,
AND HIS
WIFE:

Who were taken by Pyrates, and carried to the
Uninhabited-Part of the Isle of *Paradise.*

CONTAINING

A Description of that Country, its Laws, Religion,
and Customs: Of Their being at last releas'd; and
how they came to *Paris,* where they are still living.

ALSO, THE
ADVENTURES
OF
ALEXANDER VENDCHURCH,

Whose Ship's Crew Rebelled against him, and set him
on Shore on an Island in the *South-Sea,* where he
liv'd five Years, five Months, and seven Days; and
was at last providentially releas'd by a *Jamaica* Ship.

Written by HIMSELF.

LONDON:

Printed by *J. Bettenham* for *A. Bettesworth* and *T. Warner,* in
Pater-noster Row; *C. Rivington,* in *St. Paul's* Church-yard;
J. Brotherton and *W. Meadows,* in *Cornhill*; *A. Dodd* without
Temple Bar, and *W. Chetwood* in *Covent Garden.* 1719.
Price Two Shillings.

THE
PREFACE.

*T*HE *value of history is too uni-*
verfally allow'd to need any proof
in this place ; but as the fubject
of hiftory in general is of princes,
kingdoms and nations , with their
feveral fates and revolutions ; and that the
Biographers *themfelves, who treat only of*
particular lives, have for the moft part cho-
fen to write of men who are eminent by their
ftations, either in war or peace ; it may feem
neceffary to fay fomething in behalf of tranf-
mitting to pofterity the tranfactions of private
perfons, who have never been diftinguifh'd from
the reft of mankind by their places or dignity,
or any thing elfe but the fingularity of their
fortune.

    THERE is a double ufe of hiftory in ge-
neral, that is, one for delight, and the other
inftruction ; the principal inftruction, which is
drawn from them, relates chiefly to ftatefmen ;
that by a view of former events they may
form fome conjectural judgment of the prefent :
                      That

THE PREFACE.

That of delight reaches every one who takes any pleasure in knowing what has pass'd in the world from its beginning.

THE relation likewise of the adventures of private men is not without its advantage, either of delight or instruction; nay, I may say, that both these are more extensive in the latter than in the former; these reaching to every one, those to but few. What delight particular accounts give, is plain from the general reception of travels and voyages, and the lives of private persons, which have always been receiv'd with considerable satisfaction and applause, when they afford any thing either entertaining, surprizing, or beneficial to the active part of the world.

AMONG these, I believe I may say, that the two following relations merit as valuable a place as any that have been publish'd; but this I wholly leave to the judgment of the reader.

THE

THE
LIVES,
ADVENTURES,
AND
WONDERFUL DELIVERANCES
OF
Mrs. *MARTHA RATTENBERG,*
AND
JAMES DUBOURDIEU.

SIR,

CCORDING to your defire, I take this opportunity of one of my Lord Ambaffador's retinue going for *London,* to fend you a full account of the ftrange and wonderful adventures of our Countrywoman Mrs. *Martha Rattenberg,* and of *James Dubourdieu* her husband ; for you muft know that marriage in *France* does not take away the maiden name of the wife, and this is the reafon I call her *Rattenberg,* and not *Dubourdieu.*

B   ABOUT

ABOUT the fifteenth of *February* laft, I was over-taken with a ftorm of rain and hail, which forc-ed me into the firft publick houfe I came at, which made a much handfomer appearance than the Taverns of this City ufually do; but that was no invitation of my taking into it, for had it been much worfe, it had been fufficient to fhel-ter me from the ftorm.

WHEN I came in, the firft perfon I met with was the miftrefs of the houfe, a comely woman of about fifty : Having taken my feat and call'd for my wine, it was foon brought me by her huf-band, a man about threefcore; for houfes of this nature in *Paris* are not furnifh'd with drawers like a *London Tavern*. I ask'd them both feveral queftions, which they anfwer'd with great civili-ty, particularly of what Province they were; the man reply'd, that he came from *Burdeaux*, and the wife, that fhe was of *England*; upon which the reft of our converfation ran in the *Englifh* tongue, which the husband underftood very well, tho' he pronounc'd it ftill like a *Frenchman*. The good woman finding me an *Englifhman*, faid, fhe hop'd I would endeavour to promote their bufi-nefs, by recommending her houfe to the reft of the *Englifh* of my acquaintance in *Paris*; affur-ing me they fhould find very good accommoda-tion, both in the liquor, and in the rooms where they were to drink it. We are, faid fhe, tho' old people, but young beginners in this bufinefs;

yet

yet with a profpect of engaging my countrymen,
we have taken care to make the rooms as com-
modious as we can, and as like thofe in *London*;
upon which fhe defired me to take a view of
them, and I found them indeed much handfomer than I expected; among the reft there was
one that might pafs even in *London* it felf.

It was hung round with feveral good Prints
by *Audran Simon du Cange*, and other good
hands; but that which touch'd me moft was
a piece of painting over the chimney, not for
the exquifitenefs of the work, for that was but
indifferent, but for the oddnefs of it, the main
matter that fill'd the picture being a fea without
one fhip upon it, in the middle of it was plac'd
an ifland, much the greateft part of which feem'd
to be nothing but rocks; but the low-land, which
appear'd to be very fmall, was adorn'd with feveral beautiful trees, and fruit, and flowers as beautiful as the painter could make them. My landlady obferving my eye fix'd upon this piece, ask'd
me the reafon of it; I told her that the oddnefs of
the painter's fancy had mov'd me to enquire whether 'twas a reprefentation of any particular place,
or only a whim of his own. Ah! Sir, reply'd
fhe, that painting I caus'd to be put up here, to
put me often in mind of that fignal deliverance
which my husband and I had about ten years ago,
and which ought never to be forgotten by us.

OBSERVING

OBSERVING that she utter'd this with some concern, I call'd for more wine, and press'd her to know the story. Alas! Sir, said she, my story is too long for you to hear at one sitting, but I will do what I can to gratify your curiosity; upon which sitting down, she gave me a short account of her life and adventures, from her birth to that time; and tho' she hurry'd it over, yet it took up all that evening, and part of the night.

I have sent you by pieces several of the most extraordinary incidents of it, which mov'd your curiosity so far as to importune me for a perfect narration of the whole. In obedience to your commands I went to the *Golden Dragon*, and made my request to Mrs. *Rattenberg* that she would let me write it from her mouth for a friend in *England*; and gave her this encouragement to do it, that I would come every day and dine with her 'till it was done. The good woman made some difficulty at first of complying with my request, but I had been too good a customer since my discovery of the house, and brought too many of my acquaintance thither to let her venture the disobliging me by a denial: Having therefore got all things in order, I went thither, and began the work on the seventh of *April* last, and which I now send you just as she deliver'd it to me.

I was

I was born, fays fhe, as I have told you, in *Penfance* in the County of *Cornwal,* my Father's name was *Stephen Rattenberg*; I can't fay he was a Gentleman, but he farm'd his own eftate, which was about forty pounds a year, a pretty compe-tency in that cheap country, and with which he brought up fix daughters and one fon, all whom he faw married and fettled before he married his fecond wife, my mother, at which time he was fifty five years of age, and my mother not fix and twenty : I have been told fhe was very handfome, for I never faw her; fhe dy'd in childbed a few days after I was born, fo that I may be faid truly to have come into the world with forrow ; how-ever my father was fo fond of me, calling me the child of his age, that I could not be fenfible of the lofs of my mother.

As foon as I was capable he had me taught to read and write, and gave me all the advantages of education, which that little place and his own fmall abilities were capable of. The better to encourage my reading, he got me all the pleafant ftory books which were fitted to my age and capa-city. But had I any children of my own, I would never fuffer them to read thofe idle books, fince they fill'd my head with fo many wandring no-tions, that I have never been able to fettle my mind ever fince to my prefent condition, always feeding my felf with vain hopes of bettering my fortune by my change of place, tho' I ftill found,

at

at leaſt for the moſt part, that this change was for the worſe.

I was now come to my thirteenth year, forward and pert enough for my age; when my father growing very old and infirm, began to find by his inward decay that he was not long for this world; but all his concern at his leaving of it was, that he left me friendleſs and unprovided for, tho' he had taken care out of his ſmall income to lay up one hundred broad pieces of gold, all my mother's apparel, and all his houſhold goods, except what he had already diſpoſed of to my brother and ſiſters: He left alſo a particular charge on his death bed to my brother, to take as much care of me as if I were his own child, and that with ſuch bitter imprecations and curſes on him if he wrong'd me, as make me ſtill tremble to think how that evil ſon of a good father could have ſo little regard to them.

Now began the ſcene of my ſorrows to open, and no ſooner was my father dead, but I found a ſtrange alteration in my condition; for I who 'till now had been miſtreſs of the houſe, could after my father's burial ſcarce be admitted to any ſhare in it; for my brother and his family coming now into poſſeſſion of it, left me but little to do there: I found ſome ſmall civility at firſt from both brother and ſiſter, but that was only the better to deceive me, and c eat me of all I had.

I told

I told you that my father had fav'd together a hundred broad pieces of gold for me, thefe he deliver'd into my cuftody fome time before he dy'd, and therefore mention'd them not in his will, by which he only bequeathed me his houfe-hold goods, and this was that which gave a co-lour or pretence to him of cheating me of all my money; pretending, that as heir to my father, whatever money he had left was his: In fhort, by fair means and foul he got the money into his poffeffion, and then turn'd me out of doors with only my cloaths to my back, and fome other ne-ceffaries which he own'd to be mine. I had a near relation liv'd in the fame town, whither I retir'd, and was kindly received by him, with af-furances that he would ftand by me againft my cruel brother; but I knew his abilities were too fmall to engage with him, and therefore was wil-ling to get as foon as I could to *Plymouth*, where I had an unkle, who was a man of fubftance and reputation, and might, if he would heartily en-gage in my caufe, eafily bring my brother to reafon.

ACCORDINGLY I got letters from my coufin in *Penfance* who had fo kindly receiv'd me; which letters fully inform'd my unkle of all that had pafs'd between my brother and me. Out of the wreck of my fortune I had taken care fecretly to convey five broad pieces into my pocket, and which I did not own even to my kind coufin, who

who fent his fon to convey me to *Plymouth*; where without any remarkable adventures by the way, we arriv'd in three days thro' the worft road in the world, and not to be rode with any horfes, except fuch as are bred in that Country, with any tolerable fafety to the rider's neck.

My young coufin foon found out my unkle, who at firft received me tolerably well; but when he heard that my father was dead, and by the letters found all that had pafs'd between me and my brother, I found a vifible alteration in his countenance, and he fpoke in a more furly tone than before. Well, faid he, niece, what would you have me do in this affair? Would you have me go to law with your brother for you? No, no, forfooth, I have fomething elfe to do with my money, than upon your ftory to throw it away on law. I have a great family of my own, and a great deal of bufinefs to mind; befides, how do I know that what you tell me is true, I ought to hear your brother firft; come to me again when I have heard from him, and I will tell you more of my mind. Come to you again, Sir! faid I, whither would you have me go, or where refide but with you, my unkle, in a ftrange place, where I know no body? Why did you come then, fays he, to a place where you knew no body? I have no room in my houfe for ftrangers, I don't keep an Inn, nor have I victuals enough for my felf and my family: Pray, mi-ftrefs, walk and be gone. With that he took
me

me by the arm, and made my coufin and I walk out before him, I with my eyes full of tears, and my coufin pale with anger and grief; and had not my unkle been a very old man, I believe he would have beat him luftily: However, we return'd to the inn where we left our horfes, and there got fome refrefhment for our felves. Having cry'd out my cry I began to recover my fpirits, and fed pretty heartily; my coufin did all he could to perfuade me to go back with him to *Penfance,* affuring me of his father's kind reception of me at my return; but I told him, I could not think of being a burthen to him who had fo large a family of his own, nor would I give my brother a triumph in the ill fuccefs of my journey. After many arguments on both fides, we went both to bed to our reft.

WE rofe early in the morning, and as forrow never lay long at my heart, fo there was no figns of any grief to be found in my face, but all was jocund and cafy, as if nothing had happen'd. That day we fpent in viewing the town, particularly the caftle and the docks, at the laft of which I heard fuch a character of my unkle, (for he was a mafter fhipwright) that I did not wonder at the ufage I had met with from him; for the workmen told me and my coufin, that he was the moft noted mifer in *Plymouth,* a mifer to that degree, as to make a proverb, *As covetous as old Rattenberg;* that he had almoft

C   moft

moſt ſtarv'd his family, tho' very rich, forcing
two of his ſons to go to ſea as common ſailors,
for he would make no proviſion for them, by
putting them out apprentice to any trade, ſince
that requir'd money, which he did not know
how to part with on any account whatſoever;
that he yet kept himſelf in pretty good plight,
by eating and drinking at other mens coſt.
Coming home to dinner, we choſe to give my
landlord ſo much a-piece to dine with him and
his family; where, giving an account of all that
had happen'd to me, both at home and at *Plymouth*, the good gentlewoman of the houſe
ſeem'd mightily mov'd with my ſtory, and ask'd
me if I had a mind to go to ſervice? I reply'd,
very willingly, provided I could get a place eaſy
enough for my age and my ignorance; that I
was willing to learn, and to accept her good offices with thanks, if ſhe could help me to any
ſuch ſervice : She gave me hopes of recommending me to a rich old Gentlewoman, whoſe buſineſs would not be very great ; that in the mean
time I might ſtay at her houſe, and pay her when
I was able. Thus another day paſs'd on, and my
couſin ſtay'd to the utmoſt extent of his time and
money, eitherto perſuade me to go back with
him, or ſee me well fix'd in *Plymouth* ; but not
being able to do either, the third morning he
ſet out for home; we did not part without
Tears, nor would he leave me, as he thought,
entirely without money, and therefore divided
his ſtock betwixt us, which amounted to no more
than

than a crown a-piece. I manag'd my crown fo
well, that with the credit I had in my inn, I
made it laſt 'till I got into ſervice, which was a-
bove a fortnight.

In the mean time, I had been three times
with my new miſtreſs, and ſhe had made me
read to her, and ſhew her my writing, both
which pleas'd her very well, aſſuring me, that
for the reſt I was to do, ſhe would take care to
inſtruct me, and told me, that my buſineſs with
her would be very eaſy, ſince I had nothing to
do but to provide and dreſs her victuals, make
her bed, dreſs and undreſs her, and waſh her
linen, and my own, for which I was to have
thirty ſhillings a year; which ſmall wages ſhe
promis'd to encreaſe according to my care in plea-
ſing her.

The old Gentlewoman had above fourſcore
pounds a year, for her life only, and that in ſmall
tenements in the town, beſides money, which
ſhe let out from twenty ſhillings to twenty pound,
at legal intereſt, and to perſons whom ſhe knew
to be good pay-maſters: The maid ſhe had juſt
parted with was an old peeviſh creature, who
refus'd to humour her in any thing, but I being
now come to her, took care to do every thing to
her ſatisfaction, to ſtudy her humour, and when
I was acquainted with it, to prevent even her
deſires in the very minuteſt things about her;
particularly to make much of her little dog and

cat,

cat, of which she was very fond ; so that in less
than two months time, I had won the heart of
the old Lady entirely. The cold weather now
coming on, I was very solicitous that she should
lie warm in her bed, and therefore profer'd my
self to be her bedfellow. By these, and other
arts, I had made my self mistress of her affections,
so far, as she began to use me and love me as her
own child, for she was a woman of a great deal
of good nature and humanity ; and I began to
think my self so happy, that the memory of my
past misfortunes wore out, and I thought no more
of my brother's cruelty and injustice, 'till my
good mistress told me, she was resolv'd to make
my brother do me right. I assur'd her, that I
was not in the least pain about it, since the
wrong he had done me had produc'd so happy an
event, as I esteem'd the being in her service to be.
Upon which, she embrac'd me and kiss'd me,
and told me she would take care that the being
in her service should indeed be a happiness to me ;
to begin which, she would order her attorney,
the most considerable in the town of *Plymouth*,
to commence a suit against my brother in my
name. I return'd her a thousand thanks, and
tho' I had but little reason to regard my brother's
good, I yet prevail'd with her to send to him,
and demand the restitution of my goods and
money, of which I had kept an inventory, made
by my father before his death, in my pocket,
with my five broad pieces, which were now
laid up in a box my mistress had given me,

with

with fuch cloaths as fhe had beftow'd upon me.

My brother had a pretty numerous family, and had not been fo good a husband as my father had been before him, fo that he was but ill provided for a fuit at law, which muft bring daily expences upon him.

My miftrefs therefore praifing my good nature, made her attorney fend his chief clerk, who was a *Cornifh* man, and born within three miles of *Penfance*, to make a legal demand of my due. When he came to my brother, and had inform'd him of his bufinefs, he feem'd not at all concern'd, but asking where I was, and how I did, told him, That he had done nothing by me but what was juftifiable by law, and did not doubt but that, if I was fo mad as to commence a fuit with him, he fhould be as able to defend himfelf, as I fhould be to attack him. The young man reply'd, Do not depend too much upon your fifter's inability, for fhe has a miftrefs, who is a very rich woman, who is refolv'd to let her want for no money to carry on her caufe, and at whofe expence he was come fo far to make this demand ; but he gave him till the next day to confider and give a pofitive anfwer, and fo he left him and went home to his father, who, as I told you, liv'd about three miles from my brother, to whom, when he return'd the next day, he found him very much alter'd in his note, telling him, That he had too much love for me

to

to put me to the charge of a suit, which I must be sure to pay, if I prevail'd in the cause, and would perhaps find it difficult to find money to pay cost and charges if he should cast me, of which, he said, he had not the least doubt; but since he had a love for me, as being his father's daughter, and much belov'd by him, he would give me fifty pounds, in full of all demands, which, as it was all he could any way raise, so it was entirely out of his own pocket. The young man told him, That tho' he had no authority to make a composition, yet, if he would send his offer in writing, under his own hand, he would deliver it to me, but could not promise him any success, the case appearing so barbarous on his side, not only by my account of the matter, but by that of our common relations and neighbours here at *Penfance.*

In short, he writ so mournful a letter to me, that I prevail'd with my mistress to suffer me to accept of his proposal, which I was the more ready to do, by his appearance at *Plymouth* two days after the return of the attorney's clerk, when he made the condition of himself and family so deplorable, that I had certainly forgiven the whole, had not my mistress obstinately oppos'd my folly, nor would she let me so much as take his bond for the money; so that he was oblig'd to make a mortgage to my miserly unkle, and pay me the fifty pounds, and take my mistress's receipt, I having chosen her for my guardian on this occasion;

so

ſo he left *Plymouth*, and I heard no more of him till I ſaw him three years afterwards in a very poor condition at *London*.

Now fortune ſeem'd to ſmile, and gave me nothing but agreeable proſpects. I put my money into my miſtreſs's hands, who plac'd it out on good ſecurity for me, and I went on every day encreaſing in her favour; and having liv'd with her about a year, ſhe, to my unſpeakable ſorrow, dy'd, but in her will, bequeath'd me fifty pounds more, for my faithful ſervice; ſo that now I was once again miſtreſs of one hundred pounds, beſides my five broad pieces, which I always kept by me untouch'd, and was very well furniſh'd with cloaths, both linen and woollen. Having put my ſelf in mourning, I return'd to my old friend, the inn-keeper's wife, into whoſe hands I put the money my miſtreſs had left me, and by her perſuaſions call'd in my own fifty pounds, in order to put it all out on ſuch advantageous terms, that if they had anſwer'd, would have kept me without going any more to ſervice; but I found it was neceſſary to manage this, that I ſhould chuſe a guardian, for whom I nam'd the inn-keeper; ſo that he was now maſter of near one hundred pounds of my money.

Whilst I liv'd with my miſtreſs I had much time upon my hands, which I ſpent in reading; but the books that diverted me moſt, were travels and voyages; and they had ſtirr'd up in me a
mighty

mighty defire of feeing the world; which defire, fince my miftrefs's death, grew greater and greater every day, and that which compleated my refolution, was, the arrival of a Gentlewoman at our inn, at leaft of one that appear'd to me to be a Gentlewoman, tho' fhe had been a few years before a fervant to that inn; whence going to *London*, and falling into the fervice of a rich citizen, was marry'd by him, and fo made miftrefs of a plentiful fortune: She was now come down to *Plymouth* to fee her friends, and among others, paid a vifit to her miftrefs, the inn-keeper's wife, where fhe talk'd fo much in the praife of *London*, that I was fully refolv'd to go thither out of hand; but I had much ado to prevail with my new guardian, 'till I affur'd him I would ftill leave my money in his hands, to be manag'd for my advantage in my abfence, excepting twenty pounds, which I thought neceffary for my journey; all the difpute now lay, whether I fhould go by land or by fea, but that was foon determin'd, by information that there was a fhip going off of about 200 tuns, in three or four days time: My guardian therefore agreed with the mafter for my paffage, and I went on board the very morning fhe fet fail.

There was nothing happen'd in this Voyage worth taking notice of, but the Weather being fair, gave me a mighty love for the fea, for we pafs'd our time very pleafantly, being moft commonly upon deck; where, among the Paffengers,

gers there was one who play'd mighty well on
the violin, an inftrument which before I had
never heard in that perfection; the mufician
was young and handfome, and had been a voyage with a captain of a man of war up the
Streights, and the fhip being now laid up, he
chofe rather to go this way to *London*, than
to ride poft with the captain; I know not what
he faw in me, or I in him, but he pretended to
be very much in love with me, and I was very well pleas'd to think him fo; thus betwixt love and mufick, mirth and good company, our fhip brought us to *Portfmouth*,
where fhe was oblig'd to touch, and make a
ftay of fome days; which opportunity the mafter of mufick and I took, as well as the reft of
the paffengers, to fee the town, and divert
our felves afhore. Mr. *Geeting*, for fo was
my mufician call'd, took care to give me all
the diverfion he could, ftill preffing his love
with all the earneftnefs imaginable, and his
profeffions being fo honourable as marriage, I
confefs I heard him with fo much fatisfaction
that I could not difguife it to him, but promis'd to marry him as foon as we arriv'd at
London; but this would not anfwer his ends,
and therefore he contriv'd to keep me afhore
when the fhip fhould fet fail, which he brought
about by this means; under pretence of riding
to view the country, he carry'd me fo far,
that when we came back we found the gates
of the town fhut up, which oblig'd us to go

to a little publick houfe not far from it, there
to pafs the night till the gates fhould be open'd
in the morning.

THERE my falfe lover left nothing unattempt-
ed to gain his ends, but I .refolutely oppos'd
them, and render'd all his efforts to no purpofe;
when I was angry he us'd all his art and fubmif-
fion to appeafe me, and when once I was appeas'd, he us'd all his force to anger me again;
but I remain'd unconquer'd in fpight of opportunity and importunity, from the man whom I
found I lov'd but too well, forgiving him all
he had done, on his promife of never attempt-
ing the like again, and of marrying me that
morning before we went on fhip-board. Terms
of accommodation being thus agreed, we enter'd the gates of *Portfmouth* as foon as they
were open'd, but I was ftrangely confounded
when coming to the place where we left the
fhip, I found fhe was fail'd away without me,
and my lover had much ado to appeafe me by
affuring me, that he would fee me fafe to *London* time enough to meet the fhip there on its
firft arrival; which with finding a letter from
the mafter at our Inn, where they generally
were when on fhore, made me pretty eafy.

My lover now began to prefs me farther for
favours, which I affur'd him I would never
grant till marriage had made them lawful; but
that to pleafe him I would confent to marry
that

that very morning; he therefore went and got a ring, and a parſon ready, who while he was performing his office, was ſtopp'd by a pretty young woman, who it ſeems had follow'd us, among others, into the church, and claim'd my falſe lover for her husband. This had been enough to have put a man of tolerable modeſty out of countenance, but he not at all concern'd flies to her, takes her in his arms, and kiſſes her, crying out, And art thou alive then, my dear *Betty?* I had news in the *Streights* that you dy'd ſoon after I left *England.* No, you villain, reply'd ſhe, I am ſtill alive to plague you, tho' I might have dy'd, nay, been ſtarv'd to death, for what care you took of me, and now I find you endeavouring to ruin another woman, had not fortune brought me ſtrangely hither, to prevent her unhappineſs. Many more words of this nature paſs'd betwixt this happy pair of whore and rogue coupled together; for I underſtood afterwards that ſhe had been a common jilt in *London*, and was now come to *Portſmouth* with a company of ſtrolling players, who enter'd that town but the very night before, as if it had been on purpoſe to preſerve me from deſtruction: I left the church in ſome confuſion, and made what haſte I could home to my Inn, there to conſider what I had to do in my preſent condition.

I found my ſelf all alone, in a ſtrange place, without any friends to adviſe or aſſiſt me; I
had

had indeed money enough in my pocket to carry me to my journey's end, and letters of recommendation from my guardian at *Plymouth* to his friends in *London*, to take care of me; I therefore call'd for my landlady, and defir'd her to get me the moft fpeedy paffage fhe could; which fhe did, by taking me a place in the *Portfmouth* coach, which fet out the next morning. Tho' I was vex'd at my forwardnefs in liftening to the love of a ftrange man, whom I had never feen before, yet I was not without a fecret fatisfaction that I had behav'd my felf with fo much virtue and courage againft all his villainous attempts, and was heartily glad that I was got rid of him fo; but it feems I was not fo clear of him as I defir'd to be, fince before the evening word was brought me, that there was a Gentlewoman wanted to fpeak with me; I order'd her to be admitted, but not knowing any one that could have bufinefs with me there, I order'd the maid to fend up her miftrefs to be with me whilft I receiv'd this vifit, but fhe could not come fo foon as the ftrange Gentlewoman enter'd my room, whom I prefently knew to be the wife of my gallant, and whofe timely coming into the church had done me fuch fervice: I receiv'd her with all the civility I could, but fhe having taken her feat according to my defire, fhe began to accufe me of keeping company with her husband, and threaten'd me, with very high words, to give me trouble for it, as well as for the money I had

made

made him spend upon me; by this time my
landlady came in, who sitting down, and hearing
from me what had pass'd between us, took her
up very roundly; Come, *Betty*, says she, how
dare you venture to put any of your tricks upon a guest of mine, since you are sensible I know
you too well to suffer an innocent country girl,
who has suffer'd too much by the rogue your
husband, to be your bubble too? with much
more of this she tam'd Mrs. *Betty* entirely. However I then interpos'd, Mrs. *Betty*, said I, I believe that my club, in his expences with me,
will come within ten shillings, and scorning to
be treated by such a villain, there is half a
piece for you; tho' the mistress of the house
would have hinder'd her taking it, but that I
press'd it so earnestly: on which she put it in
her pocket, and gave us a full account of the
rogueries of her husband's past life, by which
she shew'd him to be a compleat villain, tho'
not two and twenty; but these things having
nothing to do with my story, I shall pass over
in silence.

THE next morning I set out from *Portfmouth* in the flying-coach, which then went
through in a day; so that I arriv'd at *London*
late the same evening, which made me take
up my lodging that night in the Inn where the
coach set up.

ABOUT

ABOUT nine the next morning I took a porter with me to fhew me the way to St. *Catharine's*, where my guardian's friend, to whom I had letters, liv'd, who upon reading my letters, receiv'd me with a great deal of civility, and went with me to find out the fhip, which at laft we found very near the *Cuftom-Houfe*, and the mafter happening to be on board, deliver'd me my things, and made an apology for his failing without me: My friend took care to have them all convey'd to his houfe, where I continu'd for fome time.

THO' I had a pretty good ftock of cloaths, yet all being made in the country, they were too unfafhionable for this town, fo that I was oblig'd to have fome of them alter'd, and drew a bill upon my guardian for ten pounds more, in order to furnifh my felf compleatly, but receiv'd a letter of advice, to manage my money with a little more prudence, fince my ftock was too fmall for me to pretend to follow all the fafhions: However, by a repeated importunity I prevail'd with him to fend me five pounds, which was all that ever I had of my money, my guardian, foon after, breaking for a confiderable fum.

THERE liv'd an old maid in the houfe, who being fifter to the mafter of it, manag'd all his domeftick affairs: With her I went about to fee the town, even from *Wapping* to *Weftminfter;*

ſter ; and indeed ſhe ſhew'd me every thing that was worth a ſtranger's curioſity, thro' its whole extent.

BARTHOLOMEW Fair coming on, ſhe carry'd me likewiſe to ſee that ; tho' the Drolls and other Shews gave me diverſion enough, yet the *Royal Oak Lottery* was what took moſt with me ; for having always a mind to raiſe my fortune, I was ſtill ready to catch hold of every appearance of doing it ; wherefore being inſtructed by looking on, I was reſolv'd to venture what little money I had about me ; I took my place and ſat down, and did not get up till my good luck had prov'd that my hopes were not in vain. My companion finding that I had won about twenty Guineas, was for hurrying me away, for fear the chance ſhould turn, and leave me worſe than it found me.

THIS good fortune tempted me to go again, which I did ſeveral times during the Fair, and generally came off a winner ; inſomuch, that by the end of the Fair, I had got together by the Royal Oak, near one hundred pounds, which was not every bodies fate with that lottery. This ſucceſs made me purſue the ſame courſe during the time of *Southwark* Fair ; but my landlord and his ſiſter repreſented the great odds againſt me ſo effectually, which ſhe confirm'd with particular inſtances of numbers daily ruin'd that way, that I ſat down contented

ed with what I had got, and only confider'd
how I might with fafety improve my gains:
The late lofs of my money in my guardian's
hands, made me afraid to truft it out of my own
cuftody, and yet to keep it by me was not the way
to improve it, and the fum it felf was too fmall
for me to pretend to live upon, which left me
under a neceffity of feeking out for fome credi-
table fervice, which would at leaft hinder me
from impairing it: In order to this, I fet my
felf to learn all thofe qualifications which were
capable of recommending me to the moft beneficial places that a fervant could hope for; I
learn'd therefore to raife pafte, to diftil, and
make all manner of confectionary ware, as well
as the art of cookery in general, and had gain'd
a pretty fmattering in the *French* tongue, by
converfing with a *French* Gentlewoman who
lodg'd in the houfe, who having an acquaintance at the other end of the town, at laft
got me to be waiting-woman to a Lady of
quality, where I had twenty pounds a year, befides a fhare in my Lady's old cloaths, who being young and gay, made that perquifite pretty
confiderable to me.

In this poft I might have been happy enough
if I could have been contented; but to be fubject to the will and pleafure of another, I began foon to think intolerable, and therefore
all my thoughts and invention were taken
up how to make my way into fome condition
of

of life which was more free and independent.

THERE was one Mr. *Rogers* who paid his court very conftantly to my Lord, he kept his chariot, and a handfome equipage, and made as great a figure as if he himfelf had been a man of quality; but I underftood that his father was a fhoe-maker, of *Exeter*, and not being able to live by his trade, on the firft peopling of *Barbadoes* went thither, and had rais'd a very confiderable eftate, which was now come to the fon, and had made him a Gentleman, and companion for Lords: This reviv'd my old inclination for travel, efpecially to that country, where thofe people who went beggars, return'd home mafters of fuch confiderable riches; but being a woman indeed was fome check to thefe imaginations; yet being young, and not difagreeable, as I thought, I flatter'd my felf that I might, as well as other women that went over fervants, come back wife to fome wealthy planter: However the difficulties feem'd too great for me at that time to ftruggle with, and I had fome other ill fortune to go through, before I could be entirely wean'd from my love to my native country.

WALKING one evening in the park with my Lady's houfe-keeper, there was a handfome Gentleman would needs talk to us as we walk'd there, and was mafter enough of that tittle tattle which generally takes with our fex; tho' he talk'd

E   to

to us both, yet his chief application was to me;
we had no way to get rid of him, but by leaving the park, and going home; he seemingly
took his leave of us, but order'd chairmen to
watch us, as he told me afterwards; and having
thus got knowledge of our abode, he soon
found out who and what we were; and by pick-
ing an acquaintance with one of my Lord's gentlemen, found means of coming into my company, and of making his addresses to me; and
made such an intimacy with my Lord's gentleman, that he prov'd his perpetual advocate in his
absence: I told you that his person was handsome,
and his talk agreeable, which, joyn'd with the
importunity and the solicitations of his friend in
the house, made me at last agree to marry; in
order to which, I gave my Lady warning, much
to her dissatisfaction, for she had a particular
kindness for me: I assur'd her Ladyship, that
it was not out of any disgust to my place, but
that I was engag'd to alter my condition, by
marrying a Gentleman who had made honourable addresses to me for some time. My Lady
examin'd very nicely into the matter, by which
she found that I could not give an extraordinary
account, either of what or who he was: I told
her in general, that I had good assurance that
he was a Gentleman of an estate, as well as a
man of honour. She shook her head, and
wish'd that I might not repent of a folly, to which
I was hurry'd by my youth, (not being yet eighteen
years old) and by my ignorance of the town. I
had

had too great an opinion of my own underſtand-
ing, to think I could be impos'd upon in this
matter; and ſo taking leave of my Lady, I went
into private lodgings, whence I and my Lord's
gentleman, my future husband and another
friend, went out of town, and was marry'd in
the country, with all the appearance of joy in
both faces. I liv'd with him two months with
a great deal of pleaſure, he infinitely fond, as I
thought, and I therefore not a little happy. He
came home one evening extremely out of humour, not with me, but with ſome diſappoint-
ments he had met with that day: I preſs'd him
mightily to know the cauſe of his chagrin;
and with much ado he ſeem'd to force himſelf to
comply with my deſire; and pulling a letter out
of his pocket, (which I knew was not his hand
writing) ſhew'd it me; there appear'd upon the
outſide ſomething like a Poſt-mark; the contents
were to aſk his pardon for not returning the
two hundred pounds he had order'd till a month
after: I endeavour'd to pacify him, but to no
purpoſe, for he ſwore he would turn his ſtew-
ard out of his place for a neglect, by which he
was like to be a great ſufferer in his honour. I
told him that if one hundred Guineas would prevent that, I thought it my duty not to let him
be uneaſy. After ſome pauſe; Well, my dear
Patty, ſaid he, you infinitely oblige me with
this ſupply; that will be ſufficient to ſave my
honour, tho' not anſwer all my occaſions. So
having embrac'd me, and taken the money, he

went

went away, as if to anfwer thofe demands that were on him; but I never faw him nor my money afterwards.

I fat up all the firft night, thinking that he might be engag'd at a Tavern amongft his friends; the day came, but no hufband; and the people of the houfe being all of them up, I ventur'd to go to fleep, and lay till eleven o' clock; nor had I been up half an hour, when my Lord's gentleman, who had fo great a hand in the making this fatal match, came, as he ufually did, to fee me and my hufband; he was furpriz'd to hear he had not been at home all night, and was afraid that fome mifchief had befall'n him; which fear had tormented me from twelve o' clock till I went to fleep: I told him that he went out with a charge of money about him. My Lord's gentleman faid, that he would go to all the haunts of his that he knew, to endeavour to find him out. In about two hours he return'd again, but with a melancholy countenance, the fight of which put me into fuch a fright, that I thought I fhould have fwooned away, crying out, What news, Mr. *Barton?* (for that was the Gentleman's name) What news? Tell me quickly, or I dye away with the frightful imagination? Where is my Husband? Is he well? Alive or dead? Be not frighted, fays Mr. *Barton,* for Mr. *Macknamar* is, for ought I know, in good health, but where he is I know not, but where he ought to be I am loth to fpeak: In fhort, Madam, you

and

and I have been both deceiv'd in the man who
has marry'd you; for seeking after him at every place where I thought he might be found, I
was at last directed to an alehouse in the *Minories*, where they said I should be sure to hear of
him. Coming thither, the man of the house inform'd me that he was gone the night before
down to *Gravefend*, on board a ship that was
bound for *France*, but he was afraid it would
set sail before he could arrive there ; if so, he
will certainly come back to this place to night.
I seem'd so much concern'd at the news, that
the man ask'd me if he had bit me of any
thing? I reply'd, no ; but I cannot believe that
he would go out of *England* without acquainting his wife one word of the matter. His wife,
cry'd out the woman in the bar, which of his
wives? for I believe there are in this town of
London, many who pretend to that name, and it
is confidently affirm'd, that he is actually marry'd
to no less than twenty. He never made scruple to marry any woman whom he had a mind
to lie with, or had any hopes of getting but
twenty pounds by the match. These words of
Mr. *Barton* interrupted his narration by my
swooning away : he presently call'd the maid,
and did all he could to revive me, and bring
me to my self; which when he did I was too
impatient, and too much troubled to hear him
any farther at that time ; so that he was going
to return to the *Minories* in order to secure
the villain, if he should come back that night ;

but

but at that very inftant we heard a woman running up ftairs, and crying out that fhe would fee him, ay that fhe would, and tear out the whores eyes who kept him from his wife; fo into the room fhe came, and had certainly fallen upon me had not Mr. *Barton* interpos'd with more than ufual roughnefs to hinder her; in fhort, he let her underftand that I was really his wife, and that he was prefent at the marriage; with other words, which brought the Lady to a better temper, who then told us that fhe was marry'd to him about half a year before, and that having got two hundred pounds of her money, he left her about three months after, under pretence of going out of town upon earneft bufinefs; but that having had no letter from him all that time, a friend of hers met him in the ftreet, and dogg'd him to that lodging but the night before; that upon this information fhe had procur'd a warrant to take him up, which had delay'd her too long to let her find him at home. In fhort, we let the Gentlewoman know the whole matter, and that he was gone on board, in order to leave *England*; yet there was fome hopes remain'd, that he might be driven back again that evening. She readily offer'd her felf to go with Mr. *Barton* to the place where he was expected: When they were gone I order'd the maid to let no body elfe come up till Mr. *Barton's* return, and that if any one enquir'd for Mr. *Macknamar*, fhe fhould tell them that he was gone out of

town

town the day before, and take no notice of what
had pafs'd ; 'and it was well I did fo, for there
was no lefs than three women more came that
very day, upon the fame errand ; for his ftay-
ing fo long in that lodging as two months,
and the little caution he took in going out and
in, had made it known to fuch who were e-
very day upon the hunt after him.

Though this was a terrible fhock, and e-
nough to affect any one in my circumftances
with pain and confufion, yet I, with whom grief
and uneafinefs never dwelt long, after crying
about an hour, or thereabouts, dry'd up my
tears, and began to confider what was now to
be done to avoid thofe evils with which my
own rafhnefs and folly now threaten'd me ;
almoft all my money was now gone at once,
he leaving me not above three guineas, about
five pounds in filver, and my own old hoard of
the five broad pieces I have mention'd : I had,
indeed, a pretty large ftock both of *linen* and
apparel, a *cheft of drawers*, and a *toilet* hand-
fomely fet out, but what was this for my fupport ? I thought I might, indeed, return to my
Lady, fhe having not yet provided her felf to
her fatisfaction ; but I was too much afham'd
of what had pafs'd, to think of entering that
family any more, and I found that *London* was
not the place where I was to raife my fortune
to that degree which was agreeable to my defires ; I refolv'd therefore to leave *England*, and

go for *Barbadoes*, efpecially if my Lady would get me letters of recommendation from Mr. *Rogers*, which I did not at all doubt. Being come to this refolution, my paffions were pretty well appeas'd, having nothing to fear but that I might be with child: Thro' all other evils I thought I faw a very eafy way, and of that I was not extremely apprehenfive, having had my fortune told me, that I fhould never have any children; for tho' there may be nothing in the art of foretelling, yet fome things having happen'd, as I thought, according to the prediction, I concluded that all the reft would do fo too.

THE firft thing I did towards the fettling of my diforder'd affairs, was to enquire of my landlady, how our accounts ftood with her, in order to remove to fome cheaper lodging, and found that he had not paid one farthing fince we had been in the houfe; this, with a fcore we had at a neighbouring tavern, made up three pounds, which was a great deal out of my fmall ftock, however I difcharg'd the whole.

IT was near nine o'clock at night before Mr. *Barton* came back, and told me that there was no news to be heard of the fugitive villain, againft whom he fwore the utmoft revenge whenever he could find him; but that was but little comfort to me, or any redrefs of the evils

I lay

I lay under; so putting off that discourse, I gave him an account of the resolution I had taken of leaving *England*: He endeavour'd to dissuade me from so hazardous a voyage, assuring me that he was confident that my Lady would be very glad to receive me again into my former place; but finding all he could say was to no purpose, he undertook to manage my affairs according to my desire, and so he took his leave for that night.

Mr. *Barton* broke the business to my Lady by her housekeeper, who was mightily troubled at my misfortune; for I behav'd my self so well in the family, that I had the love of all my fellow servants. My Lady said she pity'd me, but that I was a rash and obstinate girl, and had brought this mischief on my own head, of which she her self had forewarn'd me; but however, she was so really concern'd for what had happen'd, that she would make it her endeavour to do her all the service she and my Lord could; and she was as good as her word, and got me such effectual letters of recommendation from Mr. *Rogers*, that they must have been of very great use to me had I ever arriv'd at *Barbadoes*. Mr. *Rogers* likewise gave a particular charge to the master of the vessel I went in, to take particular care of me during my voyage. My Lady farther added a present of twenty guineas, and my Lord gave ten, to buy such things as would be convenient to carry with

F   me,

me, which yet I manag'd fo ill as not to leave
my felf money enough, without three of my
five broad pieces, to pay my paffage; fo that
when I came on fhip-board, I had no more than
the two broad pieces, and fix fhillings in filver,
left me; nor indeed had I any occafion for money, having every thing provided that I could
want during my voyage.

My Lady would needs fee me before I went,
and it was with the utmoft confufion that I beheld her, and not with a few tears that I parted
from her. When I came on board I found
four other young women, a Gentleman and his
wife, and an elderly Lady, who were to be my
fellow paffengers. At *Gravefend* we took in two
young women more, and one man; not touching any where elfe till we came to *Plymouth*,
our company was there encreas'd with three
young women more, and then we purfu'd our
voyage with a profperous gale, and very fair
weather, which continu'd with little variation
for a month together; tho' moft of the other
young women, efpecially when the fea went a
little high, were fick, I was perfectly well all
the way; and the mafter told us we were within fourteen days fail of *Barbadoes*, if the wind
continu'd fair. When my fellow voyagers had
recover'd their feafoning, and were now become
converfable, I diverted my felf fometimes by
enquiring into their fortune, and the caufe of
their undertaking fo long and hazardous a voyage;

age; two or three of them frankly own'd that love was the caufe, others confefs'd that the hopes of riches, or at leaft a better fortune than they left behind them, gave them courage to venture fo far.

We kept an exact account of the days after the mafter had told us how long we were to continue ftill at fea; and now being about three or four days from the end of our voyage, in the morning early the boy at the *top-maft-head,* cry'd out, *a fail,* and about two hours after they difcover'd two more, which gave not the leaft concern or fear, becaufe it being profound peace they were not in any apprehenfion of danger; when the fhips came nearer, we had the comfort likewife to fee that two of them carry'd *Englifh* colours: it was almoft night before they came up with us, and then our *mafter* began to fear that they were *pirates,* and to wifh that he had made more *fail* when he had firft difcover'd them; for though they fail'd much better than we, we might in all probability have had at leaft a chance of efcaping them; but now in the dusk of the evening, they firft took down the *Englifh,* and clapt up *Spanifh colours,* and then fent off a long boat, with about a dozen men with fmall fire arms, who made directly to our fhip. The mafter propos'd to his men to fight, but they faid it was to no purpofe, they having no *guns,* nor any thing fit for an engagement with an enemy that was

vifibly

vifibly fo much their fuperior, both in force
and number. You may imagine that we were
all in a confternation, expecting nothing but the
moft cruel and barbarous treatment from fo
lawlefs a crew, made up (as the mafter told us,
and as we afterwards found) of people of all nations; however our ufage prov'd much better
than we expected; for the men in the boat being admitted, kept only poffeffion of her, without any diforder, till the next morning, when
the commander in chief came on board us;
and finding the women in a great confternation, he very affably defir'd us to lay afide our
fear; affuring us, that as foon as ever he could,
with fafety to himfelf and his men, he would
take care to put us on fhore. We were glad
to find the chief officer an *Englifhman*, and to
perceive fo much humanity in him; they only
enquir'd into the *cargo*, and the provifions, the
latter of which they had fome occafion for;
and leaving us fcarcely enough for five or fix
days fubfiftence, they remov'd the reft, with all
our wine, into their own fhips; and I believe
had fo difmift us, had they not wanted our veffel
for an hofpital or ftore-fhip; for having feveral
of their men fick, they remov'd them on board
us, with about half a dozen prifoners *Frenchmen*, whofe fhip they had funk but three days
before. Befides this they took away all our feamen and our mafter, and divided them amongft
their own fhips, and put as many of their men
on board us, as were fufficient to work our
fhip;

fhip; and they had directions to make the beft
of their way to a certain ifland in the *South
Sea*, which was the place of their rendezvous;
the name of which I have forgot, tho' I remember that they faid fomething of *Cape Horne*,
fo that I fuppofe this ifland was not far from
that Cape.

OUR new mafter and his men examining into what ftores of provifions we had left, found
themfelves under a neceffity of demanding of
their comrades as much as they thought their
voyage would require, tho' they were contented
with but fhort allowance. All things being
thus fettled, the *pirates fhips* were foon out of
fight, tho' ours crowded all the fail fhe could,
that they might be able to make their voyage
whilft our provifions lafted. We fail'd two or
three days in pretty good weather, and our new
feamen found leifure enough to make their addreffes to the young girls; fome of them indeed
were very handfome, and frefh colour'd, and
being wholly at their mercy, were oblig'd to go
with them into what part of the fhip they pleas'd;
for my part I examin'd not what paft betwixt
them, being fufficiently fatisfy'd that I was not
fo agreeable in their eyes as to be made the vi-
ctim of their luft; tho' my felf, the Gentleman's
wife, the old Lady, and two others, were all
that efcap'd them; and how long we had done
fo I know not, if their conftancy had not held
them to their firft choice, till the enfuing ftorm
found them other employment. AND

AND indeed a moſt terrible tempeſt, with a
violent wind, and frequent hurricanes, turn'd our
ſhip even where they pleas'd, and at laſt I
found quite out of their knowledge. All the
hands we had were fain to be employ'd to
keep her above water; this tempeſt having
continu'd for ſome days, which was made more
terrible by the prodigious claps of thunder, ſuch
as I never heard in all my life, and ſuch flaſhes
of lightning, that made us ſeem to ſail through
fire it ſelf: But at laſt the winds began to abate,
and a calmer ſea to enſue, to our very great comfort: Yet another evil now came upon us, which
we did not much think of during the ſtorm,
and that was, the fear of ſtarving, for our proviſions and water grew ſo low, that it was impoſſible we could ſubſiſt above three days longer;
beſides, our ſhip had ſuffer'd ſo much in the
paſt ſtorm that ſhe was very leaky, ſo that
three or four men were continually forc'd to
ply the *pumps*; and the maſter having made
his obſervations, found, that tho' he was in the
South Sea, he was yet gone ſo many leagues beyond his deſtin'd port, that it was impoſſible
he could go back, both for want of proviſions,
and the crazineſs of our ſhip. But the ſecond
day after the ſtorm we were all reviv'd to hear
the cry of *Land* from the top-maſt head; our
maſter therefore ſteer'd directly towards the land,
tho' perfectly ignorant of what coaſt it ſhould
be; and a briſk gale riſing up ſo exactly for
us, that our ſhip ſail'd before the wind. The
next

next morning we found our felves within a few leagues of a coaft that look'd like a perpetual range of vaft high mountainous rocks, without any place where there feem'd a poffibility of getting on fhore; but one of our men who had a telefcope, perfuaded us, that he difcover'd to the weftward of thofe rocks, a flatter fhore, fo that we immediately fteer'd to that part, where we found a little *creek*, into which we run our fhip, with a great deal of joy to all our company, as well *pirates* as others, never confidering what country we were caft on, whether inhabited or not, and if inhabited, whether by a people civiliz'd, or barbarous; or if not inhabited, what we fhould do to fubfift, fince our provifions were now quite fpent.

NOT confidering, I fay, any of thefe difficulties, we all went on fhore, by the confent of our new mafters; and going a few fpaces up into the country, we were fo lucky as to meet with a pretty fpring, of whofe waters we all took our fill, and found them the moft delicious that ever we tafted in our lives, at leaft they appear'd fo to us who had been fo long ftraiten'd in our liquor: We had each of us about half a bisket left, and after we had quench'd the violence of our thirft, we fell to eating of that, as if it had been the beft food in the world.

AFTER this repaft, our mafters began to mufter up, and to call over their people, and found

found that in the ftorm we had only loft three of
the fick *pirates*, who, I told you, were put on
board us; moft of the reft were very weak, and
more likely to dye than to live; the *Frenchmen*,
and we, were all pretty well, and I was extremely glad to find the old Gentlewoman, who was
very good humour'd, and whom I thought the
leaft capable of going through thefe hardfhips,
the moft brisk and jolly of us all. Our mafter
detach'd three or four of his men, arm'd
with fmall guns, up into the country to make
difcoveries, and the reft went on fhip-board,
with fome of the men prifoners, to bring on
fhore fome conveniences for his fick men to lye
on, and to examine into the condition of the
fhip, now the tide was out, and not above ten
foot water in the *creek*. About five o' clock in the
afternoon our fpies return'd, and brought us word
that they had been feveral miles up the country, but
could difcover neither man nor beaft; but told us
that the country it felf was certainly a new *paradice*, the air all around being perfum'd by the
odoriferous flowers and herbs that grew wild
there in great abundance; that the trees were
loaded with delicious fruit, of various fizes and
colours, but whether good for food or not
they durft not try; all that they ventur'd to
take was fome bunches of grapes, which were
the largeft and moft beautiful that ever we
faw; and the fpies having tafted them before,
we all ventur'd to do the like, that is, as foon
as our company had brought us a good hand-

fome

fome ftock of them. Thefe refrefhed us extremely, afforded a fort of nourifhment, of
which we had then very confiderable need.
They ventur'd likewife, at their requeft, to give
fome of them to the fick men; to whom they
were fuch a cordial, that we prefently difcover'd new life in their eyes. It grew now towards night, and upon a private debate among
themfelves, our mafters agreed, that thofe that
had a mind to it, might lye on fhore, but within call of the fhip. The prifoners were all willing to venture themfelves on land, being fufficiently tir'd with the paft voyage: However, they
permitted us to take all the neceffaries we found
in the fhip, for our accommodation in the night:
For my part, I did not much care how I lay,
not fearing to catch cold, or any other mifchief,
fince I expected to dye of hunger in a few days,
which was far more terrible than any diftemper
I could apprehend from this conduct. The next
morning the *pirate* went out again on difcoveries, and fo did three or four of the *French-*
men, who having been kept fo fhort in their
allowance on fhip-board, were too fharp fet to
be very cautious in trying the fruit they found
on the trees, and by good luck found many of
them, not only very favoury, but very nourifh-
ing, appeafing their hunger, and fatisfying their
appetite as well as they could wifh, and finifh-
ing their banquet with fome of the grapes that
grew there in great abundance; they loaded
themfelves as well as they could, and brought

G   them

them to us women; fome of the fruit look'd
like chefnuts, tho' of a much finer flavour, and
richer tafte; fome had the appearance of very
large oranges, but upon cutting them they prov'd
folid, and yielded a very noble food: Some of
the young laffes, and the Gentleman's wife, were
afraid to touch them for fear they fhould be veno-
mous, even after they had feen me eat heartily
of them, being willing (they faid) to fee what
effect they had on me and the *Frenchmen* who
had eaten; fo they contented themfelves with a
few of the grapes, which they had before expe-
rienc'd to be good and wholfome.

THE night coming on, the remaining pirates
were under a great confternation when they found
their companions not return'd, and more fo, when
the night fhut in without any news of them; and
indeed it alarm'd us all, and made us think of
returning into the fhip for fafety; but it being
dark, it was a difficulty not to be got over by
the women, who were therefore forc'd to remain upon the land, and the men prifoners ftaid
with us and watch'd us all the night, for fear of
any furprize from the fuppos'd natives of that
place. When the morning came and fully fatif-
fy'd us that we had been afraid of mere imaginary
enemies, no creature appearing yet amongft us;
we all ventur'd to walk up into the country, men and women: The *pirates*, not much
caring what become of us, employ'd themfelves
entirely in refitting their fhip, ftopping all the
leaks,

leaks, and mending the fails and mafts, which had fuffer'd very much in the ftorm : They oblig'd us, however, to bring back with us grapes, and other fruit, enough for their fupport. This day alfo pafs'd, and no news of the *pirates* who went to view the country the day after our arrival; and indeed it was the fixth day, almoft night before they came back, when they brought an account, that they had gone, to the beft of their judgment, fifty miles an end, and met with no living creature; they faw indeed fometimes feveral birds, but came within fhot of none; that they found the low-lands of the country edg'd all along on one fide with thofe rocky mountains which we faw by us, and on the other, by the fea; that when they had gone about half way, they beheld a high hill, from whence they hop'd to have a profpect of the whole place, which made them proceed in their journey, tho' they found it much farther in their going, than they imagin'd when they faw the hill, to the top of which, they had a pretty eafy afcent for above two miles together; and when they were got up to the very higheft part of it, all they could difcover, for want of telefcopes, was, that the reft of that country feem'd nothing but hills and rocks, and a vaft fea beyond them, as well as all round them; by which it was plain, that this was an ifland, and no continent; fo defcending from the hill, they made what fpeed back they could; that the valleys, or low part of the ifland, was, as they guefs'd, no where

G 2   broader

broader than feven miles, but every where di-
verfify'd with little woods or groves, fprings
and fmall brooks of delicate water, and a great
quantity of fruit of various kinds, with which
they fupported themfelves very well in their journey : We were indeed all furpriz'd, that a place
fo adapted for convenient and happy living,
fhould be wholly without inhabitants; and fome
of us concluded that we were ordain'd to people it; and the young laffes, with whom the
pirates had already been familiar, as I told you,
feem'd to leave no ftone unturn'd to contribute
their part towards this work; for we had little
of their company whenever our mafters were at
leifure from refitting the fhip, to divert themfelves, and pafs their time in fuch pleafures as
were agreeable to them; and we wifh'd indeed
that they would have kept them always with
them, for when they were with us they were
extremely troublefome, thro' that infolence and
impudence which they had contracted by their
vices, affuming a fort of authority from their fa-
miliarity with our prefent mafters, efpecially
one of them, of whom, it feems, the mafter,
or captain, was fo fond, that the others call'd
her Governefs; her name was *Betty Higham*,
at leaft the name that fhe affum'd; fhe was tolerably handfome, and fung pretty well, and was
befides an excellent mimick, had a very good
ftock of affurance, and by her converfation plainly difcover'd her former courfe of life; and
that notwithftanding her pretences of being
the

the unfortunate relict of a broken merchant of that name; it was too evident that she had publickly intrigu'd, and was forc'd, in all probability, by being an old face in *London*, and quite out of credit, to seek a new fortune abroad where she was less known.

FURNISH'D with these qualities, she had render'd her self mistress of the inclinations, as I have said, of the principal of our masters; and I from the beginning determin'd to make my advantage of the interest she had in him, and therefore much against my will, made my court to her, and perfuaded her to engage our captain, not only to furnish us with all that was necessary for our lying on shore, but to let us have such trunks and boxes as were able to furnish us with materials to keep us at work; which she the more easily yielded to, by my promising that she should have a large share, not only in my cargo of linen, but in my work to make it up. She having so good success in this, and understanding that in the ship were found several *hatchets*, and other tools fit for a joyner or carpenter, we flatter'd her and her comrades so effectually, as to get them for our *French* fellow-prisoners, who were engag'd to me, who was the only person that spoke *French* among us, to build some little huts, which might protect us better from the rains than that shelter which the trees afforded us. The *French* consisted of three joyners, two priests and a surgeon;

geon; who was afterwards that husband whom
I now have. About three or four miles farther
up in the country, they had found out a
much more pleafant abode than that in which
we now were, and to which we got our Governour's permiffion to retreat, It was a pretty o-
pen fpace, furrounded with groves or woods;
in the midft, there was a pretty large fpring,
which fed a little brook, that in its courfe run
quite thro' the woods northward.

In this little plain, our builder defign'd to fix
our new habitations, which they purpos'd to
make of a tree they had found out, that was
as foft as fir, but of a much finer nature, and
which they found would fplit with abundance
of eafe. Of this they made a fort of boards,
and foon erected four little dwellings; one for
the Gentleman and his wife, and another for
me and Mrs. *Wright* (for fo was the old Gentlewoman call'd) another for the three young
laffes that continu'd with us, and a fourth for
themfelves; but as for the reft we took no manner of care, fince they chofe generally to lie on
fhip-board with their lovers. Thefe little huts
they cover'd with the broad leaves of a certain
tree that grew thereabouts; thefe leaves were as
thick as the canvas of which our fails were made,
and about half a yard over. They fix'd up our
hammocks, and difpos'd our baggage within our
little apartment; they found the greateft difficulty to make us doors, having no hinges nor
locks;

locks; but this they fupply'd by making ledges above and below, and fliding the door into them, which was eafily faften'd by a pin on the infide. We were all mighty glad when this work was finifh'd, as having never till then pull'd off our cloaths, or fhifted our felves. Mr. *Walker*, the marry'd Gentleman, gave each of our *French* workmen a clean fhirt, for he had with him a large ftock, which we had now all on fhore. We had alfo prevailed with our Governefs, as we call'd her, to get her Lords to change the rags in which they had cloath'd them upon their being taken, for their own cloaths again. Madam having done us all thefe favours, we very ungratefully, and impolitickly too, began to flight and affront her and her fifterhood, which had like to have been fatal to us all; for one of the *Frenchmen* having prefs'd the grapes, and made fome of the moft delicious wine in the world of them, prefented the *pirates* with a tafte of it, who liking it extremely well, order'd them to bring on fhore half a dozen empty casks, in which we had had fmall beer; and beating out the tops of them, and ftopping the bung-holes with cork, commanded us to wafh them, and fill them with the fame juice. All hands were immediately fet to work, the men to gather them, and bring them to us, and the women to fqueeze them into the veffels; which was not fo very laborious a task, becaufe they took care to gather no bunches but what were

fully

fully ripe; and we had, befides, the hands of all the madams to help us on this occafion.

THE veffels being all full, we had immediate orders to remove two or three of them towards the fhip, which with much ado was at laft effected; and the *pirates* having been a great while without wine, had no patience to ftay till it was fine, but fell to drinking of it upon the *lee.* This opportunity *Betty Higham* took to be reveng'd upon the affronts (for fo fhe call'd our flighting and avoiding her company) and made her complaints with the utmoft inveteracy againft all of us; intimating, that fhe wonder'd that fince we were flaves as well as they, that they did not take the fame privilege with us, but leave us the vanity of our fuppos'd virtue, to infult them for their willing obedience to their mafter's commands. The *pirates* being warm with the wine, and vitious in their own nature, approv'd the hint, and thought four or five frefh women would compleat their entertainment; they therefore fent immediately two other women to command our attendance, who perform'd their meffage in a moft haughty manner; telling us, that we fhould no longer pretend an excellence above them, fince the *Governefs* had found this way to humble us; but when we made a difficulty of obeying, they plainly told us, that if we would not go with them, we might expect to be dragg'd thither by fome of the men, and perhaps murther'd when they had had their

will

will of us. This frighted the three young laſ-
ſes that remain'd with us ſo far, that they went
with them. When they were gone, Mr. *Walker*, Mr. *Wright* and I, went directly to our men,
who were at work a little farther in the woods,
to conſult with them what we ſhould do on
this occaſion; who advis'd us, by all means, to
to go up farther into the country, and hide our
ſelves, as well as we could, in the thickets, to
avoid their fury at leaſt that night, hoping that
the next day, when they were ſober, they might
be prevail'd on to take more gentle reſolutions;
ſo we all together went farther on, about two
mile, and bending towards the mountains, we
came to a little wood that was ſo thick with
under-wood that we could not get into it; but
one of our guards going round it, he found at
laſt a little inlet, through which, by the help
of their hatchets, they might be able to get us
in one by one; which they did, with ſome
difficulty; and the better to ſecure us, they
trampled about for a quarter of a mile farther,
to leave the print of their footſteps, to miſlead
our purſuers to the next coppice, where they
ended. By that time all this was done, and
we got into our place of ſafety, we heard three
or four of them come running and hallooing,
ſwearing and curſing; but ſtriving in vain to get
into our little wood, they ſwore bloodily that
we could not be there, ſince there was not
room for even a mouſe to get in; ſo they
went on to the coppice I ſpoke of, where ha-

ving fufficiently torn their cloaths, and fcratch-
ed their hands, legs and faces, we heard them
return curfing us to hell, fwearing they would
feek no farther after us that night, having whores
enow already to ferve 'till next morning.

WE were glad to hear them go back again,
but kept our felves clofe in our lurking place
till good part of the next morning was over;
but certainly never was fo dreadful a night
pafs'd, not for the thunder and lightning, for
we had much greater in the ftorm at fea; but
for the ftrange noifes that feem'd to come out
of the ground, which it felf appear'd to tremble beneath us.

WHAT I am going to tell you, Sir, may
feem incredible to one that has not been us'd
to read the feveral alterations that happen in
the earth; the fea fometimes fwallowing up
whole countries, and fometimes cafting up,
as it were, whole iflands in a night, where
there was no land before. This, if I may give
credit to the accounts I have read, has happen'd in the *Archipelago*, and feveral other
parts of the world; which, with the finding of
fea-fhell in the inland countries, has made fome
believe that the fea and the earth have chang'd
places; but be that as it will, I am witnefs to
this which I am going to tell you, and owe to
it one of the greateft deliverances that ever I
had in my life.

I told

I told you juſt now of our retreat into the thicket, to avoid the rage and luſt of the *pirates*; but having ſtaid there the next day 'till near noon, without hearing any thing of them, it was agreed to ſend one of our party out to gain intelligence how things ſtood, and MONSIEUR DUBOURDIEU proffer'd himſelf to be the man; he return'd again in a little more than an hour, full of amazement, and telling us that we might all quit our lurking place, ſince our enemies, in all probability, were no more, but ſwallow'd up, ſhip and all, in the earthquake that we felt ſomething of laſt night, or were overwhelm'd with that vaſt quantity of earth that had riſen up and cover'd all that part of the iſland where they were, and reach'd even as far, within a few furlongs, as our laſt ſettlement. Upon his aſſurances, full of thanks for our eſcape, we all came out into the open country, and went back to ſee the ſtrange revolution in our little world; and were ſtricken with unſpeakable terror and wonder at the ſight we beheld, finding that all the country, from our ſettlement to the ſea, had entirely chang'd its face; and that in the night, in the midſt of thoſe terrible noiſes which we heard, the ſea or earth had thrown up prodigious mountains for twelve miles together; that is, from the moſt *Weſterly* point of thoſe rocks. We ſaw at our coming hither, even ſix miles beyond the main land of the iſland to the *Weſt*, by which jetting out into the ſea there was

form'd

form'd a fort of a haven, or calm road, pro-
tected againft all winds but the *Weft* and
Northweft; that from the heighth of thefe
mountains, in all probability, there had tum-
bled down fuch vaft quantities of earth, as to
have cover'd all the low-land, and part of the
fea, for betwixt three and four miles broad,
and fo rais'd the furface by an eafy afcent up
to the mountains themfelves.

WE view'd all this fo long, that we were almoft ftupid with the confufion which it gave
us; bleffing our good fortune that had made
us fly fo far from this dangerous neighbourhood; and tho' the *pirates* and their Ladies
were a parcel of moft profligate wretches, we
could not but pity their terrible fate, which
had fo on a fudden funk them in the midft
of their fins; but our own proper fears foon
banifh'd thefe confiderations, and made us
think of removing to fome other fettlement,
farther from this direful place; but fince we
could not prefently carry away our effeds, we
were content to go only with our hammocks
fome few miles from it, 'till we had fix'd upon a convenient fituation: And upon a full
debate of the matter, we came to this refolution, that we would fettle as near as we could
to the middle of the ifland; fo our Gentlemen, in a few days, found out a pleafant hil-
lock or rifing ground, fomething more than
two miles from the *Weftern* fea, and above
three

three from that range of rocks which ran cross
the country to the *East*; and much about the
mid-way, between the *North* and the *South*
side of the island. Near this we fix'd our
hammocks, under the shelter of the adjacent
woods, 'till we could be provided with better
lodgings; which our Gentlemen went about
with the utmost expedition, every one of them
labouring hard to contribute to the finishing of
the work. But the first thing they did was to
frame four sorts of carriages, to which the
joyners made broad low wheels, as well as
they could; and with these, in a little time,
brought away our baggage, and what other
things were necessary for our work. They resolv'd now not to make four different huts, as
before, but one contiguous building; and tho'
they labour'd with a great many difficulties for
want of iron-work, yet, with a great deal of
industry and pains, they supply'd that defect,
and in about three month's time compleated a
tolerable habitation, and we settled in our new
abode with a great deal of satisfaction.

OUR house being thus finish'd, our men, to
keep themselves employ'd, and make our habitation the more convenient, went upon furnish-
ing it with tables, and such seats as they could
make, 'till we had all things that were absolute-
ly necessary for our accommodation.

Mr.

Mr. *Walker*, his Lady, and the old Gentlewoman could speak no *French*, nor could the *Frenchmen* at first speak any *English*, but in time they came to speak it intelligibly; 'till when, most of the conversation run thro' my hands, I being interpreter to them all, tho' they were every one full of the complaisance, so usual in those of that nation; yet *Monsieur Dubourdieu* discover'd a more than ordinary civility to, and care of me, nor did he at last make any scruple of declaring, that he had a peculiar love for me.

One day when the men were gone out for provisions, or a walk, and we women were left alone, Mrs. *Walker* discover'd a very great uneasiness at her present condition, and express'd her fear that she should never get from this place. I did what I could to comfort her, and told her, that I thought our present state something better than that of our first parents after the Fall, they being more solitary for several years together, since there was no other people in the world but themselves, nor could expect any 'till their children were grown up fit for conversation; but we were a pretty jolly company, and were not without hopes we might be deliver'd by the chance arrival of some ship. True, said she, but that is very uncertain, since I find, that the *pirates* themselves, who are us'd to these seas, knew nothing of this island; so that there

is

is more probability of the decreafe than the increafe of our company. Oh, Madam, faid I, as long as you live, I hope we fhall every now and then increafe by a li.tle one from you, fince I find, at laft, an inftance of it from your being with child. That will be but flow work, interpos'd Mrs. *Wright*, unlefs you add to the number of our breeders, by marrying *Monfieur Dubourdieu*, who has long exprefs'd his love for you. I would fain have diverted the difcourfe, but the old Gentlewoman went on; you find, faid fhe, that he is the only perfon among the fix men whom you can make choice of for a husband; the three joyners you hear, are, by their own confeffion, marry'd men; and the two priefts, you know, according to their Religion, can have no wives: Nor, faid I, is *Monfieur Dubourdieu* like to have one in me, he is too much a ftranger for me to entertain any fuch thoughts about him, and I have fuffer'd too much already, by being credulous of the profeffions of mankind.

THIS was the fum of that day's difcourfe, which Mrs. *Walker* told her husband, and in that, the reft of the company; as foon as they came to us, *Monfieur Dubourdieu* return'd them thanks for their good offices, and defir'd earneftly that they would renew them, nor give over 'till they had vanquifh'd my obftinacy: They perfectly comply'd with his defire, nor would let me alone; 'till having had fuffi-

cient

cient experience of his good temper, and verily believing that I should have better fortune
with him, than I formerly had, either with
the *Englifh* or *Irifhman*; in the beginning of
the third year, I confented to become his wife,
and the ceremony was perform'd by the elder
of the two priefts, who could fpeak the beft
Englifh, and who was forc'd to fatisfy me, in
performing it over again, according to my *Com-
mon-Prayer Book.*

THIS year was remarkable, not only for my
marriage, but for the birth of Mr. *Walker's* child,
tho' the laft was as melancholy an incident, as the
firft was merry; for tho' we brought the child alive
into the world, it liv'd not many days; and
the mother, to the unfpeakable forrow of the
husband, dy'd before the end of the month;
we buried her with all the folemnity that we
were able, but could never appeafe Mr. *Walker's*
grief as long as he liv'd, which was not many months after his wife: His death happen'd
in the following manner.

THE men having work'd themfelves entirely
out of employ, knew not what to do with themfelves, but rambled up and down every day,
from one part of the ifland to another. The
pirates about two days before their miferable
cataftrophe, had been rowing about in the long
boat by the North fide of the ifland, in hopes
to difcover fome other part of it; but having
                                            row'd

row'd about twenty miles to no purpofe, they came back again, and doubling the Weftward point, they put on fhore in a little creek that run about a quarter of a mile within the land, where they faften'd her in about two foot water, defigning the next day, or a day or two after, to renew their enquiry, and go farther on the Northward coaft, but were prevented, I fuppofe, by fome other thoughts, and fo never went again. This boat was found in the fame place by fome of our company, almoft three years after, and it was agreed among them to go out the fame way from her, which the *pirates* had gone, to try to make fome difcovery, and the rather, becaufe when they had been fome time upon the North hill, formerly mention'd, they either heard, or thought they heard, the found of trumpets, or fome inftruments like them : Accordingly the three joyners, one of the priefts, and Mr. *Walker*, putting provifions enough on board to ferve them two days, efpecially a large quantity of grapes, they row'd away, but how far they went, or what became of them, we could never learn, for they return'd no more to us : This was a great diminifhing to our little company, which was now reduc'd to four perfons; *viz.* the prieft who had no mind to go upon this expedition, the old Gentlewoman, my husband, and my felf.

WE had nothing remarkable for above two years more, the fame things happening to us every

I

ry

ty day over and over again, with very little variation, which afforded nothing worth relating;
we eat of the fruit, and drank of the purling
stream, sometimes moderately improv'd with the
juice of the grape, which we got and preserv'd
in little vessels, with which nature furnish'd us;
for there grew a sort of fruit upon a stalk which
lay upon the ground, much like our pompions
in *England*, tho' near as large again as any that
I ever saw; the outer rind was pretty hard, so
that they were forc'd at first to use hatchets to
cleave them open, in order to see what they contain'd; besides this outer rind, which was something like the shell of a nut, tho' ten times thick-
er than any that I know of, there were two
other rinds, about two inches thick each, and
near as soft as that of a melon; under all these
there was a very pleasant food, of which one of
the joyners ventur'd to taste, invited by the fine-
ness of its smell, and we all follow'd, he having made the experiment; and it is observable,
that we never met with any thing noxious a-
mong all the fruits and herbs, which were in
plenty in this place, most of which, some of us
tasted at one time or other; the upper rind of this
fruit was as easily clear'd of all it contain'd,
when open'd, as a nut-shell is of the kernel;
our workmen therefore, instead of splitting them,
as at first, saw'd off the head, and so made compleat vessels that held about three or four gallons,
and these we fill'd with the juice of the grape,
of which we made two sorts, one, by laying a
great

great heap of bunches full ripe upon one another on a clean table, and the weight of the grapes prefs'd one another, whilft our veffels beneath caught the juice as it fell ; and when no more came away by this means, we fqueez'd them with our hands, but kept thefe two juices afunder in different veffels, for there was indeed a great deal of difference in the wine; but to preferve our liquor the better, they digg'd a pretty cave in the fide of a bank, and there we plac'd our wine, having firft cover'd it with the upper part of the fhell, around which was fix'd a fort of a hoop, and in the middle of it a handle to take it off and put it on: There was fome of this wine left, which we made in the fecond year, even when I left the ifland, for it was of a very ftrong body, and would have kept, I believe, twenty years, fixteen I am fure it did, for fo long after it was, before I was deliver'd from this folitude. I have already told you how our company was reduc'd ; but fortune was not yet fatisfy'd, nor was I come to the height of my tryal, 'till I was left quite alone: The next two that I loft, was the prieft and my husband, tho' it was above two years after before I had that affliction.

THE prieft, and Mr. *Dubourdieu*, went daily out a walking, either to the fea fide Weftward, to fee if they could difcover any fhip, or fometimes to the North-weft hill on the fame errand, but it was long before they ventur'd upon the new

hill

hill that was rifen upon the South-weft part;
but at laft feeing it all over green, they went
up to the top of it, and from its height look'd
out for fhips, but to no purpofe; this being too
far for a day's walk, without a great fatigue,
they would not venture to ftay long for fear of
frightening us by their abfence, without letting
us know of it beforehand; but they agreed to
go on purpofe to ftay a day or two, in order
to fearch it from one end to the other; accordingly, in about a week's time, they went, and
return'd in three days after, giving us this account; That the hill thrown up in the night,
was about twelve miles long, and three miles
in the declivity; that going to the moft eafter-
ly part of it, they came within ten foot of the
mountainous rocks that were there before;
that being there by day break, they heard the
moft harmonious mufick, both vocal and inftrumental, that could be imagin'd on this fide heaven: The prieft, who had been in *Italy*, and
prefent at all the performances of both voices,
and mufick, which were eminent in that country, declar'd, that they were all infipid and flat,
in comparifon of what he had now heard; and
they both told us, it feem'd to them to pafs
on like a proceffion, tho' it was of fome hours
continuance.

THIS had rais'd our curiofity fo far, that we
refolv'd to take a journey with them, to par-
ticipate of the fame pleafure: Accordingly, we
walk'd

walk'd the firſt day to our former habitation, and reſting there all night, began our walk to the top of the hill by the very firſt appearance of daylight; but nothing could we hear of their boaſted harmony, except ſome diſtant ſounds of wind inſtruments, which was ſo faint that we could not determine whether it was really ſo, or only the effect of fancy; ſo that tir'd with our waiting to no purpoſe, we came down again, and ſpent the reſt of the day in the ſhade, and the night in our old huts, and the morning following we ſet forward for home.

THE prieſt and my huſband, notwithſtanding our bantering them, and endeavours to perſuade them that all they had told us was nothing but a pleaſant dream, they perſiſted in the fact; and, upon many deliberations, concluded that it muſt be the inhabitants in the mountainous parts, who were that morning, when they heard the muſick, performing ſome ſolemn feſtival perhaps to the *Moon*, ſince it was much about the *new Moon* when they heard it, and therefore they reſolv'd to be at the ſame place the next change of the ſame planet.

THEY went accordingly, but were again diſappointed, hearing nothing but thoſe diſtant ſounds which we had imagin'd that we alſo had heard: All which had heighten'd their cu-

rioſity

riofity fo far, that they refolv'd to endeavour
to make a difcovery of what was conceal'd in
thofe mountains. All the difficulty was how to
get upon them, for betwixt the new mountains
and the old ones, there was a fort of a gap or
chafm, which they judg'd to be about ten or
twelve foot over, and above fifteen deep; they
concluded therefore to lay a fort of a bridge
a-crofs it: And in order to it cut down one
of the light trees, whofe body was above fifteen foot high, but fo fmall, that when they
had cut it out it was not much above half a
foot broad; however, with a pole of the fame
length, and each his *hatchet* ftuck in his girdle,
they went upon this new expedition, much a-
gainft my inclinations, and contrary to my defires.
The day after they were gone I had a mind to
follow them, but my old Gentlewoman was
taken fo ill, that fhe could think by no means
of fo long a jaunt, nor could I think of leaving her alone when fhe was not well; fo I
determin'd to wait with patience the return of
our men. Mrs. *Wright* grew worfe and worfe
every day, and I more impatient to know what
was become of my husband: In fhort, in a
little more than a week's time, worn out with
age and her evil fortune, fhe gave up the ghoft.
But before fhe dy'd, obferving my grief, fhe
took me by the hand, and begg'd me not
to give too much way to forrow, but preferve
my felf for better fortune; which, in time, fhe
was confident would be my lot, at leaft if I
thought

thought it better fortune to be reftor'd from this folitude to a more habitable part of the world; but as for her part, fhe was very well content to die in thefe unknown regions of the earth, being as near to heaven there as any where elfe; fo charging me not to throw away hope, and commending her felf earneftly to her Maker, fhe expir'd.

IT was with fome difficulty that I digg'd a hole capable of receiving her body; which, however, I at laft effected juft without our little houfe, and putting her into it, cover'd her up.

I was thus left all alone to bemoan and lament my unhappy ftate, which I did for fome days; but this irkfome folitude growing more familiar to me, and grief, which feldom lay long in my bofom, wearing off, I refolv'd to go towards thofe parts whither my husband and the prieft were already gone, and where my fondnefs gave me hopes that I might find fome footfteps of them. I had no great care as to taking provifion with me, fince the trees every where afforded me food as I went along; and the fprings, which were very frequent, all the liquor I defir'd; putting therefore a little goblet in my pocket, with a knife, I loaded my felf with the lighteft hammock I had, and fet forward by break of day; and refting all the heat under the fhade of the trees, I went

on

on again till the evening; when fixing my hammock on two trees, I refted very heartily all night, being fufficiently tir'd with my walk, tho' not above ten miles. The next morning I proceeded on my journey, and that day reach'd ten miles more, as well as I could guefs, that is, within two miles of the foot of the mountain; there again I fix'd up my hammock, and refted as before. As foon as day appear'd I got up, gather'd fome fruit to eat, and fome grapes to fupply the place of drink; and putting them in my handkerchief I went on, and got at laft up the mountain, which was an eafy afcent for about three miles together; where refrefhing my felf with eating the viands I had brought with me, and refting a while I turn'd towards the *Eaft*, and went forward 'till I came to its extremity; but all that I could find by this great fatigue was a pole and plank laid acrofs that gap in the mountain which I formerly mention'd; on the left hand of which there was nothing dreadful, fince it was not above fifteen foot deep; but to the right a moft fearful precipice, which was the only thing that hinder'd me from purfuing them over the plank, the very fight of the precipice making my head giddy; I was therefore forc'd to fit down and bewail my misfortunes, the very beft I having to hope, being that they were got fafely over; tho' doubtlefs, by their long ftay, they muft be fallen into the hands of the inhabitants of that country, if any,

with

with whom, what fate they had met, was now
my only fear; fo after fome hours I return'd
down the hill, and came to my laft lodging.
I could not be fatisfy'd without returning next
morning by day-break, to the very fame place,
refolving to try to pafs the plank my felf, but
when I came there I was furpriz'd by that
heavenly mufick which my husband and the
prieft had fo often talk'd of, and which, ftill paffing forward, continu'd till near noon, and
went from me by degrees, till quite out of my
hearing; then I look'd again at the paffage,
but being quite dizzy with the profpect, I
was fain to throw my felf immediately back-
ward, or I had fallen down I know not how many fathom deep. Being come to my felf I began to confider of what I had heard, and drew
thence this comfort; that if there were inhabitants in that part of the ifland, they were
certainly of a very humane kind, fince they
could not have that charming mufick among
them, and yet retain any thing barbarous and
cruel; wherefore I determin'd to return to
my own home, and wait with patience the
coming back of my husband and his friend,
which I perfuaded my felf would be as foon
as they could find any means of efcaping; fo
I went back again, and refted my felf that
night; the next morning I fet forward, and by
eafy journies reach'd again to my houfe; where I
divided my time betwixt prayers and fuch o-
ther employment, as was neceffary for my fub-

K   fiftence.

fiftence. I fpent much time in reading thofe few books which I had by me, efpecially the Holy Bible, in which I found great comfort; fometimes I took pen, ink, and paper, of which I had a ftock by me, brought out of *England* for my own ufe in *Barbadoes*. The fubject of my writing was to give an account of all that I could remember had happen'd to me during my whole life, to that very time; which I did partly for an amufement, and partly that if any one elfe fhould come upon that coaft after I was dead, they might find my ftory.

It was above three years before I faw my husband again, and the greateft uneafinefs I had during all that time, was, that I fhould lofe the ufe of my tongue by fo long a filence; but to prevent that evil, (for fuch a woman thinks it) I frequently talk'd to my felf; I often fung both *French* and *Englifh* fongs : And when I took any books in my hand, I always read aloud, and pronounc'd my words as diftinctly as if I had other auditors to hear me.

During thefe three years of folitude I had nothing happen'd to me that deferves a particular narration. When the three years were over, and fome odd months, fitting at my door towards the evening, under the fhelter of fuch trees as had been planted about it, I was not a little furpriz'd and frighten'd, to fee two naked men make towards me; I immediately ran in a-doors, and faftned my felf as well as I could,

could, and was, with some difficulty perfuaded
by my husband and his friend (whofe voices
at laft I knew) to open the door and come out
to them; however I immediately got fuch linen garments as I had formerly made, and
gave them my husband out of the window,
and when they were cloathed came out to
them. I need not tell you the joy of our
meeting, after fo long an abfence, and when
I had given over almoft all thoughts of ever
feeing him again. After our firft embraces
were over, I gave him my fciffers to cut off
his beard; for he had no other inftrument all
the time fince our fhipwreck, or landing on
that coaft, to perform that office; the prieft
was refolv'd to let his beard grow 'till he
came into *France*, which he faid he verily believ'd he fhould do before he dy'd.

This night of our meeting, feem'd the moft
comfortable that ever I knew in my Life, folding
in my arms the husband I lov'd, and who lov'd
me entirely. After I thought him loft, you
may be fure I was inquifitive enough into their
adventures fince they left me; particularly what
fort of inhabitants they had found, and what
had detain'd them fo long from me. They told
me that they had certainly been in *Paradice*, that
the inhabitants were perfect *Angels*, and yet
nothing kept them fo long away but their being under a fort of confinement till the hour
of their return. The particulars of all this I

fhall

ſhall refer to my husband's account, who was better able to deſcribe what he had ſeen with his own eyes, and heard with his own ears, than I, what I only had by relation.

HERE my landlady made an end, and having inform'd her husband how far ſhe had gone in their ſtory, deſir'd him to give a full account of all that paſs'd afterwards, 'till their arrival and ſettlement in *Paris*; but this was reſerv'd 'till the next day, when after dinner my landlord *Dubourdieu* thus began.

I have nothing to acquaint you with, Sir, relating to my ſelf or family, or any of my affairs in *France*; they contain nothing remarkable enough to deſerve your notice; let it ſuffice, that my father being a citizen of *Bourdeaux*, had me bred a Surgeon, hoping to prefer me to his Majeſty's ſervice ſooner that way than any other; however, meeting but with little Practice, I reſolv'd to take the opportunity of a ſhip bound for *Martinico*, hoping in that new ſettlement to make my fortune: It being a time of peace, tho' our ſhip was a pretty good burthen, and carry'd fifteen guns, yet expecting no enemy, ſhe was but ill provided with ammunition and men fit for an engagement, yet ſhe made a pretty good defence againſt the three *pirate ſhips* which attack'd her, and had it not been for an unlucky ſhot which took her betwixt wind and water, I believe we had made

made our efcape, but now finking in the midft
of the fight, all her men perifh'd, except fix of
us, who were taken up by the *pirates*, and put
aboard one of their fhips. The day before, the
Englifh fhip, in which my wife was, fell into
their hands; all that paft afterwards, to the time
of my return to my wife, fhe has given you
an account of; I fhall therefore begin my narration at our paffing the gap in the mountains,
of which fhe has told you.

WHEN the prieft and I were got over
the plank, and fix'd our footing on the o-
ther fide, we had fome difficulty to get
down a fteep place of about five or fix yards,
and which, like a wall or rampart, furrounded the inhabited part of the ifland; but having got down on the firm land, as I may call it,
we advanc'd to the brow of the hill, whence
we had a full furvey or profpect of the moft
beautiful and charming country that our eyes
ever beheld; hence we began our progrefs down
thro' pleafant groves, or frequent groupes of
trees, for above a mile together; proceeding
on ftill, near the end of another mile, we were
furpriz'd, and frighten'd too, to fee at our backs
three huge animals, that at firft appear'd to us
to be *Lyons*, but coming up with us, they did
no more than take hold of the lapet of our
coats, or linen garments we had on, and thus
led us down to the foot of the hill, above half a
mile farther; they at laft brought us into a plain,

where

where there were thousands of people, some in
an adjacent pool or pond, and others on its
banks, men, women and children, and all stark
naked; the men were all tall, and seem'd to us
of a larger size than generally our *Europeans* are,
but of a perfect symmetry, and their eyes seem'd
to carry a perfect awe and majesty in them;
their hair was generally of a light brown,
curling in ringlets a little below their shoul-
ders; that of the women something more
yellow, and falling down even to their wastes;
not without frequent curles, which made it the
more grateful. The women were all crown'd
with chaplets of beautiful flowers, and the
men had no weapon in their hands but a
sort of a white staff, about seven foot in length,
at the end of which was fixt a sort of cutting
hook, with which I found afterwards they
shear'd and trimm'd the trees. As soon as our
Lyons had brought us into their presence, they
let go their hold, and about a dozen men surrounded us without coming very near us. The
whole company seem'd as much surpriz'd at our
company, as we were at theirs: And one of them
spoke to us looking with a stern countenance,
but we understood not what they said; but we
was inform'd afterwards they demanded of us
who, and what we were? Whence we came?
And how we got thither? Their country being
surrounded by vast and unpassable seas, as they
then thought them. All that we could do was
to make shew of an humble submission, and
signs

figns of our begging their mercy and protection; fo they feparating again pointed to the
Lyons, and utter'd fome words, upon which
two of them came and feiz'd us by the garments, as before, without doing us any farther injury. One of the company went on
before, and beckon'd us to follow him, which
we did, being ftill held by our guardian *Lyons:*
As we pafs'd on, the whole company open'd
to the right and left, to let us go thro' them,
without touching of them; which, it feems,
they thought an abomination before we had
been purify'd, according to the cuftom of that
country, or rather according to the precepts of
their laws, fince that can fcarce be call'd a cuftom which had not been done before in the
memory of any one then living. Our guide
conducted us fome miles to a little plain, or open
fpace, furrounded by a fort of quick-fet hedge,
or dwarfifh trees; in the midft of it there was
a fort of a fountain, or little pond, very clear,
and about half the depth of a man: As foon
as we were enter'd this little plain, our *Lyons*
let us go, in obedience to a nod from our
guide, and plac'd themfelves on each fide the
entrance; and then our guide leaping into the
fountain, wafh'd himfelf, and went out on the
other fide; when he was out he made figns to
us to do the fame, which ftripping our felves
we foon did, to the great amazement of the
native, who, as we afterwards underftood,
thought we had pull'd off our outward skins,
having

having no manner of notion of cloaths. By
that time we had done this, there came two
other natives with little baskets of fruit, which
they set down, and jumping into the fountain
as the other had done, they went out likewise
on the other side, making signs to us to eat
and refresh our selves with the fruit they had
brought; which, while we were doing, they all
three went away, without coming near us, but
left our guard at the entrance, who kept their
posts without ever stirring away. By that time
we had done our repast, and got up to look
about us, we found the whole enclosure surrounded by those terrible animals, tho' not one
of them ever attempted to come nearer to us;
the fruit they brought us was the most delicious
in the world, much more excellent both for
taste and flavour, than what we had met with
in our part of the island. In the middle of
this hedge that surrounded us, there was a
small bower, which entering; we found above
two foot thick of the most sweet fragrant flowers that could be found; and this place we concluded was to be our nightly abode.

ABOUT an hour before night we had more
provisions brought us, and our former baskets
remov'd; which, as soon as the bearer had set
down, he plung'd into the fountain, wash'd
himself, got out, and went away. It being
now dusky, we heard that heavenly harmony
all around us, of vocal and instrumental musick,

fick, made up by the voices of men, women, and children; but such voices that are not certainly to be found any where in the world but here: And we having said our Prayers retir'd into our bower, and throwing our selves upon our bed of flowers, after a little discourse, we went to sleep, notwithstanding the evil neighbourhood of those creatures which surrounded us.

In the morning, by break of day, we were awak'd by the same divine musick; which about noon we heard again, as we did also at night, and so for every day while we stay'd among them. We had constantly fresh food brought us three times a day, and a sort of little cups, out of which we drank our water; not from the fountain, or pond, which I mention'd to be in the middle of our enclosure, but from a little brook which empty'd it self into that pond; whose waters were kept at a certain height, by emptying themselves into another little channel on the other side, in proportion to what they receiv'd from the former.

We had observ'd that whoever came to us, not only never approach'd us, but as soon as they had set down what they brought, leap'd into the pond, wash'd themselves, and went away, and three times a day made us do the same; from which we concluded that they

L took

took us for a fort of impure animals, which were not to be convers'd with 'till we were fufficiently purify'd by the waters of that place; and which indeed was the only fuperftition that we ever difcover'd amongft them. One thing was remarkable, that our guard of beafts always left us as foon as it was day, and came again juft before the clofe of the evening, excepting two, which were always found at the entrance of the enclofure.

IT was two months before ever our human keepers vouchfaf'd to fpeak to us, except by figns; but after that, we had generally one or other with us, except at the time of morning prayer, and repaft at noon-tide prayer and dinner, 'till evening prayer and fupper call'd them away. In thofe intervals they did what they could to make us learn fomething of their language; but we found it fo difficult, that it was almoft two years before we became mafters of it. By that time we had been there two months, our linen garments being pretty much fully'd, we agreed to lay them by, and go naked, as the natives did; hoping by that means to ingratiate our felves more with them, by following their manners, than by being tenacious of our own. And by this time our beards were grown to a great length, as well as the nails of our toes and fingers, befides the face and head, and all thofe parts where hair generally grows. The prieft's whole body

was

was extremely hairy, tho' mine was not fo, which gave our new mafters a frefh furprize: Indeed we made but a fcurvy figure, a very mean appearance, in comparifon of the natives. They were tall and handfome, finely limb'd, and no hair about them but on their heads: We were both little men, our heads and faces almoft cover'd with hair, and his body all o-ver fo, that they fcarce look'd upon us to be of the fame fpecies: Tho' now they began to converfe a little with us, it was at fome di-ftance, as if they fear'd fome contagion from us, if they approach'd nearer; however they feem'd very defirous to make us underftand them; and we employ'd all our apprehenfion to gratify them on our part; but ftill when-ever they left us they leap'd into the fountain, wafh'd themfelves, and went away. When we were alone we walk'd round our enclofure, to view, as far as we could, the country about us, and we faw perpetually paffing by us men, women and children, all naked, and without the leaft covering about them. The women were extremely beautiful, both as to face and fhape; the colour of their skins was not fwar-thy, as might be expected, from their going naked in fo warm a clime, tho' there was a fort of an olive tincture in them; their eyes were brisk and penetrating, their limbs exactly proportion'd, without any deformity among them. We were about breaft high, cover'd with the hedge or dwarfifh trees that went a-

bout

bout our enclofure; fo that all they faw of us was very hairy, which was what they never faw before in their lives. We perceiv'd very plainly, that tho' they endeavour'd to conceal it, they all caft a fide-long glance at us. After we had continu'd about five months, we were led back to that pool which we firft faw at our coming down the hill, but no body about it but the three natives; who, with our *Lyons,* conducted us thither, and there we were oblig'd to wafh our felves for two hours together, and found in our fwimming about that the water was brackifh, and therefore muft have fome fecret communication with the adjacent fea. This pool, we perceiv'd afterwards, was by cuftom, or fuperftition, a place in which all the inhabitants of the ifland purify'd themfelves twice every year.

FROM thence we were re-conducted to our lodging, but our mafters then ventur'd to come clofer to us, and every day endeavour'd, with abundance of diligence, to inftruct us in their language; and when we could underftand them tolerably well, they feem'd very inquifitive to know what we were? Whence we came? And how we got thither? In all which we endeavour'd to give them what fatisfaction we could, with that little part of their language which we underftood; but being at laft good mafters of it, we gave them an account of our country, religion, and manners, and alfo of our voyage

to

to that place. We had much ado to make
them underftand what a fhip was, and how it
was poffible for us to pafs fo many worlds of
feas as fhould take us up near feven months in
our paffage, and that without feeing land once
in all that time; but they feem'd amaz'd not
only at fo ftrange a paffage where no tract
could direct them, but that men fhould venture their lives in fo fmall a machine fo far
from their own country. They frequently afk'd
us what could be the motive to fo hazardous an
undertaking? And faid that furely we inhabited fome miferable climate, that we fhould
chufe to fly from it thro' fo many dangers.

WE did all we could to make them underftand
that it was in purfuit of gain and riches for
which we did this; but we could by no means
make them comprehend what gain and riches
were. They afk'd us whether we wanted food
in our own country, and were forc'd on
that account to feek it abroad? We told them
it was not that, but the earneft defire of having more than what was abfolutely neceffary, that made us venture fo far; fince large
poffeffions and great abundance did not only
gain the refpect and veneration of thofe who
had not the fame advantage, but even an authority over them. This likewife feem'd to
puzzle them, for they could not form an idea
of any pleafure and fatisfaction that there fhould
be in thofe things; but to give them the better

cer notion of it, we proceeded to give them
an account of our manners and condition:
That envy, malice, ambition, avarice and luft,
rul'd abfolutely in our parts of the world; and
that he who was not in fome meafure a flave
to any of them, was look'd upon either as con-
temptible, or indeed very miferable.

I find, faid one of them, that you are of the
number of the children of wrath, of which we
have an obfcure traditionary account, tho' we could
fcarce believe it, 'till your words now confirm
the fact. Oh! wretched generation, with whom
reafon has fo little power, and paffion fo much.
How happy are we, who want nothing that's
neceffary to life, nor have any defire or wifhes
for what we do not want.

AFTER fome of thefe converfations we were
admitted to more liberty, and allow'd a greater freedom of going among the natives in general, at leaft in thofe parts which were not
far from our firft lodgings, whither we were
every night conducted and guarded with our
Lyons. I call them *Lyons*, not that they were
really fo; but becaufe their heads and manes were
more like *Lyons* than any other creature I know
of; but by their temper and condition they might
rather be call'd dogs, tame and domeftick animals, and were much more terrible in their
afpect than in their nature: As for their food,
they liv'd not upon flefh, but upon the fruit
and

and herbage of the country, and therefore their teeth were not made like thofe of *Lyons*, or dogs, or any other voracious animal; they were mighty tractable and obedient to the beck of their mafters, and were bred fo, that they every day went their rounds about the hills; by which means we firft fell into their cufto-dy. We faw feveral other animals, both birds, and four-footed beafts, tho none of them like any we have in our parts of the world; they were all tame, and would come to the hand.

THERE was one thing remarkable among one fort of the birds, and that was, whenever any vocal or inftrumental mufick began, they conftantly joyn'd in the chorus, and that with a very agreeable voice. They were very like our parots, but much larger; and by the fre-quent repetition of the morning, noon, and e-vening fongs, they had learn'd the very words, and fung them.

BY a frequent converfation, I found that the people of this place had no form of govern-ment among them, but liv'd like that colony of the *Sidonians*, mention'd in the book of *Judges*; that is, without magiftrates, or any rule, which might contradict the inclinations of every particular or individual. And indeed there was no occafion for magiftrates, when there was no ground for contention; there be-ing no property among them, but a perpetual
and

and uninterrupted courfe of a perfect love of one another. What the earth produc'd was a fufficient ftock, plentifully to provide for their fubfiftence; and their cultivation of thefe products was fo far from being laborious to them, that it was only their exercife and diverfion. In the cool of the morning, after the firft prayers were over, and their firft repaft, the men went all out to prune the trees, and them into fuch forms and figures as they thought fit; and which they did with thofe white ftaves, headed by a fort of hooks, as I defcrib'd them at my firft coming down. Thefe hooks were not made of iron, but of a certain ftone, very hard and clofe, and wrought to an edge; fo that they cut very well, and did the bufinefs as well as any of our gardiner's tools can do; the natives managing them with extraordinary dexterity, as will be plain from what I fhall tell you hereafter.

WHILE the men were thus employ'd, the women were taking care of their children, to inftruct them both in the principles of religion, and what other duties were neceffary for their future conduct; but their duties not being many, the precepts they were to learn were but few.

THO' I have faid they had no property, yet that muft be underftood in the lands, or in the product; for in their women, or wives, they

they had, and that fo facred, that no one ever
invaded it, fo that adultery was a crime unknown among them. I obferv'd that every
man had but one wife, fo that in all probability the births of males and females were pretty equal; as there was this exception to what I
told you of their having no property, fo there
is another to what I faid of their having no
magiftrates, tho' this indeed is fcarce an exception. The oldeft men among them were the
heads of their families, or little tribes, and to
them there was a refpect and deference paid,
and all publick actions were directed by them;
as general meetings, approbation of matriages,
the order of all folemnities, and who fhould
fpeak or dance in them. They alfo had the
chief place in their publick meetings, or feafts,
and deliver'd to them their thoughts and fentiments in religious matters, fomething after the
way of our fermons; the fubftance of which
was upon God, and exhortations to mutual
love, and their duty to one another; and this
was generally done after their temperate meals
were over, fo that they fhould be at perfect
eafe to attend to what they heard. When
there were none of thefe difcourfes, and the
talk was promifcuous, the converfation ftill run
upon the difcoveries they had made in their
contemplations, and then hearing fuch doubts
and difficulties as the younger fort propos'd;
and this held them 'till the heat of the day
was pretty well over, and then the young men

M   went

went to their task of pruning and cultivating
their trees and ground, and the women to inftruct their children; the virgins often accom-
pany'd their lovers in their work, and there
heard their addreffes. When a young man
and virgin were agreed to marry, they then
propos'd it to the father and mother of both;
whofe confent having obtain'd, as well as the
approbation of the elders of their tribe, neither of which was ever deny'd, a day was
fix'd for the publick folemnization of their nup-
tials, at which their whole tribe were always
prefent. The ceremony of their marriage was,
as well as I can remember, in the following
manner.

IN the morning, after the firft prayers were
over, the bridegroom, attended by all the
young men of the tribe, with mufical inftruments, and their heads crown'd with chaplets
of flowers, came to the bower or lodging of
the virgin who was that day to be marry'd;
and after he had fung and danc'd for a little
while, came forth, attended with all the young
virgins and girls above twelve years of age, a-
dorn'd likewife with chaplets of flowers; from
whence hung down, both before and behind,
ropes, as it were, of flowers and odoriferous
herbs. The bridegroom receiv'd her with great
expreffions of joy, and having kifs'd her lips
and her eyes, march'd on with her towards
the publick hall of the tribe; he follow'd by
the

the young men, and fhe by the virgins and
girls. The publick hall is a fort of an amphitheatre, above an hundred yards over; round
which was planted, inftead of walls, lofty and
beautiful trees, whofe branches fpreading far,
and joyning artificially in their growth, compos'd a very agreeable canopy of green, inter-
mingled with beautiful flowers of an admirable
fcent; and which fufficiently fhaded, tho' not
cover'd, the whole fpace of the amphitheatre
or circle; the middle of which was open to
the air all round: Clofe to the bodies of the
trees there were three ranges of feats made of
banks cover'd with herbs and flowers; which,
like camomile, was the better for being fit on.
On thefe feats fet all the marry'd men and women, and the elders of the tribe; the chief of
which fet on feats exalted above the reft. The
bride and bridegroom, with their trains, being
enter'd, came up to the feat of the chief elders, where the parents, of both fides, ftood
ready to receive them. The bridegroom made
a fpeech, and the whole company joyn'd in
prayers to heaven for a bleffing on the new
marry'd pair, then the nuptial fong began, in
which every one bore a part; during the folemnity the father and mother, of each fide, deliver'd to the chief elder the hands of their
fon and daughter, which he joyn'd together;
after which the bride and bridegroom embrac'd
one another, and after fome kiffes feparated a-
gain, and began to dance, fometimes by them-

felves, and fometimes in company, with all
the reft of both their trains: When they had
fung and danc'd for fome time, they all went
to their repaft in a long room, arch'd over entirely with the branches of the trees on each
fide, fo artfully interwoven, that the cieling
feem'd perfectly folid; but they went not to
dinner before they had all joyn'd in the noon-
tide prayer, and which was never omitted upon any account whatfoever. After dinner the
young ones went again to dancing, and the
old ones to talking on what they thought fit:
Thefe revels continu'd till evening prayer, after which the bridegroom led his bride, attended as before, to the bower of blifs, I mean
to that arbour where they were to confummate
and reft the whole night. The boys and girls,
in the mean while, had ftrew'd the way, from
the publick hall to this bower; and on each
fide, as they pafs'd, ftood the old women
ftrewing on their heads odoriferous flowers:
When they were enter'd, the whole company
difpers'd, every one to his own home. This
is the ceremony of their marriage, but what that
of their funerals was I cannot tell, having not
feen one during the three years time of my a-
bode among them.

I could not obferve that they made any difference of days, or diftinguifh'd *Sunday* from
the reft; but upon our mentioning that we
fet apart one day in feven, as a day peculiar
for

for the fervice of God, which we therefore
call the Lord's-day, they cry'd out, in a fort
of a wonder, Why is not every day the day of
the Lord, and dedicated to his fervice either in
prayer, or fuch duties and exercifes as he has
ordain'd? But when we faid we did it in commemoration of God's refting from his labour,
after he had in fix days created the heavens
and the earth, and all things in them; they
ftopp'd their ears, and cry'd out, Blafphemy;
efteeming it fo, in calling whatever God did,
labour; and expreffing it in fuch a manner, as
if tir'd with his foregoing work he wanted reft,
like man, to refrefh himfelf. We were at
laft admitted to their converfation after dinner,
and there, to the whole company, gave an account of the cuftoms, laws, manners and vices
of our part of the world; particularly of our
wars, and the many thoufands flain in battle,
with the vaft devaftations and defolation which
the ambition of princes brought upon their
people, all which feem'd to ftrike them with
the utmoft horror: However, this was the occafion that we were fent from tribe to tribe
round the whole ifland, and oblig'd to each
tribe in feveral particular and general affem-
blies to rehearfe the fame account, and always
met with the fame horror and deteftation in
every one of our audiences. This progrefs of
ours took up the reft of the time that we
ftaid among them; but before we were permitted to go away, there was a general affembly
of

of the elders of all the tribes, at which were
prefent likewife many of the younger fort;
the place in which this affembly was held was
about the middle of the Ifland, where, in a
fpatious plain, there arofe a magnificent building, if I may call that a building whofe walls
were all vegetables, for they were compos'd
of feveral lofty trees fet at convenient diftances,
the fpaces between each being fill'd up with
fmaller plants, which being interwoven, each
within the other, feem'd a fort of a green
wall which did not rife up to the roof, but
left feveral openings like windows to let in
both the air and the light; the roof being
form'd out of the branches of the tall trees
feem'd fupported by them as by fo many pil-
lars; the roof of this was much the fame with
that I defcrib'd; and here likewife was fuch
another amphitheatre, tho' much larger, and
capable of holding a far greater number of
people. In the midft of this there grew another lofty tree, whofe branches fpread far and
wide, and help'd to compleat the canopy that
kept off the fun and weather from incom-
moding the affembly. Beneath this middle
tree, there was a bank all rais'd up behind it to
fuch an eminence that it overlook'd the audience, and from it were made fuch fpeeches as
were addrefs'd to the whole company; and here
it was that we were to have our audience of
leave, as I may call it; and where my good friend
the Prieft had like to have fpoil'd all by an un-
timely

timely zeal for propagating the Gofpel among them; for being mounted upon this eminence, after he had given thanks for the human treatment we had met with among them, he went on, and firft prais'd their happinefs in their knowledge of the true God, as well as in the place of their abode, and the ftrength and finenefs of their reafoning; but, faid he, there is ftill one thing wanting to render your felicity compleat; that is, to hinder its expiring with your life, for I do affure you, there are much greater bleffings in the eternal kingdom of God, which can only be obtain'd by the means of Jefus Chrift: In return therefore of all our obligations, and in obedience to the dictates of my confcience, I fhall offer you another religion, which is yet in fome meafure built on th which you already profefs. Here the audienc would not let him proceed any farther, and ic of the eldeft of the company fpoke thus to nim. Stranger, let not thy ignorance of what we believe, put thee upon a fruitlefs trouble to wafte our time in hearing what can never have any agreeable effect among us; therefore before you proceed, hear an account of our religion, and then if you can offer any thing better you fhall have leave to fpeak. Upon this we were ordered to defcend and ftand among the audience; and a young virgin of about fifteen, was commanded to mount the eminence in our room, and thence to give an account of their religion. They did this for two ends; firft, to fhew how well their young

ones

ones were inftructed; and next by way of contempt, by putting fo young a creature to open
the argument againft us. When fhe was got up,
bowing her felf, and putting one knee to the
ground, fhe implor'd heaven to enable her to
fpeak in fuch a manner as was agreeable to the importance of what fhe had to utter. O *Affa,* (which
by interpretation fignifies Thou Being without a name) 'tis thou whom we adore, thou who
haft produc'd, by thy infinite power and wifdom,
all things that fill the univerfe ; thou who art infinite and every where; thou who doft by thy
providence fuftain every thing that is, and which
only and wholly fubfifts by and in thee ; thou
who hadft no beginning, but didft give beginning to every thing elfe, to thee are all our
prayers and our praifes due and daily paid, as
our eternal benefactor and fource; and to thee
be praife for evermore.

THEN ftanding upright fhe thus proceeded.
This great God has implanted in us certain laws,
which are equally evident and beneficial, and
of which reafon is our teacher; a teacher who
can never deceive us, fince this great God has
given us no other guide either to him or of our
own actions. As reafon leads us to the being of a
God, fo it tells us, that we have a perpetual
dependence upon him, and receive perpetual
favours from him in the life which we enjoy ;
and therefore, that our prayers and praifes fhould
be likewife perpetual, it farther tells us, that
                                         fince

since this great Being has created human kind
with a beneficent intention, for eternal good-
ness could have no other; it follows, that we
are oblig'd to do nothing that may injure that
happiness which he defign'd his creatures should
enjoy; but the surest way of avoiding whatever
may disturb our tranquillity, is to love one a-
nother; for whilst we love one another, we
can never do any thing to hurt our selves;
for hurt is the effect of hate, and not of love;
our religion therefore is very short, and not
burthen'd with many articles, since it only commands that we love and adore our eternal Benefactor, who is entirely and every way lovely
and adorable; but as a testimony of this love
and adoration, we ought publickly to pay to
him our thanks and our praise, and for all
those things which we daily receive from his
bounty; and to give infallible proofs that this
profession and publick worship has its foundation in our hearts, we must always, and in all
things, act according to what love requires of
us to one another, and this is the sum of our
religion.

HAVING said this, she made another bow,
and descended from the eminence; and then
the priest was order'd to go up again, where
he began to tell them the whole history of
Adam and *Eve*, and the *Fall of Man,* which
had corrupted the whole generation, and made
all the progeny of *Adam* to be born in ori-

N   ginal

ginal fin, which excluded them from that eternal happiness hereafter, for which their Maker had defign'd them; and that therefore it was necessary that there should be a Redeemer to restore mankind to the grace and favour of God; but that could not be done by any one man, who was merely a man; therefore one person of the Godhead took upon him human nature, and was born of a virgin, did many miracles, and at last dy'd an infamous death, to make atonement to heaven for the sins of all mankind; who were by that means made capable of entering into heaven, whose gates he open'd; where rising again from the dead, he ascended into heaven; and therefore no one can follow him thither who are not let into this congregation by baptism, and acknowledge him, as well as the Holy Ghost, to make up one Godhead with the Father.

THE priest was proceeding to the worship of the virgin *Mary*, and the saints and angels; but his discourse had seem'd too shocking to the assembly to let them suffer him to go on any farther. One of the elders told him he should say no more, since their ears could not hear of the Deity's being divided into three; and that a man who he confess'd dy'd, was however the ever living God; so directing the priest to come down, he got up in his place, and turning himself all round to the people, cry'd out, O happy generation, who are separated

rated fo far from thefe children of wrath, as
to have no communication with them; they
are rebels to reafon, and God, and by that
means are the moft miferable of men; always
fubject to fears and mifchiefs, created by their
own folly; and for this reafon were thefe two
fons of wrath permitted to go round our country; that hearing their account of their own
wretched ftate and condition, you might have
the greater relifh of that tranquillity and happinefs which heaven has made our lot.

You have read, I doubt not, all of you, the
accounts our hiftories give of thefe children
of wrath, which we find now confirm'd by
themfelves; we may therefore blefs that eternal power, who at once to fecure the children
of love from the infection and evil machinati-
ons of the children of wrath, funk fo many
vaft tracts of land to divide us from the reft of
this wicked world, and feparate us to felicity
founded on innocence; ye fons of wrath, therefore with fpeed retire from among us, left
your longer ftay fhould infect our bleffed bow-
ers.

With that we were conducted out of the
affembly, and fet directly towards the place
where we enter'd this happy habitation; but
the day was too far fpent for us to go out
that night, fince we had five and twenty miles
to walk from the affembly to their utmoft

N 2   bounds;

bounds; we were therefore conducted again to
our firſt lodging, where we reſted that night,
having our uſual guard about us, which we
had not had ever ſince we left that place 'till
we return'd thither again; we had however the
converſation of two or three of our firſt guides
and acquaintance, of whom I enquir'd what
was meant by the diſtinction us'd by that elder who ſpoke laſt in the aſſembly of the
children of wrath, and the children of love.
We have, reply'd one of them, a hiſtory a-
mongſt us, that begins before the creation of
the world, and reaches down to our ſeparati-
on from the reſt of mankind; but though we
do not build any faith upon this account, it is
yet receiv'd with a great deal of veneration for
its antiquity; it being written on the very firſt
foundation of our nation. By this account the
creation of the world is attributed not immediately to God, but to certain ſpirits made by
God of wonderful power and wiſdom, much
beyond our comprehenſion; that every one of
the ſtars, as well as the ſun, were made by
theſe immortal ſpirits; that the ſpirit who
fram'd the earth, was belov'd by God above all
the reſt; and therefore when he had made the
birds, and the beaſts, and the reptiles, he ani-
mated them with life by fire given him from
the ſpirit who had form'd and govern'd the ſun;
that when he had made man with wonderful
œconomy in his body, he pray'd God to enli-
ven it with a rational ſoul; in compliance with
which

which prayer, God infus'd reason into man, who by that reason was likened to its divine cause, and has this difference from its body, that it never dies, but is eternal; that is, endures for ever, since nothing that is the immediate work of God himself can ever perish: The body indeed dies, but that was only the work of the great and wonderful spirit before mention'd. This new made man having likewise a woman joyn'd unto him, begot their like; whose race for many years kept up to that purity and innocence in which they were first made, and which they preserved by keeping up to the directions of reason; but afterwards they began to neglect that duty, and follow the direction of their passions; which gaining head, soon depos'd reason, and with it lost all knowledge of God, and their own original. They left their delicious abode, being driven out indeed by angels, or some ministers of the great spirit who made them, and from that time call'd them the children of wrath, but yet his children; and those who remain'd innocent, who were in all but four, he call'd the children of love; and to keep them from being seduced by the children of wrath, he sunk all the ground about this place, or happy abode, and surrounded it with vast unpassable waters; here they encreas'd to the number which you now find. This history does describe the children of wrath much in the same manner as you have describ'd the

people

people of your countries; which will add a great authority to this book, at least in that particular; but yet not enough to make us add any thing to our religion, either as to mingling some other worship with our adoration of the one God, or those maxims which direct our conduct to one another. And you may thank our principle, which forbids us the killing of any living creature, that you escap'd with your lives, for offering such absurd notions of three Gods; a man God, or one that dy'd as man. This, and much more, he urg'd against our religion, as propos'd by the priest. To put off the discourse, I ask'd what the meaning of that procession was, which I found they perform'd four times a year; the whole nation going round the mountains that encompass their whole country, singing hymns or songs of praise to God for some great deliverance: He told us that it was in commemoration of their being separated from the children of wrath, which they counted the greatest blessing that heaven had bestow'd upon them. The evening coming on they left us, and we retir'd to our bower to rest; the next morning, as soon as prayers were over, they came to us again, and led us up the hill to the place where we enter'd, and where we found our plank and rails still remaining; so parting with our children of love, we pass'd it, and came into our old territories, and by night got to

our

our habitation, in the manner which you have heard from my wife.

I ſhall only add concerning the people, that notwithſtanding they were all naked, we never could obſerve the leaſt look, word, geſture, or motion, which had any favour of immodeſty; which, for all that I know, beſides the temperance of the people, might proceed from their going naked; for that making all things familiar and conſtant to the eye, took away all curioſities, which our garments hiding, promote. When we told them that we wonder'd at leaſt that they cover'd not thoſe parts which we thought modeſty requir'd they ſhould; they ſeemed to laugh at our folly, in thinking the parts of generation ought more to be cover'd than any other part of the body. In ſhort, their life ſeem'd wholly celeſtial, being ſpent in the praiſe of God, and the love of one another. They had no trades among them, for every one made what inſtruments they wanted themſelves; and the children of each family wove, as I may call it, thoſe little diſhes and plates or trenchers, in which they ſerv'd their fruit at meals; wove, I call it, becauſe they were made of a ſort of ruſhes, twiſted ſo cloſe together, that they would even hold a liquid, and of the ſame material; and the ſhells of certain nuts they form'd their drinking cups of: What and how they made their muſical inſtruments, I do not know, tho' I have heard

a great

a great variety among them, for they were wonderful proficients in the art of *mufical* numbers; they were all likewife poets, but their poetry confifted only of hymns and love fongs.

BEING return'd home again to my wife, I was forry to hear of the lofs of the reft of our company, but glad to find her ftill alive. All that I had learn'd during my abfence, which could be any way beneficial to her, was the cooking, as I may call it, of the feveral fruits which grew amongft us; particularly in making of oyl, or fqueezing of it out of a fruit which we had before not minded, and which was of an excellent flavour and relifh, and very much heighten'd feveral of our difhes. But no fhips yet appear'd, and very little hopes we had that we fhould ever efcape from that folitude to our more peopled world. The prieft and I every day walk'd out fome where or other, yet generally we went but a little way, becaufe we would not leave my wife alone. One day taking a turn towards thofe mountains, or high rocks, which run crofs the country, and feparate us from the children of love, we chanc'd to fee, at the foot of them, a certain reddifh fand, which we fancy'd to be gold; and taking it up, perfuaded our felves that it really was fo, being wafh'd down from thofe rocks by the great fhowers which had been all the day before; we took two or three handfuls, and carry'd with us to my wife; who

perfuaded

perfuaded us to fetch all we could find of it,
and fill thofe chefts and trunks which were
now empty'd of all our linen and cloaths,
which by this time were pretty well confum'd,
fhe faid, fince we had little elfe to do: And
that fince we might fome time or other meet
with a conveyance from that place, if we could
in the mean time get any ftock of this fuppos'd
gold, it might be of great ufe to us if it prov'd
right, in our return to our own country. Accordingly we went and brought all we could
find at the firft place; but that was foon ex-
haufted, there being no fupply except after violent rains, which we fuppos'd wafh'd it down
from the mountains; fo we were careful to go
always after the rains, not only where we found
the firft, but all along wherever we could come
near them for the woods. We had now pretty well fill'd one of our boxes, when an accident happen'd that put an end to our raking
together what we did not know would be of any
real value; or if it was, it could be none to
us while we remain'd where we were, and
therefore not worth the running of any rifque;
for whilft we were one day gathering this glittering fand, we heard a moft prodigious noife,
and looking up we faw part of the mountain
or rocks about half a mile from us tumbling
down, and covering the country about it; we immediately, being fufficiently frighten'd, run full
fpeed to our own habitation, where only we

O thought

thought our felves fafe, being above three miles from the mountains.

Nothing elfe happen'd that is worth relating, during our ftay in this place, which was above two years longer. At laft taking our walk to the fea fide, we thought we faw a fhip, and found before it was dark that it was really fo, and that fhe was making what fail fhe could towards our ifland: We went home with this good news to comfort my wife, who had been extremely uneafy at our ftay fo many hours more than we us'd to do. The next morning we all walk'd again to the fea fide, and found the fhip juft entering our port or road; and that which was a greater fatisfaction to us, we perceiv'd that fhe carry'd *French* colours. The fhore was very *broad,* fo that the fhip came very near land, and at laft laid her fide clofe to the fhore; and feeing us they hail'd us, and made feveral figns, as if they thought we were natives of the place, and underftood not their tongue; but the prieft ran nearer to them, and call'd to them in *French,* telling them they might fafely come afhore; which was very agreeable news to them, fince they had above eighteen of their men very fick, whom they brought all on fhore, in order to the recovery of their health: The fhip likewife was pretty much fhatter'd in a ftorm, which had driven them into thofe parts. Now my

my ſtore of wine, which had continu'd by us
ſome years, was of conſiderable uſe; for giving the ſick ſeamen ſome of it in ſmall quantities, and mingled with water, it contributed
very much to their recovery. The ſhip's name
was the *Barfleur*, and the captain of her was a
gentleman of *Bretagne*; to whom we gave an account of all our adventures, and who, with ſome
of his crew, perſuaded the prieſt and me to be
their guide to the place where we had made
our former entry into the territories of the children of love; he reſolving, if he could, not
only to ſee the place, but to take ſome of
the inhabitants, and carry them into *France*;
but when we came there we found not only
our plank gone, but the breach or gap, from
ten foot, as we left it, widen'd to above threeſcore yards, and not much leſs in the depth;
which, whether it was done by accident, or
by the natives, to prevent any more viſits from
the children of wrath, as they call'd us, I know
not. We ſtaid in thoſe parts two or three
days, in hopes, at leaſt, of hearing ſome of that
heavenly muſick, of which both the prieſt and
I had told them, but to no purpoſe; ſo that
returning back to the ſhip, the captain made
all the haſte he could in refitting her, and refreſh-
ing her with freſh water, of which they had
been in great need. And the men being now
all recover'd, and our baggage carry'd on board,
and the wine that yet remain'd drawn off into
bottles, of which the *captain* had a pretty good

ſtock,

ſtock, tho' all empty'd in his voyage; putting
likewiſe on board plenty of the moſt laſting fruit
of the iſland, we all enter'd the *Barfleur*, and
put out to ſea.

I need not give you any relation of the ſeveral ſtorms we met with, or the other common
accidents which happen to ſea-faring people;
I ſhall only obſerve, that after many months
voyage, as we came almoſt to the chops of the
channel, we met with a *Dutch* man-of-war,
who attempted to take us; but being a ſhip
of pretty good force, and maintaining her ſelf
with a great deal of bravery, bringing the
Dutchmen's main-maſt by the board, we ſheer'd
off, being too weak in guns and men to pretend to take her: We made all poſſible ſail,
and ſoon got out of danger, and reach'd
the firſt port we could in *France*, which was
Bayonne; having loſt a dozen men in the fight,
among which was the captain, as well as many wounded, in the number was my ſelf, for
there I loſt my right hand; and the ſhip being very much batter'd, the prieſt, my wife,
and my ſelf, were very glad that we were
once more got on ſhore in *Europe*, proteſting
we would never again ſeek our fortunes by
ſea; and I believe my wife, though ſhe has a
great mind to ſee her native country, *England*, will never do it, becauſe we muſt paſs
ſome part of the ſea to arrive there.

WE

WE ſtaid at *Bayonne* 'till my arm was quite
cur'd, by the ſurgeon of the ſhip; and here
we made tryal of our gold duſt, and found
in the experiment, that there was indeed a
great deal of that valuable metal amongſt it,
to our great ſatisfaction; for it not only ſup-
ported us while we ſtaid there, but enabled us
to get to *Paris*; where being furniſh'd with
better tools to ſeparate the ore from the
droſs, we found that we had of pure gold to
the value of more than two thouſand *Louis
d'Ors*; which the prieſt propos'd to divide into three equal ſhares, of which he took one
to himſelf, and gave us the other two; and
with his ſhare he purchas'd himſelf a good be-
nefice about twenty miles from *Paris*. He
ſtill wears his beard, and eats no fleſh nor fiſh,
and is now alive, hale and jolly, coming once
a year to *Paris*, where I am ſure of his company; and who, when he comes, will confirm
the truth of all I have told you. As for my
wife and I, we try'd many ways, and ſpent a
great deal of our money to little purpoſe, 'till
I ſet up a Tavern at the other end of this city; but my wife knowing that the *Engliſh*
very much frequented this part of the town,
choſe this houſe we now live in; and where
we hope, by your means, that ſhe may frequently converſe with her own countrymen.

HERE

HERE my landlord made an end, with a-
bundance of proteftations of the truth of all he
had told me; being ready, if I defir'd it, to
confirm it with his folemn oath before a ma-
giftrate. The prieft arriv'd here a few days
after, and confirm'd every part of this account, from the time of their being taken
by the *pirates*, to their coming away in the
Barfleur, proffering to give me an atteftati-
on of the whole in writing under his own
hand; or, if I requir'd it, his oath: Which tho'
I then refus'd, with abundance of thanks for
his civility, I will yet procure it, if you requeft
it, of him, for he is ftill in this city. I fhall only add, that I am,

Your moft fincere friend and fervant,

AMBROSE EVANS.

THE

THE
ADVENTURES
OF

Alexander Vendchurch,

AND OF HIS

Ship's Crew Rebelling againſt him, and ſetting him on ſhore in an Iſland in the *South-Sea,* &c.

THE
ADVENTURES
OF
Alexander Vendchurch,

And of his

*Ship's Crew Rebelling againſt him,
and ſetting him on ſhore in an
Iſland in the* South-Sea, &c.

 Was born in the city of *Edinburgh*
in *Scotland*; my father was a ſub-
ſtantial tradeſman of that kingdom,
with whom I liv'd 'till I was about
twelve years of age; when being
unable to bear the ill temper of my mother-in-
law any longer, I run away from my father; and
getting on board an *Engliſh veſſel* that lay then
in *Leith* road, I ſail'd in her for *London*, and
to diſcharge of my paſſage, I took upon me the

A   office

office of a *cabin boy* ; in which I pleas'd my master so well, that at my request he got me a
place in the family of a considerable merchant ;
though it was only to run of errands, clean
the *shoes*, and be an assistant to the cook-
maid. I had in *Scotland* got a pretty good
smattering in the *Latin* tongue, and writ a tolerable hand for my age; which, when my master was inform'd of, and finding me very tractable and good humour'd, he put me out to
school to perfect my writing, and learn such
accompts as might render me useful in his business ; my diligence and application was so great,
that I soon made a considerable progress in
both; so that I was taken into the Compting-
house to copy letters, and such other things
as boys are generally employ'd in. My master
had a daughter, who played upon the *lute*, and
I having a mighty fancy always for *musick*, I
ingratiated my self so far with her master as to
give me now and then a lesson; in which I
was such a proficient, that I believe he would
have taken me on my young mistress's recommendation, for an apprentice ; but I had other
things in my head, which flatter'd me with
greater prospects than that way of living; however, I improv'd my writing so well, whenever I
had the least leisure from my master's business,
that my young mistress having heard my performance, gave me a *lute*, and paid her master
to instruct me in the notes, that I might not
play all by rote, but be able to take off a tune
when

when I faw it before me; in two years time I play'd tolerably well, and by conftant application, in two years more, was a perfect mafter: For I never loft any time, as lads of my age very often do; but when I had no bufinefs in the Compting-houfe, I was always thruming on my *lute*. Having liv'd with this merchant about five years, or fomething more, he was fending a factor to *Cadiz*; who being willing to take me with him, I prevail'd with my mafter to let me go: Among others of my new mafter's acquaintance in *Cadiz*, there was a *Spanifh* merchant, who was very intimate with him, to whom afterwards I ow'd a great deal of good fortune, though at laft it had like to have prov'd my deftruction.

I was always for improving my time, and therefore employ'd all the leifure I had in learning the *Spanifh* tongue; in which I got fuch a maftery in a fhort time, that I could almoft have pafs'd for a native *Spaniard*. I would no more fing any *Englifh* fongs, or play any *Englifh* tunes, but got all the *Spanifh* mufick and fongs that I could procure; for which reafon, when the merchant I juft mention'd drank with my mafter, I was call'd to entertain him with a *Spanifh* fong on my *lute*; which pleas'd him fo much, that when my *Englifh* mafter was to return to *London*, he did all he could to detain me at *Cadiz*; proffering me fuch encouragement, that I thought fit to accept of

it:

it: And being now come into a *Spanish* family, I foon grew a perfect *Spaniard*; and finding that my mafter lov'd to hear the *guittar*,
I foon learn'd to play on it, though it is but a
poor inftrument in comparifon of a *lute*; however my bufinefs was to pleafe my mafter,
which I did to fuch a degree, that he lov'd me
extremely; nay, as much as if I had been his
own fon, but he was a batchelor, and a great
marriage hater.

My mafter having a very confiderable
fortune fallen to him at *Panama*, in the
Weft-Indies; and thinking that he could the
better fecure it by going thither, he refolv'd
upon that voyage with the next *Flota* that fet
out from *Cadiz*. The only difficulty that he had
was, what to do about me; for to take me
with him was dangerous, at leaft to me, none
being permitted to go into thofe parts but native *Spaniards*; and yet he could not think of
going without me. I told him that I was willing to run any hazard rather than ftay behind
him; that I was grown fo much a *Spaniard*
in every thing, that no body would take me
to be of any other country, who did not know
the contrary. This pleas'd my mafter wonder-
fully, and the better to difguife me, he made
me take upon me his own name, which was
Gonzalvo de Toledo, only inftead of *Gonzalvo* he call'd me *Roderigo*, and made me pafs
for a near relation of his when we came to
Panama.

Panama. All the difficulty that now remain'd, was how to get me on ſhip-board, ſince I was ſo well known in *Cadiz* to be a *Scotchman*; this likewiſe we got over, by pretending to part with me, and my ſeeming to ſet out for *Madrid* about a month before the departure of the *Flota.* My maſter *Gonzalvo* furniſh'd me with money ſufficient for this expedition, and gave letters of credit to ſome of his cor-reſpondents in *Sevill,* with whom I negotiat-ed ſome affairs of my maſter's, and then went on board a veſſel that went to joyn the *Flota,* which was ſail'd a few hours before our ſhip arriv'd, and therefore we made all the ſpeed we could after it, without ſtaying at *Cadiz,* of which I was very glad: It was near two days before we came up with the *Flota;* when my maſter was over-joy'd to ſee me come on board the ſhip in which he was. There was nothing material happen'd during this voy-age, but the whole *Flota* arriv'd very happily at the ſeveral ports to which they were bound, and we got ſafe to *Panama,* a very fine and populous city. *Gonzalvo* negotiated his affairs with great ſucceſs, and in leſs than a year's time might have return'd again into *Spain* with all his effects; but being now very old, he had no mind to undergo ſuch a voyage, merely to die in *Spain:* He therefore reſolv'd to ſtay there during the reſt of his life, and for my part, I eſteem'd no country more than that where I was likely to be a gainer; and that

was

was with my new unkle, as he call'd himself, who grew every day more fond of me.

OUR bufinefs not being very fatiguing, I had much time upon my hands, fome of which I fpent in making my addreffes to the Ladies, but without any pain or difquiet to my felf. I ferenaded fometimes one, and fometimes another, with my *lute* or *guittar*, and fuch difmal ditties as that place afforded: But I was not long to enjoy this tranquillity, for being one day at church, I kneel'd next to a Lady whofe fhape and hand infinitely pleas'd me; I made my addreffes to her with fuch fuccefs, that fhe took an opportunity to let me have a fide view of her face; which was the moft tranfportingly beautiful that ever I beheld in my life, and quite ftruck me to the heart; but my comfort was, that my perfon had not been wholly indifferent to her, and I prevail'd with her to let me know who fhe was, and where fhe liv'd; fhe inform'd me that her father's name was *Don Henriquez de Tortofa*, one of the moft eminent citizens of *Panama*; in return I let her know mine, and my unkle's name; which, with fome fhort proteftations and vows of love on my fide, concluded that converfation, the place admitting of no long conferences, tho' I went home extremely pleas'd with the fuccefs I had met with. When I began to reflect, I remember'd that *Don Henriquez de Tortofa* was the greateft enemy that
my

my unkle had in that city, and that he was equally hated by him; this made me conclude that I muſt manage my amour with *Donna Elvira* with the utmoſt caution and ſecrecy, to keep it from the knowledge of both the old Gentlemen.

My unkle had before now talk'd with me about marriage, aſſuring me, that if I fix'd my affections on any woman, in order to make her my wife, he would take care to give ſucceſs to my choice, by making ſuch a ſettlement upon me as ſhould be ſufficient to anſwer her fortune; but I always told him I would imitate him, and continue a batchelor, at leaſt as long as I ſhould be happy during his life, and that I could not think of dividing that love which I bore him with any other; but as for thoſe addreſſes I made, they were only amuſements, mere effects of gallantry, without the leaſt tincture of love. He gave me ſome prudent cautions for my conduct in thoſe affairs, putting me in mind of the danger which thoſe addreſſes very often brought upon us; I thank'd him for his care of me, and aſſur'd him that I would not carry matters ſo imprudently as to run any riſque in the purſuit of my gallantries, which were too general to draw any particular jealouſie upon me; but I never durſt tell him, as long as he liv'd, one word about my paſſion for *Elvira*, being afraid of offending him; for a *Spaniard's* hatred is never to
be

be appeas'd, and therefore I very well knew
that on her father's account he would never
indulge, or even pardon my inclinations for
the daughter: However, I took care to find
means of conveying a letter to her, by brib-
ing, with the help of a friend, the *Duenna*,
or governefs, who had the immediate guardi-
anfhip of *Elvira*; fhe being the only daughter of *Don Henriquez*, and very much belov'd by him, was permitted more liberties
than the young *Spanifh* ladies are generally allow'd.

I fhall not here pretend to give you copies
of the feveral letters which I fent her, or of
her anfwers, they being all loft at the fame
time that my wealth was ravifh'd from me;
it muft fuffice that they were really paffio-
nate on both fides, and the effect of a true
and violent paffion. By the help of the *Duenna*
I had feveral interviews with my miftrefs, in
which we both deplor'd our mutual misfortunes,
in the hatred that was fix'd betwixt her father
and my unkle; but yet we fometimes comfor-
ted our felves, that they were both very old,
and very infirm, fo that if either dropt, we
imagin'd that the other might eafily be brought
to give his confent; but we were out in this, for
want of confidering, that when a *Spaniard*
hates One of a family he hates them All.

My

My unkle, who had never well recover'd his voyage from *Spain*, was now taken ill of his laſt ſickneſs, and took care to leave me ſo plentiful a fortune, that if I had been really his nephew, I could not have deſir'd more. He bequeath'd a conſiderable legacy to one of his near relations in *Spain*, and left me a particular charge to remit it to him; which afterwards prov'd a great damage to me in the poſſeſſion of that fortune which *Gonzalvo* had left me, and which, after all legacies and funeral charges were paid, amounted to upwards of one hundred thouſand pieces of eight, a very handſome ſtock for a young merchant to begin the world with.

Some time after my unkle's death, my deſire was too eager to have *Elvira* to my wife, to ſuffer me to conſider things calmly; I therefore, by a common friend, made motions to *Don Henriquez*, of an accommodation; and to cement our new friendſhip, made him propoſe me as a husband for his daughter. On this motion *Don Henriquez* flew out into the moſt extravagant paſſion in the world, uttering the vileſt abuſes, both againſt me and my unkle, that an inveterate malice could prompt, and ſwore bitterly that he would ſooner give his daughter to an *Alguazil* (a hangman) than to me; telling him, that if I ever made any addreſſes to her, or came near his houſe with that deſign,

B   he

he would take care that I should be treated like an invader of the honour of his family; but having no notion of that affair which I had so long had with his daughter, he did not abridge her of those little liberties which he before allow'd her; he thought it sufficient only to tell her of the proposal that had been made, with his own answer; adding, that he hop'd he had no occasion to threaten her with his curse, if she ever listen'd to any solicitations from him; which indeed he did not expect, supposing that this proposal was only an effect of the care of my own interest, and not of love.

THIS discourse, though it struck *Elvira* to the heart, yet she knew her father too well to suffer either her looks or words to give him the least suspicion of the truth. We both long'd to see one another, but how to accomplish it was a difficulty which neither of us could presently think of surmounting.

THERE was in *Panama* an old Gentlewoman named *Donna-Bianca*, who was a widow, and a very near relation of *Don Henriquez*; and on that account, as well as for the love she express'd for his daughter, was always well receiv'd at his house, and *Elvira* was allow'd by him to make frequent visits to her at her house. The engaging this widow entirely in our cause, appear'd the only means of an interview between us. *Bianca* was not
only

only covetous by nature, but render'd more fo
by age, which open'd a way for me to make
her my own; but even that was not to be
done without fome caution and addrefs; I
therefore made ufe of an acquaintance of hers,
who had fome dependance upon me, and
foon brought matters to bear, for by pro-
mifing large rewards, fhe allow'd her houfe
to be the place of our rendezvous: Accordingly at laft we met there, to the infinite fatisfaction of us both. It would be endlefs and
fuperfluous to give an account of the joys and
tranfports of our meeting, it is enough for any
one to confider what might pafs between two
young people, equally poffefs'd with a violent
paffion : We met often, and every time produc'd new warmth, and new defires, which
neither party had power to check, or any
thoughts of doing fo; on the contrary, every
meeting feem'd to encreafe our love, and thofe
familiarities which hearts perfectly united make
little fcruple of; but whatever they were, they
were not fufficient to fatisfy our defires; we
therefore confulted how to bring matters to
fuch a conclufion as might make us both happy in one another, which nothing could do
but marriage; but that we knew was not to
be accomplifh'd in a publick manner, and by
her father's confent, who was my irreconcile-
able enemy; nor was it to be done privately,
becaufe after the confummation, and her fet-
ling with me, it muft be known, and by con-

fequence draw upon us both fuch a revenge, as would not end without fomething very fatal and dreadful; the only means that we could find out, was, that I fhould call in all my effects in thofe parts, and return to *Spain*, taking her with me. This therefore was refolv'd upon, and I immediately began to fet in earneft about it. If we had kept this refolution to our felves, I believe it had met with fuccefs; but taking *Bianca* into our council, being, as we thought, neceffary to our accomplifhing it, fhe privately betray'd us; for confidering that by our departure, there would not only be an end of her profit, which was what made her our friend, but that fhe fhould be left alone to ftand the fury of *Don Henriquez's* refentment, fhe refolv'd to play another part, fecretly to reveal fo much of our affair as might difappoint our defigns, and render what fhe did acceptable to *Elvira's* father; telling him, that he had beft have a watchful eye over his daughter, fince fhe had certain information, that fhe not only met me under pretence of coming to vifit her, but that matters were brought to fuch a head, that our marriage was fuddenly defign'd. The old Gentleman was in a prodigious fury at what he heard, 'till *Bianca* advis'd him not to depend entirely upon her information, but to have her watch'd whenever fhe went out: *Don Henriquez* took her advice, and accordingly provided not only fpies to watch her, but *Bravo's*

to

to put an end to his fears by my death. The next time of our appointed meeting I happen'd to come firſt, and was extremely ſurpriz'd to find *Bianca*'s doors faſt, and that they would not be open'd by my knocking, or any noiſe I could make: I began to ſuſpect that we were betray'd, and therefore taking the two men I always had with me, for fear of accidents, I went a little forwards in the way that I knew *Elvira* muſt come; and accordingly met her not many paces from *Bianca*'s houſe. I told her what had happen'd, and the cauſe I had to fear that our ſecret love was made known to her father; ſhe was ſtruck with an inexpreſſible grief and concern at this unhappy event; but while we were conſulting how to manage our affairs for the future, there came up half a dozen men, two of them ſeiz'd upon her and her *Duenna*, and hurry'd them away, the other four at the ſame time made at me; but retiring a little way, I drew out my pocket piſtol and ſhot among them, which forc'd them a little to retire; but finding they were none of them hurt, they came on again with greater violence; in which interval I retreated back to my two men; we all drew our ſwords, and behav'd our ſelves ſo well, that we made them leave the place, and ſo got home; but in the ſcuffle I receiv'd two wounds, which for ſome time were thought to be very dangerous, and ſo bad that it was given

out

out I fhould die of them; and indeed it was
fome time before I perfectly recover'd.

You may be fure that I made it my endeavours to enquire after the fate of my miftrefs,
and of what treatment fhe had met with upon this difcovery; all that I could hear was,
that her father had fent her away from *Panama*; fome faid to *Portobello*, and fome to
Spain, but moft were of this latter opinion;
but for fear of a miftake I difpatch'd a friend in
whom I could confide, to *Portobello*, to make
a ftrict enquiry whether fhe was there or not,
but could not hear the leaft news of her; fo
that I refolved to haften the calling in of my
effects, in order to go into *Spain* after her:
But this was not to be done with any manner of convenience, without taking up a
confiderable time. However, having at laft
fettled my affairs, I freighted a fhip with
all my own cargo; defigning very fuddenly
to fet out from *Panama*, which I was the
more expeditious to accomplifh, becaufe I had
not only been frequently attack'd by the par-
tifans of *Don Henriquez*, but was more ter-
rify'd by the arrival of *Lorenzo de Toledo*,
a near relation of my fuppos'd unkle; to
whom he had left the handfome legacy I
before mention'd: But he, not fatisfy'd with
that, was come to *Panama*, to examine who
it was that had depriv'd him, of the poffeffion of the whole; for *Roderigo de Toledo*
was

was a perſon of whom he had not the leaſt knowledge. When he arriv'd, I was almoſt ready to go on board, but his coming put a little ſtop to it; for when he ſaw me, he remember'd that I was *Alexander*, his relation's ſervant, and not *Roderigo* his nephew; and therefore made his complaints, that either I had forg'd the will, or that it was invalid, ſince I was mention'd there in a wrong name, and not being a native *Spaniard*, but an *Engliſhman* (for they make no diſtinction between *Scotch* and *Engliſh*) and, as he ſuppos'd, an heretick, I could be neither heir nor executor, in prejudice to a native *Spaniard*, and a true Catholick. You may be ſure I deny'd the whole charge, ſince not only my fortune, but my life, might in ſome meaſure depend upon it. *Don Henriquez*, tho' he hated all my unkle's family, yet having a greater averſion to me, and in hopes to embroil our affairs, he plainly eſpous'd the cauſe of *Lorenzo*, and I had ſecret information that they were endeavouring to get an order to ſeize both me and my ſhip; I was therefore advis'd to put in my appeal to the Courts of *Spain*, and immediately to get on board, and put off to ſea; which accordingly I did, but not ſo ſoon but that *Lorenzo* had found means to get a creature of his on board my ſhip, as a common ſailor, who ſhould accompliſh my deſtruction, which he brought about in the following manner: This creature of his was a cunning fellow, and

had

had foon infinuated himfelf into the good graces of the reft of the failors, affuring them that they would not only do God good fervice, in deftroying an heretick, but fecure to themfelves moft of the fhip's cargo by throwing me over-board; which had certainly been done, had not a fmall ftorm, for a while, deferr'd the mifchief they intended me. This ftorm had driven us very near an ifland in the *South-Sea*; which, tho' once inhabited, they knew was now quite depopulated; which however mov'd the mafter, who ow'd his employment to me, to move them rather to fet me on fhore upon this defart ifland, than to throw me into the fea. Accordingly the mutiny being now ripe, they told me that as I was a heretick, they could not hope to profper in their voyage whilft I remain'd in the fhip; and though they intended to caft me over-board, yet by the mafter's mediation, and the appearance of that ifland, they chang'd their refolution, and were determin'd to fet me on fhore with fuch provifions and neceffaries as they could fpare. I did all I could to pacify them, and recover them to their duty, but to no purpofe; I might as well have talk'd to the fea or the winds, for bigotry and defire of gain had made them entirely deaf to all I faid; I therefore fubmitted to a fate I could not prevent, and was fet on fhore with fuch provifions and utenfils as they were pleas'd to allow me, and which they would not fo much as

carry

carry up into the ifland for me, but juft fet
them on fhore a little above the high water
mark, and fo went off. I ftood with melancholy eyes to fee them fail away with all my
fortune, and all my hopes, leaving me on a
defolate ifland, with no more provifions than
would, well manag'd, ferve me about two
months. .They left me indeed a gun, fome
fhot, and fome powder, a little kettle, and
fome few tools, which might be neceffary for
building me a little hut, for my refidence and
protection againft the injuries of the weather;
fo that if the ifland it felf fhould afford me
no affiftance, my life could not be of a very
long date: But I found it was in vain to
grieve and repine at what I had loft, or the
condition in which I was. And fo when I
had look'd at the fhip 'till fhe was got clear
out of fight, I went a little farther up into the
ifland to fearch for a convenient place, whither
I might tranfport, by degrees, that little ftock
of neceffaries which the villains had left me,
of which I valu'd nothing more than a poor
hammock, which, with much intreaty, I had
obtain'd of them; for being always us'd to lie
well, I was very apprehenfive of having fo hard
a lodging as the cold ground. I had not gone
many paces before I difcover'd a little fort of
a hut, tho' almoft dropping down, for want
of care to repair it; however, fuch as it was,
I was refolv'd to enter into it, and fee what
convenience it afforded for my felf, and what

C   I had

I had to place in it; I was likewise willing to
shelter my self against the violent heat of the
sun, for it was then but just turn'd of noon;
and there I resolv'd to remain 'till the cool of
the evening should enable me to fetch my
things thither. With these thoughts I enter'd
the hut, and making to the most shady part
of it, which was likewise the darkest, I
threw my self down on the floor, in order,
if I could, to take a little nap; but was very
much surpriz'd when I heard a human voice,
tho' in imperfect sounds, as from a person a-
sleep, crying out in these words, *Oh! Roderigo*,
several times repeated, and attended with many sighs. I could not immediately tell what
to do, but to satisfy my self drew nearer to
the sound, and found that there was some body asleep there, but who or what I could by
no means so much as guess; my motion and
feeling about, at last, awak'd the sleeper; who
affrighted to find some body near her (for it
was a woman) started up, and was running a-
way; but I soon stopp'd her, and taking her
by the hand gently, enquir'd, Who she was?
Whence she came? And what brought her thither? But what amazement where we both struck
with when I saw that it was *Elvira*, and she
beheld in me her unfortunate *Roderigo!* We
both a while stood gazing at each other, when
all I could utter was, Sure it is impossible that
this should be my *Elvira!* And all she could
say was, Oh! heaven, is it possible! Can it be!

Is

Is this my *Roderigo!* We both at once cry'd, Yes, yes, and flew into each other's arms; nor could our embraces and kisses soon find a cessation, but our first extacy being over, we began to ask and enquire of each other, how we came thither? I gave her a full account of all that had pass'd since the time of our separation to that day: But, concluded I, I will no longer complain of fortune, since if she had not frown'd in this manner upon me, I had not now had the blessing of clasping my dear *Elvira* in my arms; nor will I, said she, complain of mine, since it has brought my beloved *Roderigo* to mine; so after an interval of repeated embraces, she gave me the following account of her adventures.

WHEN I was forc'd away from you, said she, near *Bianca*'s house, I was hurry'd back by the Ruffians who seiz'd me (one of whom was my brother) to my father's house, but was not admitted into his presence; for my brother told me that his indignation was so great, that he had sworn never to see me more, left his rage should transport him to use me with such severity, as he might afterwards repent. He let me know that *Bianca* had betray'd me, in revenge of which I told him that she had been my confidant in the whole affair; and for the sake of money had given us the use of her house, with all imaginable freedom; which my brother said he would take care to let my father know

as

as foon as his paffion was a little more abated;
in the mean time he advis'd me to write a
fubmiffive letter, which perhaps might make
way for a reconciliation, tho' he fear'd not. I
writ not only one, but feveral letters to my
father, in hopes to revive his former tendernefs to me, that I might by that means gain
a little more liberty, in order to find out fome
way of letting you know the pofture of my
prefent affairs; but my *Duenna* being turn'd out
of doors, and I put under the fevereft confinement, could not poffibliy accomplifh it. My
brother at laft brought me word, that I muft
immediately prepare for a voyage to *Spain:*
This news ftruck me to the heart, efpecially
fince I had no means of letting you know it;
but it was in vain to ftruggle, my father was
inexorable, nor would he fo much as admit me
into his prefence, even fo much as to take my
leave of him; but fent me on board fo guarded,
that it was impoffible for me to give you the
leaft notice of my condition. In fhort, we fet
fail in an evil hour; for we had not been out many days before we were attack'd by a *French
privateer*, and were taken by her: But not
much caring for the fhip, they were contented
with its plunder, fcarce leaving us the cloaths
we had on our backs. This misfortune was
foon after attended with another; for when,
upon a confultation, it was refolv'd to turn
back again to *Panama,* as having neither provifion nor cargo left to proceed on our intended

ded voyage, they thought it the beſt courſe they could take; but, as I was ſaying, a ſtorm juſt then aroſe, which prov'd ſo violent, that it drove us farther from the coaſt for ſeveral days together, inſomuch that our lives were in danger; becauſe the ſhip, by the fight ſhe had ſuſtain'd with the *French*, was very much ſhatter'd, and grown ſo leaky, that they almoſt deſpair'd of keeping her above water. The on-ly comfort we had in all this diſtreſs was, that we had diſcover'd land, being the iſland where you now find me; but that which leſſen'd this ſatisfaction was, for fear that the ſtorm which yet continu'd, ſhould daſh us to pieces on ſome rocks, which they either knew, or concluded to be about this coaſt: However, being now within a league of the ſhore, they were in hopes that they might reach it in their boat if the ſhip founder'd, as they expected every minute it would, and which ſoon after it did. They had but juſt time to get me, three other paſſen-gers, and themſelves into the boat, but the ſhip ſunk.

THE number of us in the boat was about two and twenty perſons, that is, the maſter, my ſelf, three other paſſengers, one of which was my maid, and, as near as I can remember, ſix-teen or ſeventeen ſeamen, of whom many were very much wounded in the fight. Thus with a great deal of difficulty, and every moment ex-pecting to be ſunk by the waves which perpe-

tually

tually broke in upon us, we got within a quarter
of a mile of the shore, when the boat was
dash'd to pieces against a rock, and we all set
on float in the water, so that every one took
care of themselves; and I must certainly have
perish'd had not one *Diego*, an old servant of
my father's, and who was an excellent swim-
mer, caught hold of me, and bidding me hold
my breath as much as I could, bore me so
near the land that he could wade but up to
the middle in water; where finding me quite
spent, he carried me on shore in his arms;
and then making me cast up all the water I
had swallow'd, he in a little time brought me
to my self. Another did the same by my
maid, but I know not how it was, when she
was brought on shore, either by the fright she
was in, or by the great quantity of salt water she
had swallow'd, she was so far suffocated that she
never came to her self. There were about
half a dozen more of the seamen that got to
land, the rest who were so much wounded as
I have said, were render'd incapable, as we
suppose, of struggling with the waves; for they
and the two Gentlemen passengers were all
drown'd; and indeed our condition was very
little better, for being cast upon an island
where we expected no subsistence, and were
entirely destitute of all support, we could
not expect to live many days. The men having first stripp'd my maid, threw her into the
sea; they had no instruments to dig a grave for
her

her on the shore; they after, hung her cloaths a
drying, and her linen prov'd very useful to me
afterwards.

WE all soon remov'd farther up into the island,
and the men went out to see what provisions they could get for our relief, leaving with
me *Diego*, that I might not be wholly alone.
They found at last a small cottage, though very ruinous, in which there were two rooms
pretty entire; and searching on, they found
two or three acres of ground, some planted
with turnips, and others with potatoes, and
they all having knives in their pockets, made
use of them to dig up these Roots; which
they plac'd in the cottage, and came to fetch
Diego and me to their new habitation. But
how to prepare this food for our eating, still
remain'd a difficulty with us, since we had no
convenience of dressing them, though there
was a chimney in this cottage; but then we
had neither firing, nor a pot to boil them
in; but searching about the house they found
three or four pieces of flint, wherewith they
did not doubt but with the help of their knives
they might be able to strike fire: Yet there
was still wanting some very combustible matter to receive those sparks of fire which they
should strike from their flints, so they went
out to see if the place afforded any thing which
would supply that defect. They found at last
                                    a dry

a dry rotten tree, fome parts of which receiv'd the fire they ftruck as well as any tinder; they then gather'd together all the fuel they could find, confifting of part of this rotten tree, and other things of the like nature, with which they made a good fire, and try'd to roaft, fince they could not boil their roots; which, confidering our prefent circumftance, we all being pretty hungry, prov'd tolerable food. The next care they had, was how to provide a lodging for me, but they could find no other way than cleaning the floor as well as they could, and laying my maid's cloaths under me, with a fmall log of wood for my pillow; which, after my fatigue, prov'd fo good a bed, that I flept very foundly all the night. I forgot to tell you that juft without the cottage there was a fine fpring of water, which ferv'd us for drink; tho' our hands were all the cups we had, 'till we had found a fort of fruit very like a lemon, but its juice was fo four, that we could make very little ufe of it, but fcooping them clean, they made us tolerable drinking cups.

THIS ifland is about feven leagues long, and three broad, and abounds with feveral inoffenfive animals, left there by the inhabitants, who had lately quitted it, particularly goats; which we were at prefent but very little the better for, and in no way of taking or killing them. There were likewife fome hogs, but
all

all thefe were at the farther part of the ifland, and out of our power to make food of: However, one day three of our men brought in a couple of young kids, one of them they made a kind of pen for, out of the old pieces of boards they found about the place, and the other they kill'd, flead and drefs'd, by broiling on the coals: And this was noble food, confidering how we had liv'd for fome days. We had no napkins or plates, but a piece of board very well fcrap'd and wafh'd, which ferv'd us both for table and trenchers. We had no bread to our dinners, but that was tolerably fupply'd by our roafted *potatoes*; of the kid's skin, when it was dry'd in the fun, they made me a bolfter, fomething fofter than what I had, and with other skins, prepar'd in the fame manner, they improv'd my bed; for they all took care to make my misfortune as eafy to me as they could. They one day happen'd to find a fow with a litter of young pigs, of which they brought away two, with a great deal of joy, and drefs'd them as well as they could.

AND indeed as long as I had my companions I bore up as well as cou'd be expected, and in three months time had us'd my felf to the hardfhips of my fortune fo well, that I was grown a perfect campaigner. We had our fcouts out every day, to fee if we could difcover any fhips, but to no purpofe; for to this minute I never heard of any 'till, your prefence

D   inform'd

inform'd me that there has been one upon this coaft.

OUR men willing to gratify me with fome variety of food, went frequently upon the ftrand, in hopes to find fome fhell-fifh, and at laft they brought home half a dozen oyfters; which I eat with fo much fatisfaction, that they ventur'd to get to a rock, when the tide was out, on which they imagin'd they faw a pretty great ftore of them; but this was a fatal expedition, there coming out of the fea half a dozen fea lyons, as *Diego* call'd them; creatures of a vaft bignefs, and terrible to behold, at leaft they feem'd fo to *Diego* in his fright; who being neareft the fhore, fled away with the lofs of a piece of the fleeve of his waftecoat, and two great fcratches in his arm made by the paw of the lyon, whilft all the others were devour'd by them. *Diego* came to me in a very great fright, and his arm all running with blood: I took him to the fpring and wafh'd his wounds, binding them up as well as I could, with the only handkerchief I had left. I was extremely concern'd for the lofs of his companions, and the more, becaufe it was partly upon my account that they run into this danger. *Diego* and I did as well as we could, I being oblig'd both to ftrike fire, and cook my victuals; that is, roaft my potatoes and turnips, which was all the food we had left, keeping no flefh by us, becaufe of the

heat

heat of the feafon ; but for potatoes and turnips they had brought a pretty large ftock into
the houfe.

I wafh'd and drefs'd poor *Diego's* wound every day, but whether there was any venom in
the creature that gave the wound, or that the
renting of the flefh caus'd it, I know not, yet
a great inflammation enfu'd, and after it a
mortification; which foon carry'd off poor
Diego, and left me all alone, with a dead body, which I had no capacity of burying. What
to do I could not tell, fince to ftay in the
houfe with him was impoffible, the ftench
that would arife from his corrupting body being too great to be borne; I therefore immediately refolv'd to remove to this little hut where
you now find me. Accordingly I firft carry'd
all my bedding, and then as many of my turnips and potatoes as I could, in four or five
journies; which I continu'd for a day or two,
'till the ftench of *Diego's* body deterr'd me
from going any more to the cottage, which
is fomething more than half a mile from hence.
I brought away with me likewife two of the
feamen's knives, the flints, and what touch-
wood we had by us, with two or three of
the cups that we had made of the rhine of the
lemon.

My ftate was now indeed very deplorable,
being in an ifland all alone, a poor helplefs
woman,

woman, who could not expect to support her
self long with that small quantity of provisions which my old companions had left me,
not knowing how to come at more when they
were spent, without the utmost difficulty. Thus
I have liv'd upwards of a week, but now heaven has sent you to my relief, which may yet
a while delay my fate, tho' I am not at all
solicitous to put off that death which in a
little time seems to me inevitable: However, I
shall die with pleasure, since it is given me to
expire in the arms of my *Roderigo*.

HERE she made an end, and after a thousand tender embraces, I bid her be comfort-
ed, and cherish better hopes, since I was now
with her to take care of her, and provide such
necessaries as the island afforded. The evening
growing cool, I went to the shore where I was
landed, and by degrees brought all my provisions and stores to the little hut; where having first refresh'd *Elvira* with what I had to
eat, and a little wine, for the rogues had been
so bountiful as to give me a gallon and no
more, having finish'd our repast, with much ado
I fix'd up my hammock, in order to mend the
lodging of *Elvira*. She made some scruples
at first of permitting me to lie in the same
place with her; but having convinc'd her that
we were really man and wife before heaven,
having pronounc'd all the obligatory tyes of
matrimony, which were the only essentials of
it,

it, she seem'd less averse. I told her that as
for the priest, and the other formalities of the
church, they were mere ceremonies, and wholly political; that the children of *Adam* were
really marry'd, tho' they had no priest to join
them, for there was no priest then in the world;
that ours was the same case, being in an island
where there was no body but our selves. It
growing now dusky, we both went into the
hammock, and slept very heartily; the next
morning we got up, and having taken our
breakfast, I resolv'd to go and bury the dead
body, that we might remove to more convenient quarters. There grew by the hut some
fine scented herbs, and taking such tools as I
thought might do the office of a spade, I went
and dug a hole large enough for the body;
and with a great deal of trouble, in the midst
of a horrid stench, I got the corpse into the
hole; I soon cover'd it up, and went to the
spring, wash'd my hands and face, mouth and
nostrils, to get away all the relicks of the stench,
and then I drank a little of the water, and return'd
again to *Elvira*; though before I came back
to her I rubb'd my self all over with the sweet
scented herbs I mention'd before, that I might
carry her no disagreeable smell. She receiv'd
me with joy and open arms, and told me how
troubled she was at the nauseous office I had
perform'd. I reply'd, that the burying of the
dead was a christian duty, and here being no
body to do this but my self, I thought I was
oblig'd

oblig'd not to neglect it; that befides the
difcharge of that duty, I had provided her
a more convenient habitation. The day growing hot, we retir'd again to our hammock,
where we repos'd till two or three a clock,
when we got up and went to dinner, and in
the evening took a walk out into the coun-
trey. We let it be three or four days, nay,
if I miftake not, a week, before we remov'd
our quarters; and I had made fires and purify'd the houfe, and ftrew'd it with fweet herbs
and flowers, and fitted up the coolest part for
my hammock, which I brought with me. When
I led my love to her new dwelling, that being
fix'd, I began to remove my effects, which
took me up above two days, working only
early in the morning, and in the cool of the
evening.

WHEN all was remov'd, and we entirely
fettled, I began to think that I was not fo unhappy as the loffes I had met with would perfuade me: 'Tis true, I was depriv'd of a plentiful fortune, but that was attended with many cares, and threaten'd with great difturban-
ces, and wonderful anxieties perpetually tortur'd
my mind, on account of my dear *Elvira,*
whom I loved with the most violent of paffion; on the other fide, I began to fet my gains
againft my loffes, and found my felf in the
poffeffion of that dear woman, without whom
I could not hope for any happinefs; that I
had

had her without rival, without any awe of parents, entirely to my felf, and full of equal love; that as I wanted the pomp and equipage of the world, fo I was on the other fide free from all its difquiets. Company I wanted none, for *Elvira* was as much as I defir'd. Thefe confiderations, and many more of this kind, made me not only believe that I was happy by my prefent lot, but perfuaded *Elvira* that fhe was fo too; and indeed fhe never difcover'd the leaft fentiments that fhe thought otherwife. We enjoy'd each other all the day and all the night too, we were never weary of being together, but always uneafy when neceffity at any time parted us but for a quarter of an hour: Thus I never went out when my walk was not beyond her ftrength, but fhe went with me. I feldom went without my gun upon my fhoulder, and going one day with her by the fea fhore we were furpris'd at the approach of three lyons, who coming out of the fea made directly at us. I being a pretty good marks-man, fhot the firft of them directly into the eye, upon which he fell down dead; and either the flafh of the fire, or the noife of the gun fo frighten'd the other two, that they turn'd about, and made all their fpeed back into the fea. I charg'd my piece again immediately, however we both took a full view of the dead monfter, which was of a vaft magnitude; but knowing of no ufe it could be to me, *Elvira* and I retreated and left

him

him upon the fand; whence the next tide, as
I fuppofe, carry'd him quite away; for when I
went that way again, I faw nothing of him.
Finding that poor ftock of provifion which was
fet on fhore with me began to decreafe, I took
care to provide for the future; and not only
fow'd again the turnip-feed that I had gather'd,
but alfo fome *Indian* wheat and rice, hoping
that in time they might yield a convenient crop for
our future occafions: I likewife look'd out for
kids and pigs, and got enough of them both
for prefent food, and to feed and bring up
tame. I having a pot, and two or three napkins, a cup or two, and fome earthen plates,
Elvira had her dinners better drefs'd and ferv'd
up than before I came.

In this manner we fpent our life, abound-
ing in nothing but love; nor had we any accidents or adventures during the three years fhe
liv'd with me: But my joys were too compleat,
for the malice of my fortune, to allow me a
long continuance of 'em; and therefore towards
the latter end of the third year *Elvira* was
taken dangeroufly ill, and the diftemper was
fo violent, that it carry'd her off in three days
time.

Nothing ever went fo near my heart as
this lofs, and had I not been preferv'd for more
evils, the grief that *Elvira's* death gave me,
would certainly have put an end to my life:
I could

I could not leave the dear body for near two days after her deceafe, but prefs'd and kifs'd it as if fhe was yet alive; but coming a little to my felf, I confider'd that fhe muft be buried, fince it was impoffible to keep her another day in this hot climate without putrefaction; I took pains, therefore, to dig a grave as deep as I could; into which, having firft kifs'd her, tho' fhe began to fmell pretty ftrong, I gently let her down in her cloaths, and cover'd her up with the earth, my eyes flowing all the while with tears. After this I led a very melancholy life for two years, five months and feven days, without any manner of occurrence worth the inferting.

On the laft of thofe days, ftanding upon the beach with my gun on my fhoulder, I difcover'd a fail about three leagues to the *South*, but directed its courfe *Northward*; I fir'd my piece (having made very little ufe of my powder) which they took for a fignal of diftrefs; but I difcharg'd it once more, and then I perceiv'd they ftood in to the land; and in lefs than two hour's time, came fo near as to be able to call to me. They ask'd who, and what I was, in a fort of broken *Spanifh*? And I finding, by fome of the oaths of the mariners, that they were *Englifh*, anfwer'd them as lamely; telling them that I was all alone upon the ifland, and defir'd them to take me in, and I would give them an account of my

E   ftory.

ſtory. They preſently mann'd out their boat, which came on ſhore and took me on board, without ever going back to my quarters, where I had left nothing worth preſerving. It happen'd to be a *Jamaica* Sloop, *William Thomas*, maſter, which had been carrying on that private trade with the *Spaniſh Indians*, which the men of *Jamaica* had found very beneficial ; though oftentimes very hazardous, becauſe it was practis'd againſt the *Spaniſh* laws, but private gain ſeldom has much regard to publick tyes. We had a proſperous voyage to *Jamaica*, where the account of my ſtory procur'd me ſuch a Benefaction as was fit to ſet me out, and bear my charges into *England*, whence I have been abſent now many years. I found means of getting from *London* to *Edinburgh*, where my father was yet alive, tho' very old and crazy, my ill natur'd mother-in-law having been dead for ſome time. My father was very glad to receive me, and at his death, which happen'd ſoon after, left me an equal portion with the reſt of his children : And here I ſhall conclude my narration, what has ſince happen'd to me affording nothing material, or any way uſeful for a general entertainment.

F I N I S.

ERRATA.

Page 3. line 9. read *Simono' du Change.* p. 33. l. 21. r. *me.*
p. 43. l. 15. for *saw by us* r. *fail'd by.* p. 45. l. 26. r. *by.*
p. 57. l. 13. r. *in.* p. 68. l. 1. r. *is.* p. 80. l. 11. add *cut.*

P. 2. l. 27. r. *musick.* p. 7. l. 15. r. *in.*